CAPITOL MURDER

Books by Phillip Margolin

Lost Lake

Sleeping Beauty

The Associate

The Undertaker's Widow

The Burning Man

After Dark

Gone, but Not Forgotten

The Last Innocent Man

Heartstone

Washington Trilogy

Executive Privilege

Supreme Justice

Capitol Murder

Amanda Jaffe Novels

Wild Justice

Ties That Bind

Proof Positive

Fugitive

PHILLIP MARGOLIN

CAPITOL MURDER

A NOVEL OF SUSPENSE

HARPER
An Imprint of HarperCollins*Publishers*
www.harpercollins.com

HarperCollins books may be purchased for educational, business, or sales promotional use. For information, please write: Special Markets Department, HarperCollins Publishers, 10 East 53rd Street, New York, NY 10022.

FIRST EDITION

Library of Congress Cataloging-in-Publication Data

Margolin, Phillip.
Capitol murder : a novel of suspense / Phillip Margolin.—1st ed.
p. cm.
ISBN 978-0-06-206988-7
1. Murder—Investigation—Fiction. 2. Washington (D.C.)—Fiction.
3. Political fiction. I. Title.
PS3563.A649C37 2012
813'.54—dc23 2011028746

---

12 13 14 15 16 OV/RRD 10 9 8 7 6 5 4 3 2 1

For Jean Naggar, Jennifer Weltz, and everyone at the Jean V. Naggar Literary Agency.

It's nice to have great agents who are also great friends.

CAPITOL MURDER

Prologue

KARACHI, PAKISTAN

Nadeem Gandapur was a slight, wiry man in his early forties who had lived his whole life in the sprawling, dusty, densely populated warren of cinder-block huts, bazaars, and winding alleyways that made up one of Karachi's largest slums. He worked construction and was blessed to have a steady income that enabled his family to live better than many of his neighbors. Nadeem believed that his good fortune was due to his devout nature, and he went frequently to the mosque that was the centerpiece of the slum.

On the evening Nadeem met the American, he did not leave the mosque until night had fallen because he and Imam Ibrahim had been debating whether Ramadan should begin when two or more Muslim men see the crescent moon or whether the start should be based on astronomical prediction. On the way home, he was still thinking about the imam's points and did not notice the two men who were following him until they shoved him into a narrow, dimly lit alley.

Nadeem stumbled backward into a mound of garbage. The humid air was heavy in the alley, and the stench of the rotting refuse made him gag. His assailants were dressed in white short-sleeve shirts whose bottoms hung loosely outside their tan slacks. One of them grinned at Nadeem while the other showed no emotion. Both men drew large knives from sheaths hidden under their shirts. A knot formed in Nadeem's stomach.

"Give me your money or I'll gut you," said the man with the sense of humor.

Nadeem could see more rubbish piled against the alley wall behind the robbers. A section of the pile appeared to move and Nadeem wondered if his fear had driven him mad.

"Quickly," commanded the man who did not smile.

Nadeem took out his wallet, praying silently that money was all the men would take from him. As he extended his hand toward the robbers, the rubbish pile rose six feet in the air and flowed toward him. Nadeem's eyes widened and he froze, the wallet halfway to his assailant. The smiling robber took a menacing half step closer to Nadeem and began to mouth another threat when a sturdy table leg appeared out of the rubbish pile and slashed across his elbow. The robber screamed and his knife dropped to the alley floor.

The second thief turned and slashed. Nadeem heard a grunt. The pile took a step back and the robber attacked. The table leg parried the thrust, then connected with the robber's face. The thief's hands leaped to his nose and the second knife fell to the ground. Blood sprayed through the robber's fingers. The table leg connected with his shin. He dropped to the ground and a blow to the head finished him off.

The first robber was doubled over, clutching his shattered elbow. The table leg smashed into the base of his skull, and he crumpled to the alley floor.

Nadeem's eyes adjusted to the dark, and he made out a man

dressed in rags with tangled, unwashed blond shoulder-length hair, blue eyes, and a shaggy beard matted with food and refuse. It was the American. Nadeem had seen him begging outside the luxury hotels and steel-and-glass office buildings that stood only blocks away from Nadeem's squalid slum. Nadeem knew the American lived in the worst part of the slum in a lean-to that stood close by an open privy. Most of his neighbors avoided him because they thought he was insane and violent. Nadeem had heard a rumor that he had badly beaten some men who had tried to extort money from him.

"Let's go," the American said in perfect Urdu. Another surprise, since the American was so silent that many thought him mute. A filthy hand gripped Nadeem's elbow and propelled him out of the alley.

"Thank you," Nadeem said when they were back on the street. Then he saw the blood seeping through his rescuer's rags.

"You're hurt," Nadeem said.

The American looked down, then said, "Shit!" in English. He pressed his hand against the wound and stumbled. Nadeem made a quick decision.

"Come with me," he ordered.

"I'll be okay," the American said. Then he gasped and his knees buckled.

"You will not be okay if you don't get medical attention."

Nadeem snaked his arm around the man's back and looped one of the man's arms across his shoulder. Together they shuffled away from the alley toward the mosque.

When Imran Afridi's houseman escorted Rafik Nasrallah onto the patio in the rear of his mansion, Afridi was sipping mint tea and watching the waves break on Clifton Beach. Karachi was stifling this time of year, but the breeze from the Arabian Sea cooled the air in the wealthy suburb where Afridi had built his estate. The Pakistani businessman was wearing a long-sleeve silk shirt that clung to his broad shoulders. When he stood to greet Nasrallah, the loose sleeves moved with the breeze.

Afridi was five feet seven with the barrel chest and thick legs of a wrestler. His straight black hair was receding from his prominent forehead, but he had compensated for his loss by growing a thick mustache below his hawklike nose, making him look vaguely like a desert sheikh in an old Hollywood movie.

Nasrallah was two inches taller and as solidly built as his childhood friend, but his full head of thick black hair and his smooth skin made him look much younger than forty. Nasrallah and Afridi were sons of wealth and had been educated at Cambridge before returning to Pakistan to work in their families' varied enterprises. They had also embraced radical Islam together.

Afridi could tell from the strength of his friend's embrace that Rafik was excited.

"We may have struck gold, Imran," Rafik said as the two men sat on either side of a circular, glass-topped table. Rafik gave Afridi a photograph.

Rafik stopped talking while his friend studied the picture. The smile disappeared from Afridi's lips and his countenance reflected intense concentration.

"He calls himself Stephen Reynolds, but I don't think that's his real name. He's twenty-three and from Ohio, where he was studying engineering," Rafik said. "Also, he has a background in chemistry."

"Go on," Afridi said when Rafik paused to make certain his friend understood the full import of what he had just said.

"A few months ago, Reynolds looked nothing like he does in this photograph. He was begging for a living, and his home was a hovel in the slum where one of Imam Ibrahim's students lives. This student was attacked by two robbers. Reynolds saved him but he was stabbed. The student took him to the mosque and the imam summoned a doctor.

"The wound was serious, and Reynolds was suffering from malnutrition. He also had a drug habit. The imam nursed him back to health. While he was at the mosque, he and the imam became close, and Reynolds told him why he was living in a Karachi slum.

"Reynolds went to a private high school that offered Arabic, and he became fascinated with Islam. He surfed Web sites and entered chat rooms. In college he continued to study Middle Eastern languages and came in contact with Muslims sympathetic to our cause. America's invasion of Iraq radicalized him.

"While he was in college, there was an incident with a woman. He was expelled and criminal charges were brought. The family paid a large sum of money to avoid a scandal, and the charges were dropped, but his father is ex-military, and he refused to pay off the woman unless his son enlisted in the army, which he did because his only other choice was prison. Though he deeply resented having to make this choice, he was smart enough to keep his sympathies hidden.

"Reynolds was a superior athlete. That and his proficiency in Afghan dialects led to his ending up in Special Forces."

Nasrallah paused dramatically. "Here is the important part," he said, stretching out the moment. "Reynolds does not exist."

Afridi's brow furrowed and Rafik grinned.

"His team was ambushed in Afghanistan while they were on a mission," Rafik said. "Reynolds was the only survivor, but he did not report back to his base and was listed as missing in action. He made his way over the mountains into Pakistan and eventually to Karachi."

Rafik leaned across the table. "He is very bitter, Imran. He rails against the United States. He feels he is a victim and he talks of revenge."

Afridi studied the picture again. The man in it was blond-haired and blue-eyed. He had the looks and build of a stereotypical fraternity jock; the antithesis of the features Homeland Security profilers looked for. There was no place he could not go unsuspected. He was a terrorist's dream and the CIA's worst nightmare.

"Are you thinking about America?" Afridi asked.

"He would be perfect," Rafik answered excitedly.

"It would be asking a lot. He grew up an American. He might talk jihad but he might not have the heart to go through with it when the time came."

"New converts are often the most fanatic believers," Rafik countered.

Afridi leaned back and looked at the sea. Nasrallah did not speak. Afridi was the deeper thinker of the two, while his friend was the man of action. The friends often passed the time playing chess. On the rare occasion when Rafik won, it was through a daring combination that had worked even though he had not thought it through completely. Imran usually won by grinding down his friend.

"I am nervous about letting this man in on the operation,"

Afridi said. "Until now, we have taken all of the right steps. The slightest error could destroy everything we want to accomplish."

"There's no risk, Imran. I will have Mustapha sound him out so there won't be any connection to us. We still have a lot of time before we begin the operation."

Afridi thought some more. Then he nodded. "All right, have Mustapha talk to him."

"You're wise to be cautious, Imran, but if he is suitable . . ."

"Yes."

"And if he is not," Nasrallah said, shrugging, "Karachi is a very big city. He can always disappear."

Part I

“May You Live in Interesting Times”

Three Years Later

Chapter One

As soon as Dana Cutler and Jake Teeny walked into the China Clipper, Dana took off her motorcycle helmet and shook out her shoulder-length hair. Brad Miller had been watching for them, and he waved from the booth in the back of the restaurant where he and Ginny Striker were waiting. The private detective and her photojournalist boyfriend were a striking couple. They had driven over on Jake's Harley and they were both clad in black leather jackets and jeans. At five ten, Dana was an inch taller than Jake, but they were both lean and athletic. Jake had wavy brown hair, brown eyes, and dark skin that had been blasted by the desert winds and baked by the scorching suns of the war zones and exotic places his assignments had taken him to. Dana's green eyes and auburn hair attracted attention from men but something hard and dangerous about her made these same men think twice before approaching her.

When the couple arrived at the booth, Brad shook hands with Jake, but he knew better than to hug Dana. Physical contact made the private detective uncomfortable, and Brad knew why. The fact that Dana was sleeping with Jake said a lot about the strength of their relationship.

Brad was five ten with a straight nose, clear blue eyes, and curly black hair, which was showing a few gray strands, the result of two straight years of heart-stopping adventures that included bringing down an American president and saving the life of a United States Supreme Court justice. Ginny was a few years older than Brad; a tall, slender blonde with large blue eyes, she'd grown up in the Midwest and spent several years as a nurse before applying to law school. The couple had met a little over two years ago when they were new associates at a big law firm in Portland, Oregon.

"How are the newlyweds?" Jake asked with a wide smile. Brad and Ginny blushed and Jake laughed. He had seen the couple a few weeks ago at their wedding. They'd had pale complexions and a case of nerves. Today they were deeply tanned and looked relaxed and happy.

"Tell us about the honeymoon," Dana said.

Ginny grinned. "Is what we tell you going to be a headline in your sleazy rag?"

Dana occasionally did investigative reporting for *Exposed*, a supermarket tabloid whose bread and butter was UFO, Bigfoot, and Elvis sightings, but which had won a Pulitzer for a series that had been a major factor in Christopher Farrington's loss in the presidential election to Maureen Gaylord.

Dana laughed. "None of what you say will find its way to Patrick Gorman's desk. Now, where did you go? You were very mysterious about your plans."

Just then the waiter came for their order.

"Justice Moss gave us an amazing wedding present," Ginny said as soon as the waiter left.

"Better than the Ashanti fertility doll we gave you?" Jake asked.

Dana elbowed Jake. "Let them talk."

"Ever since Brad saved Justice Moss's life, we've had the press all over us," Ginny said. "So she asked Tyrell Truman to let us stay at his estate in Hawaii so we wouldn't be hounded by reporters."

"The movie star?" Jake asked.

Brad nodded. "Justice Moss met him when she was with Martin Luther King. He wasn't a movie star then, just a struggling actor. They've been close friends ever since."

"Truman's on location somewhere in Asia, but he had his pilot fly us to the estate in his jet," Ginny said. "It had leather seats and wood trim. And they gave us Champagne and caviar."

"Yeah, but compared to Truman's estate, the plane was nothing special," Brad said.

"He's not kidding," Ginny cut in. "The place is amazing. It has its own private beach and servants, and Truman asked his personal chef to cook for us."

"You would not believe the food," Brad said. "It was French one night, Italian the next."

"I'm a burger and fries girl myself," Dana said.

"Even a peasant like you would have been impressed," Brad assured her. "I actually asked for a cheeseburger for lunch one day and it was the best cheeseburger I've ever eaten."

"With sweet potato fries and an amazing coffee milk shake," Ginny added.

The waiter returned with a big bowl of corn-and-crabmeat soup.

"So, what are you guys up to?" Brad asked as Ginny dished out the soup.

"I'm off to Afghanistan," Jake answered.

"For how long?" Brad asked.

Jake shrugged. "It's open-ended. We're going into a mountainous tribal region to interview warlords."

"That sounds dangerous," Ginny said.

"Danger is my middle name," Jake joked, but Brad could tell that Dana didn't see any humor in the assignment.

"How's the private eye business?" Brad asked.

"Okay," Dana answered. "So, what are you two going to do to feed yourselves?"

Brad noticed how quickly Dana had changed the subject, and he wondered if Dana's business was in trouble. She'd gotten a lot of publicity out of her role in the Farrington and Moss affairs and Brad assumed she'd be flooded with clients. He really liked Dana and he hoped she was doing well.

"You know I quit working at my firm?" Ginny said. Jake and Dana nodded. "Well, I'm going to start at the Department of Justice in a week."

"That should be different," Jake said.

"I hope so. After my awful experience at the Reed, Briggs firm in Portland, I should have known better than to go to work at Rankin, Lusk, Carstairs and White, but I needed the money. Two mistakes are enough. I'm sick and tired of being a wage slave at a big corporate law firm."

"What about you, Brad?" Jake asked.

"I've got a position as a legislative assistant on the staff of Senator Jack Carson of Oregon," Brad said. "I start next week."

"That should be interesting," Dana said, her voice dripping with sarcasm.

"You don't like him?" Brad asked.

"I've never met the guy, so I don't know what he's like personally, but his politics suck. I'll be amazed if he gets reelected the way he kisses up to terrorists."

"He doesn't kiss up to terrorists," Brad answered defensively. "He's said time and again that he backs our efforts to deal with al-Qaeda and other terrorist groups. He just wants a sane approach to our political strategy in the Middle East."

"A sane policy would involve nuclear weapons. I wouldn't mind seeing that whole area turned into a parking lot."

"Whoa, amigos," Jake interjected. "We are not going to let politics ruin a perfectly good dinner. Rancor is bad for digestion."

"I second that motion," Ginny said. "No politics at the dinner table, children."

Dana glared for a moment and gave Brad and Ginny a glimpse of the side of her personality that was truly scary. Dana knew no limits when it came to violence, and Brad was glad he was not her enemy.

Dana shifted gears quickly. "All right. I'll get off Brad's knee-jerk liberal back."

"And I'll agree to a truce with this fascist," Brad answered with a grin.

"I hope that this is the most controversy we're involved in all year," Ginny said, "or the rest of our lives, for that matter."

"I'll second that," Brad said. "I hope the rest of our lives are boring and that nothing of consequence ever happens to us again, ever."

"That's not going to happen if you're working in the Senate," Jake said.

"I meant in our personal lives. If I never see another serial killer or assassin again, it will be too soon. I've had it with excitement. That's why I married the dullest woman I could find."

"Hey," Ginny said, slapping him playfully.

The foursome joked back and forth for the rest of the meal. While they waited for the bill, they decided to go to a nearby bar with live jazz that Jake knew about. When the check came, they cracked open their fortune cookies and read them out loud. Everyone laughed when Jake's slip told him that he was going on a long journey. An inheritance was in Dana's future, and Ginny was going to meet a dark, handsome stranger, which got Jake going.

"What's your fortune?" Dana asked Brad.

"It's pretty bland," Brad answered, "It just says, 'May you live in interesting times.' "

Jake threw his head back and laughed.

"What's so funny?" Brad asked.

"You've never heard that before?" Jake asked.

"No."

"Well, my friend, that is an old Chinese curse."

Chapter Two

When Millie Reston woke up, the sun had not yet risen in Portland, Oregon, and it was well before her alarm was set to go off. She wasn't surprised. It had taken forever to get to sleep; then she'd been up every two hours. It was nerves, pure and simple, and there was a good reason for them.

When Millie was a child, her favorite fairy tale was Rapunzel. She would listen to her mother read the story and imagine that she was the beautiful princess locked in the tower who let down her long golden hair so the handsome prince could climb up her tresses and rescue her.

As she grew up, Millie became painfully aware that her looks weren't much to talk about. She was gawky. Her hair was dull brown, not gold, and frizzy and unmanageable. Millie's skin was far from smooth. She wasn't fat, but she was overweight and her figure was lumpy. Millie did have one serious boyfriend in college, but that hadn't worked out. Since then her social life had been bleak, and she had finally come to accept the fact that no one with or without royal blood was waiting for her.

Millie's professional life was as depressing as her social life.

Her grades in college had been good, but she didn't perform well on standardized tests like the LSATs, so she'd gotten into only second-tier law schools. Millie had graduated in the top third of her class, but the big firms wouldn't even look at graduates who weren't on the law review or from an elite law school. She had hoped that some of the smaller firms might want her. When they didn't, she had been forced to hang out a shingle, and she'd been eking out a living ever since, handling divorces, small claims, and court appointments.

Then Clarence Little came into her life and everything changed. Clarence had been sentenced to death three times for the sadistic murders of three young women, one of whom was Laurie Erickson, an eighteen-year-old who had been abducted while babysitting for Christopher Farrington when he was the governor of Oregon. The authorities believed that Little had actually killed thirteen women because that was the number of severed pinkies that had been found in a jar buried in the Deschutes National Forest.

After Farrington became the president of the United States, Brad Miller, an associate at Oregon's largest law firm, proved that Little had been framed for Erickson's murder. When Miller left Oregon to clerk at the United States Supreme Court, Millie had been appointed to represent Little in his postconviction cases.

At nine o'clock, Judge Norman Case would reveal his decision in Clarence's cases. Millie was certain that he would send them back for new trials and her triumph in Clarence's case would bring her the notoriety that had escaped her so far. She foresaw new clients willing to pay large fees for an attorney who had prevailed in the most notorious murder case in the history of Oregon, a case that had been covered by every major American news outlet and was front-page news all over the world.

Millie's father was a doctor, her mother was a college professor, one of her brothers was a neurosurgeon in Seattle, and the other had gone to Columbia for law school and was a partner in a Wall Street firm. Millie's parents doted on the boys. Though they tried to hide it, she knew that they viewed her as a disappointment. If she won Clarence's case, she would finally gain their respect.

More important, she would be saving the life of someone she loved. It was Rapunzel in reverse. The handsome prince was caged on death row, and Millie Reston was going to save him from the prison in which he had been unjustly incarcerated. For Millie believed with all her heart that Clarence was innocent.

The first time she went to the penitentiary to meet Clarence, she had been a wreck. The press had portrayed him as a monster who got sadistic pleasure out of torturing young women in the most hideous ways. But Clarence was nothing like the vicious beast in those news stories. He was charming, considerate, and soft-spoken. He took a real interest in her life and always asked Millie how she was doing. She had been surprised by her attraction to a man who was alleged to be Oregon's worst serial killer, but he seemed so sincere, and he was so warm and had treated her with respect that she rarely received from a man.

Clarence insisted that he was innocent, and he cited the *Erickson* case as proof that his convictions were in error. Millie had been leery of his protestations of innocence, but the more she learned about Clarence, the more she believed him. He was an educated man with undergraduate and master's degrees in electrical engineering. He had been employed by a reputable firm. His neighbors and coworkers had told the police that Clarence was a bit of a loner but he also participated in company social functions and was friendly at work and to the people in his neighborhood. No one could believe that Clarence was a sadistic murderer and many of those interviewed had assured the police that there had to be a mistake.

Then there were the murders themselves. The *Erickson* case was indisputably a frame-up, so why not the rest? The killer's victims had been abducted, then tortured in the most unspeakable ways for days on end. After meeting with Clarence for more than a year, Millie found it impossible to believe that he could do the horrible things of which he was accused. Spurred on by love and the knowledge that she was serving Justice by righting a great wrong, Millie had put together the best brief she had ever written, and everyone said she had been brilliant during the hearing. Clarence had brought out the best in her, and she was so certain she'd win that she had started fantasizing about further victories at Clarence's retrials, ending with the star-crossed lovers united with no bars or bulletproof glass to keep them apart.

Millie lived in an old brick apartment house just off Twenty-third Street. It was a little pricey because of the location, but it was one of the few luxuries she allowed herself. The furniture was secondhand and the art on the walls was reproductions or posters. There was a dining area, but Millie rarely entertained, and she ate her meals at a table in the small kitchen. Tea and toast was all she could handle this morning, but she enjoyed reading the paper because the *Oregonian* had a special feature about Clarence's case in the Metro section, and she was mentioned several times.

Millie had bought a new outfit for court and had gone to the beauty parlor to have her hair straightened to take out the frizz. After she applied her makeup, she rehearsed the speech she would make to the reporters after her victory, watching her facial expressions in her bathroom mirror to make sure they were just right. Then she dressed in a black business suit and sky blue silk shirt. She hoped she looked professional for the cameras, but more important was looking good for Clarence when she met with him at the penitentiary in the afternoon to tell him that he was one step closer to freedom.

The Marion County Circuit Court heard all postconviction cases because the state penitentiary was in Salem, Oregon's capital, and Salem was in Marion County. The Marion County courthouse, a dull white steel-and-glass building, was an example of fifties functional government architecture, and Judge Case's courtroom was as sexy as a DMV office, but Millie couldn't care less about her surroundings. The spectator section was packed with reporters and the curious, and every eye, including Millie's, was focused on the overweight, gray-haired man in the black robe who was seated behind the bench.

"The issue before me is whether Clarence Little's convictions for the murders of Winona Benford and Carol Poole must be reversed because evidence concerning the murder of Laurie Erickson was introduced by the prosecution at those trials," Judge Case began.

"This is an extremely troubling matter. I would say that it is the most troubling case I have handled in thirty-two years on the bench. The person responsible for the murders of these innocent young women is no common criminal; he is a monster and deserves the most severe punishment the law permits. But our Constitution requires that all trials be fair, no matter who the defendant is, and my job is to study what happened in these two trials to make certain that they meet the requirements of the constitutions of Oregon and the United States.

"In my written opinion, I have set out in great detail the evidence in Mr. Little's trials. There are great similarities in all of the crimes in the way these women were abducted, the method of torture, and of course, there is the signature removal of the victim's pinkie in each case. Yet the state concedes that Mr. Little is unquestionably innocent of murdering Miss Erickson.

"Laurie Erickson's case was one of the most highly publicized cases in recent history. Not only did it attract local interest, but it was reported nationally and internationally. Miss Erickson was abducted from the Governor's Mansion while Christopher Farrington was the governor of this state. Mr. Little's separate trials for the murders of Winona Benford, Carol Poole, and Miss Erickson took place while Mr. Farrington was the vice president of the United States.

"Mr. Little was prosecuted first for murdering Miss Benford and was convicted. He was then tried for killing Miss Poole. After he was convicted in that case, he was tried for the murder of Miss Erickson. Evidence from all three murders was introduced at each trial on the theory that the method used by the killer in all three murders was so similar that only one person could have committed all three crimes, something we now know may not be true.

"After a thorough reading of the record, I cannot in good conscience conclude that the evidence from the *Erickson* case that was introduced in Mr. Little's other trials did not affect the verdicts in those trials. Therefore, I hold that the verdicts in those cases must be set aside and the cases must be remanded to the circuit courts in the counties that tried them for whatever action the district attorneys in those counties deem appropriate.

"I hold further that no evidence from the *Erickson* case may be introduced at any retrial of the remaining cases."

Judge Case spoke for ten more minutes, but his words did not register. The moment the judge ruled for Clarence, Millie's heart soared high above the courtroom and she lost focus. She'd won the most important case of her life. She was a success. The horde of reporters who bombarded her with questions as soon as court was adjourned reinforced her belief that her life had turned a corner.

Millie parked her car in the visitors' lot at the Oregon State Penitentiary. Walls topped with razor wire and guarded by gun towers loomed above her as she walked down the lane that led from the lot to the prison's front door. Millie had no time to contemplate her somber surroundings because more reporters rushed to interview her.

Millie made a brief statement, then went into the prison reception area. She was enjoying her fame, but she was relieved that she would not have to give any more interviews for a while. Millie told the guard at the reception desk that she was there to meet with her client, Clarence Little. Then she took a seat on a green prison-made couch and started reading Judge Case's lengthy written opinion.

When the guard called Millie's name, she went through the metal detector. Her heart beat faster as she walked down a ramp that ended at a set of steel bars. The guard signaled to another guard in a control room, and the bars rolled aside. Millie entered a holding area and waited until the first bars rolled back in place and a second set opened to admit her to a short hallway. Millie had visited Clarence several times and she knew the routine. Her escort led her down the hall and opened a thick metal door. She entered the visiting area, but instead of being taken into a large open room with couches, tables, and vending machines, where a number of prisoners played with their children or talked to loved ones, she was led to a second visiting area reserved for prisoners deemed too dangerous to be permitted into the open area. Windows made of bulletproof glass were set in two of the walls. Visitors sat on folding chairs and talked to the prisoner on a phone receiver fixed to the wall.

At the end were two rooms set aside for attorney-client visits with death-row inmates. The rooms were barely large enough to accommodate a bridge chair. The guard ushered Millie inside one of them. Her chair faced a glass window set in concrete blocks painted institutional brown. A slot for passing papers had been built into the bottom of the window, and a metal ledge just wide enough to accommodate a legal pad jutted out from the wall beneath the window.

Millie was sick with excitement as she waited for Clarence. On the other side of the glass was an identical closet-size concrete-block room. A metal door in the back wall of the other room opened, and two guards led Clarence in. One of them unlocked his shackles, and the other handed him a file stuffed with legal papers.

Clarence was five eleven and wiry, with wavy brown hair and gray-blue eyes. Millie thought he was very handsome. As soon as he sat down, she picked up the receiver attached to the wall on her side of the glass and pressed it to her ear. Clarence flashed a big smile and she felt as if she could float.

"You look very nice," Clarence said as soon as the door closed behind the guards. "Is that a new suit? I don't think I've seen you in it before."

Millie was thrilled that Clarence had noticed. "I bought it this week so I'd look good in court."

He examined her thoughtfully. "Stand up and turn around for me."

Millie blushed. "I couldn't."

"Please," Clarence said with a warm smile. "I love to look at you."

Millie stood, but she was too embarrassed to meet Clarence's eye, so she looked at the floor as she turned slowly, the way she'd seen the fashion models she so envied make a turn on a reality television show she watched religiously.

"You did something to your hair, didn't you?"

Millie blushed and nodded.

"You look better every time I see you," Clarence said.

"You don't have to say those things. I know I'm a little heavy and . . ."

"Don't run yourself down," Clarence said angrily. "You have a great body. You're no string bean like those ridiculous women in the magazines. You're a real woman."

Millie didn't know what to say. The only other person who had ever complimented her figure was her college boyfriend. She doubted he had been sincere. In retrospect, it was obvious that he had flattered her so he could get her into bed.

Before that train of thought could travel very far, Millie remembered why she was in the prison. She broke into a grin, unable to contain her excitement.

"I have wonderful news."

"I know," Clarence said. "You won my postconviction cases. Thanks to you, the circuit court set aside my convictions."

Millie looked disappointed that her news wasn't a surprise. "How did you find out? The judge only ruled an hour ago. I rushed over to tell you."

"And I appreciate that, but the prison grapevine is better than the Internet. It's hard to keep news like this quiet. But I don't know how you won. That's what I'm waiting to hear."

"It was the *Erickson* case. The prosecutor introduced evidence about Erickson's murder when he prosecuted you for the murders of the other two women, but you were framed in that case."

"And the others, Millie," Little reminded her.

"I know, Clarence."

"Go on. Tell me how you pulled off this miracle."

"Judge Case held that the introduction of manufactured evidence from such a high-profile case was so prejudicial that reversal was required even though the prosecutor introduced the evidence with a good faith belief that you had committed the crime."

Clarence listened intently as Millie went over the judge's opinion in detail. When she was finished, he grinned. Then he pressed his hand to the glass. "You are brilliant, Millie. I knew it the first time we talked. I don't think anyone else could have won my case."

Millie blushed and placed her hand over his. There was a pane of cool glass between them but Millie's hand felt hot, as if Clarence were able to irradiate her skin with his love.

"What's next?" he asked.

"New trials in the *Benford* and *Poole* cases in which the state will be barred from introducing any evidence about Laurie Erickson."

"Can I count on you to represent me?"

Millie had daydreamed about winning acquittals in Clarence's trials but she was suddenly overwhelmed by insecurity.

"I don't know, Clarence. Maybe I shouldn't. I have very little trial experience, and trying a capital case . . . I don't know if I can do it."

"Of course you can. Look what you've done already. You're a special person, Millie, and this victory proves that you're a great lawyer."

"I'll have to think about handling the retrials," Millie said. "I'd feel terrible if I lost your case because I wasn't up to the job. If you ended up back on death row because of me, I wouldn't be able to live with myself."

"I don't want to force you to be my attorney if you're not comfortable. But when you're deciding, know that I have complete faith in you. You are my first choice."

Millie swallowed. She didn't want to let Clarence down. In her fantasies, she was Perry Mason incarnate, but when she thought about her abilities seriously, she had real concerns about handling a death-penalty murder case. Clarence leaned forward and spoke into the receiver in a low, confidential tone.

"Do you know why I want you and you alone to be my lawyer? I need you because you believe in me. Another lawyer will take the case for the publicity. He will assume I'm guilty. But you know I'm innocent, and that will communicate to the jurors. They will sense the insincerity in those other lawyers, but they will believe what you say because they will see that your words come from your heart."

"But what if . . ." Millie started. Clarence shook his head.

"There are no ifs, Millie. The woman who convinced Judge

Case to overturn the verdicts in my case is a master of the law and has no peers. How often do lawyers succeed in postconviction appeals? I'll tell you. The rate of success is minuscule. Yet you won. And you will be victorious when we go into court together." Clarence pressed his fist to his chest. "I know it in my heart."

Millie's eyes filled with tears of joy. No man had ever spoken to her like this. She was so choked up that she couldn't speak. Clarence smiled.

"Before I met you, I only had death to look forward to. Do you know what gives me hope when I'm locked down in my cell? When I start to get depressed, I think about sharing my freedom with you.

"When I'm free, we'll go away together to some warm place with white sand beaches and palm trees, and we'll lie in the sun and I'll be able to forget this nightmare. Will you be there with me, Millie?"

"Yes, I will. And we will win. I know it."

"Good girl. That's the Millie Reston I've come to admire. Be strong and we will prevail."

They smiled at each other. Then Clarence whispered, "Did you bring your legal memo?"

"Yes," she answered as she tried to keep her voice from shaking. Millie's good mood disappeared and fear gripped her. She had brought the memo at Clarence's request as she had once before. She felt sick. If she was caught, she could be disbarred. She might even go to jail.

Clarence asked a guard to step in. Millie slipped the memo through the slot for legal papers. The guard flipped through it. When he was convinced that contraband was not hidden between the pages he handed the memo to Clarence and left the room. Clarence read the memo and made several comments. Then he slid it back through the slot and Millie put it in her attaché case. They talked for another half hour before she left.

Millie thought she might throw up as she walked through the prison to the parking lot. When she was locked in her car, she rested her head on the steering wheel until the tension drained from her body. As soon as she was able, she drove away from the penitentiary. She didn't stop until she was back in Portland, and she didn't separate the pages of the memo until she was in her office with the door closed.

Clarence was a master of sleight of hand. Even though Millie had been watching him the whole time, she had missed seeing Clarence slip the envelope out of the file with his legal papers and into the memo. She remembered his warning to wear gloves when she handled the envelope so she wouldn't leave fingerprints. It was addressed to Brad Miller like the other envelope she'd smuggled out of the penitentiary.

On the evening of the presidential election over a year ago, Millie had waited in the parking lot of Miller's apartment complex in the dark with her lights off as the rain beat down on the roof of her car. As soon as Miller and Ginny Striker drove off to their election-night parties, Millie had slipped the envelope under Miller's door and driven away. There had been no repercussions then and Clarence assured her that there would be none this time. All he was asking her to do was mail a letter.

Chapter Three

Brad Miller had not been kidding when he told Dana Cutler and Jake Teeny that he hoped the rest of his life was dull as dirt. And Brad knew about dull as dirt. He had grown up and gone to college in the less than exciting suburbs of Long Island, then studied law in Manhattan. Living in New York sounds exotic if you're from Nebraska or South Dakota, but it is much less exciting if you're on a strict budget and studying most of each day. Brad had always been a straight arrow, so not once during his three years in school did he snort cocaine with swimsuit models while partying all night with the rich and famous at a new, in club. In fact, his only contact with drugs and wild goings-on occurred while reading police reports during an internship at the Manhattan DA's office during the summer between his first and second year in law school.

Brad fled the East Coast when his fiancée dumped him shortly before the wedding that was supposed to take place after law school graduation. What seemed tragic at first turned into a blessing in disguise when he met Ginny Striker, another associate toiling in Portland's modern-day salt mine, Reed, Briggs, Stephens, Stottlemeyer and Compton.

Brad also knew the flip side of dull as dirt. From the moment a sadistic senior partner ordered him to file an appeal in the sure loser, pro bono case of *Clarence Little v. Oregon*, his life had consisted of one terrifying incident after another. Once his investigation into Clarence's case brought down President Farrington, he thought he'd find peace and quiet clerking in the sedate halls of the United States Supreme Court, but once again he'd almost lost his life—twice.

So Brad was not lying when he said he craved boredom. He was madly in love with his wife, and his happiest moments were when he and Ginny, dressed in sweats, held hands while watching old movies on television.

Brad and Ginny lived on the third floor of a four-story redbrick apartment house on Capitol Hill. Their apartment was walking distance from the Senate and a longer walk or a Metro ride from the Department of Justice. They had moved in a little over a year ago, when Brad started clerking at the Supreme Court. They had been able to afford the rent because Ginny was pulling down a six-figure salary at one of D.C.'s biggest law firms. The rent was less affordable now that Ginny worked at the DOJ, but they loved the location, the exposed brick walls, and the small garden in the back.

The day after Judge Case handed down his decision, Brad was getting ready to leave for work while Ginny finished her breakfast in their roomy kitchen. Brad was slipping into his suit jacket when he saw the color drain from Ginny's face.

"Did you know about this?" Ginny asked, holding up page 3 of the *Washington Post*.

Brad leaned forward and read, COURT REVERSES CLARENCE LITTLE CONVICTIONS AND DEATH SENTENCES. His stomach did a swan dive.

"No," he said. "I haven't been involved in Clarence's case for over a year."

Brad reached across the kitchen table and took the paper from his wife.

"I'm not surprised," Brad said as soon as he finished the story. "They had to give him new trials once it became clear that he'd been framed in the *Erickson* case."

"He won't get out, will he?" Ginny asked. Brad could hear the fear in her voice.

"I don't know. They convicted him every time he was tried. The question is how great an impact the evidence from *Erickson* had on the jurors in the other trials. But I don't think we have anything to worry about even if he's acquitted. Clarence and I got along pretty well. He knows I'm responsible for his conviction in *Erickson* being thrown out. I believe he thinks of me as a friend, and he has no reason to hurt us."

"He's an insane serial killer, Brad. He doesn't need a reason. He was nice to you because he wanted you to work hard for him, but he'd kill either one of us without shedding a tear."

"That's true in the abstract, but why would he want to hurt me? Clarence kills women."

"In case you haven't noticed, I'm a woman."

Brad smiled. "Actually, I have noticed. But you're not the type of woman Clarence fixates on. All of his victims were teenagers or in their early twenties. You're an old married woman."

Ginny cast a stern look at Brad. "Are you're telling me I'm over the hill?"

"I admit that I married you as a humanitarian act."

"Oh well. Since you married me as an act of charity, I guess you won't be interested in having mind-bending, erotic sex tonight."

Brad couldn't help smiling at the thought. "It's true that I'm totally uninterested in sleeping with you, but now that we're married, I feel I have an obligation to keep you sexually satisfied."

Ginny cocked an eyebrow. "We'll see about tonight, buster." Then she got serious again.

"You really think we'll be okay?" she asked.

Brad gave Ginny a reassuring smile. "I do. And it's going to be a while before we have to think about Clarence Little, anyway. The state will appeal the judge's ruling. Then, if his decision is upheld, there will be the new trials. That will take years, and he'll probably get convicted. Don't let Mr. Little spoil your day."

Ginny put her plate and coffee cup in the dishwasher and went into the bathroom to finish putting on her makeup. As soon as she was out of sight, Brad's encouraging smile disappeared. Well over a year ago, on the evening of the presidential election, he and Ginny had returned to their apartment in Portland in a raging downpour. Ginny had gone to the bathroom to dry her hair, and Brad had started to go into the kitchen to put up water for tea when he'd spotted a white envelope on the entryway floor. His name and address had been handwritten, and there had been no return address. The letter was from Clarence Little.

Dear Brad,

I knew I was right to trust you. I've just learned that my conviction for the murder of the Erickson girl is going to be set aside and that's all due to your hard work. I'll still be executed, but I can live with that, if you'll pardon the pun. I'd invite you to the execution, but I know you're squeamish. My only regret is that I didn't get to go to court to overturn the conviction. I might have seen my lovely pinkie collection one last time. Oh well, one can't have everything. Good luck on your new job and your marriage to the lovely Ginny. She's a sweetheart. Too bad I won't get a chance to know her.

Your friend,

Clarence.

Brad had destroyed the letter immediately. He knew Ginny would be upset if she thought Clarence was interested in her. What Brad didn't understand was how Little was able to learn anything about Ginny. The letter had been hand-delivered, so the obvious answer was that the person who had delivered the letter had told Little about Ginny. Brad had decided against confronting his ex-client. It was better to ignore him.

Even locked up on death row, three thousand miles away, Clarence Little still scared the hell out of Brad. The idea that he might gain his freedom was terrifying. Brad hadn't lied to Ginny when he said he believed that Little appreciated what he'd done for him. But Ginny had been right. Little was a conscienceless sociopathic serial killer whose mood changed with the wind. There was no telling what he would do if he was released from custody.

Chapter Four

Unless you've stood for public office, it's almost impossible to appreciate the rigors of running for election. On Tuesday afternoon, United States Senator Jack Carson rushed from a session of the Appropriations Committee to Dulles International Airport for a three-thousand-mile cross-country trip to Oregon. As soon as the plane landed, he boarded a small plane bound for Pendleton, a city of sixteen thousand in the eastern part of the state. After the Pendleton fund-raiser, the senator brainstormed with his advisers in his hotel room before exhaustion forced him into a deep sleep. His six A.M. wake-up call shocked him into consciousness so he could be interviewed on a phone-in radio show. When the show was over, Carson vacuumed down an Egg McMuffin and a container of black coffee during a car ride to a local television station. Then it was five hours on the road, broken up by a lunch with supporters in a small Oregon town. During the rest of the ride, the senator's cell phone was pressed to his ear as he tried to coax money from his supporters while he was driven to an evening fund-raiser in a ballroom at the downtown Hilton in Portland.

By the time Carson finished his speech, posed for photo ops, and glad-handed the guests, he was punch drunk, starving, and running on fumes. But he still had to appear enthralled by Harry Butcher's tedious saga of his battle with the fifth hole of his country-club golf course, a tale that seemed to go on as long as an audio version of *War and Peace*.

"And when I climbed up out of that damn bunker and trekked up to the green, everyone was clapping," Butcher concluded. "The ball had hopped into the hole for a par. Can you believe it?"

Carson faked a hearty laugh and clapped Butcher on the shoulder. The $2,000 Butcher had forked over to attend the fund-raiser gave him the right to bore the senator to tears.

Carson looked over Butcher's shoulder and saw Martha chatting up a wealthy doctor and her socially connected spouse under a banner with large red letters blaring SEND JACK BACK. His wife hated these dinners, but she was a trouper. Butcher asked Jack a question about business taxes that he only half heard. As he finessed an answer, he saw a woman approaching, and the fog that enshrouded his brain suddenly cleared.

Carson had been a nerd in high school and college, succeeding in the classroom but failing miserably with women. Getting laid had been one of his main reasons for getting involved in college politics, but politics had not helped his sex life much until he was elected to national office and discovered that for certain women, being with a United States senator was an aphrodisiac.

Carson was of medium height with a slender build, curly brown hair, and pale blue eyes, someone you would pass on the street without a second glance. He had met his wife in a chemistry class at Cornell. She was attractive in a pleasant sort of way, and their marriage was conventional, with two children, a golden retriever named McGovern, and an estate in the country, purchased with part of a fortune Jack had made from software he had created during the dot-com boom.

Jack loved his wife, but he'd always harbored certain desires he could not reveal to Martha, desires that some of his mistresses were willing to indulge. Two years ago, a fling with a young lobbyist had ended badly enough to scare him straight. Lucas Sharp, Carson's childhood friend and his chief aide and fixer, had taken care of the matter. The senator suspected money was involved, but Lucas had done something else he would not discuss with Jack on the theory that what his boss didn't know couldn't be testified to in a grand jury. Whatever Lucas had done had worked, because the girl moved back to Indiana two days after Sharp met with her.

Jack had stayed on the straight and narrow after that unnerving fiasco, but the mere sight of this woman in her tight black dress caused a raft of fetishes to sail out of the senator's subconscious. If his PR firm had concocted a slogan for her, it would have been SEX, set off in blazing scarlet letters. She had high cheekbones, a dark complexion that hinted at Middle Eastern ancestry, silky black hair that fell past her shoulders, lightly muscled, long, tanned legs, and a self-confident air. She waited patiently as Carson got rid of Butcher, then walked close enough for Jack to smell her perfume before extending her hand.

"I don't believe we've met, Senator. My name is Jessica Koshani."

Carson took the hand willingly. It was warm to the touch, and he felt a slight shock of sexual pleasure from the contact.

"Pleased to meet you," was the best he could come up with.

"I loved your speech," Koshani said. "You're one of the few voices of reason in Middle East policy."

"Thank you," Carson answered, fighting the heat he felt rising in his cheeks as he struggled to keep his tone professional.

"I realize you're tired. These fund-raisers must be exhausting. But I would like to meet with you to hand over some sizable campaign donations. They're from a few of my business acquaintances who admire your work." Koshani fixed her large brown eyes on him and smiled in a way that brought more heat to another part of his body. "Would you be able to come to my home in Dunthorpe sometime this week? It will definitely be worth the trip."

The practical part of Carson's brain took precedence over his lizard brain for a second. Dunthorpe was where some of the wealthiest members of Portland society lived. If Koshani had a home in Dunthorpe, she would be connected. Jack was in a fight to the death with a well-heeled opponent, and he needed all the money he could get. He also wanted a chance to see Koshani again.

"I do happen to be free Thursday evening."

"Wonderful," Koshani said as she handed Jack a business card with her name, a telephone number, and the word INVESTMENTS.

"I've written my address on the back. Shall we say eight?"

"I'll be there."

Koshani smiled and walked away. Seconds later, Lucas Sharp was at the senator's side. Physically, Lucas was everything Jack Carson was not. The African American was a shade over six feet tall, compact and muscular, with a smooth shaved skull that made him look dangerous. Lucas had wrestled and played football in high school, but he'd also had a near-perfect GPA. Brainpower was the bond that made Jack and Lucas best friends. Sharp would not tolerate a single word against his nerdy white friend and had protected him from bullies from elementary school through high school.

The friendship had blossomed at Cornell, where Sharp's intellect was valued above his wrestling skills and he could let his interest in computer science run free. While attending law school at Harvard, Sharp had made major contributions to the software Carson had developed in graduate school at MIT, and he'd shared in the financial windfall when the patent was sold to Microsoft. Though he didn't need the money, Lucas worked as a Multnomah County district attorney for four years before quitting when Jack decided to run for Congress. Jack relished the spotlight, but Sharp preferred working behind the scenes.

"What was that about?" Sharp asked when Koshani was out of earshot.

"She wants to meet with me to discuss a major contribution to the campaign."

"Don't take it," Sharp warned.

Carson frowned. "Why not?'

"Do you know who that is?"

"She said her name was Jessica Koshani."

Sharp nodded. "Koshani's name came up more than once when I was in the DA's office. She's involved with a number of legitimate enterprises, but there was a suspicion that they were fronts for other not-so-legal ventures."

"Such as?"

"Money laundering through some of the businesses."

"For who?"

"Drug dealers, arms dealers, and she's rumored to be the silent partner in a high-end escort service."

Carson kept his features blank, but he felt the stirring of an erection.

"So there's no solid proof that Ms. Koshani is doing anything illegal?"

"No."

"Then I see no problem in meeting with her."

"There could be problems later, if Lang's people start spreading rumors."

"We need the money, Luke. You've seen the polls. Lang has closed the gap. I started ten percentage points ahead, and it's down to one. And it's the damned TV ads he's been running. If we don't come up with enough money to run our own, I could lose."

"It's not just the money I'm worried about."

"I'm a big boy, Luke. I can keep my zipper closed."

"History would suggest otherwise," his friend answered. Carson blushed and broke eye contact.

"When are you meeting?" Sharp asked.

"Thursday evening."

"Damn, I'll be in Medford."

"Look," Carson said, his tone softening, "I appreciate the warning but you don't have to babysit me. I'll be okay."

Sharp started to say something, but caught himself when he saw Martha weaving her way toward them through the round tables that the waitstaff was starting to clear. He loved Jack Carson like a brother, and he worried about him. Jack was brilliant, but he could be very stupid when it came to women.

Chapter Five

Brad was enjoying his job as a legislative assistant to Senator Carson, but he soon found that the pace of work was much faster than the pace at the United States Supreme Court. There were two gears in Senator Carson's office, fast and slow. When the Senate was not in session or the senator was not in D.C., Brad could dress casually and come to work a little later than usual, although he had so much work even in slow gear that he was at the office by eight and didn't leave until six or seven. When the Senate was in session or the senator was in D.C., he was expected to dress in a suit and tie, everything ran at hyper speed, and he might not get home until after ten.

Eating breakfast at home was a luxury Brad could not afford, no matter what the gear. Almost all of the staffers grabbed breakfast in one of the Capitol cafeterias and ate at their desks. Brad's staple was orange juice, a toasted bagel, and coffee. While he ate, he was expected to digest not only food but the contents of the *Oregonian*, Portland's daily paper, the *New York Times*, the *Washington Post*, the *Los Angeles Times*, and the *Congressional Quarterly*, a privately produced paper that covered every legislative action in Congress and that Brad found stacked at the entrance to the senator's office every day.

When he was hired, Brad had been assigned a portfolio heavy on legal issues. Lucas Sharp, the senator's chief of staff, had told him to start each day by scanning publications for issues in his portfolio. Brad was expected to be up to speed on every issue in his portfolio so he could advise Senator Carson on whether to support, oppose, or try to modify a piece of legislation. Sharp had warned Brad that the worst thing that could happen to him was to field a call from his boss about an article he had not read. In addition to reading the papers, Brad learned about each subject by talking to the staffs of NGOs, lobbyists, concerned citizens, representatives of labor and business, and anyone else who had a view on an issue.

Senators' offices were located in three buildings: Russell, the oldest; Dirksen, the second oldest; and Hart, the new kid on the block. The party in power had first choice of offices and the senators chose in order of seniority. After an election, life in the Senate was like a game of musical chairs. When a party out of power gained a majority, the losing party's senators had to move if the winners wanted their offices.

Senator Carson's office was in Dirksen. Hart was the building closest to Brad's apartment, and he usually used its staff entrance so he could get inside as fast as possible. D.C. was freezing in winter and hot and humid in summer. A corridor in Hart led to the Dirksen building and was one of many corridors and underground tunnels that connected the office buildings to each other and the Capitol.

Brad had convinced himself that there was no reason to worry about Clarence Little, but two days after reading about the reversal of Little's convictions, Brad's self-confidence evaporated. Brad rarely received personal mail at his Senate office, so he was surprised to find the plain white envelope with no return address sitting on his blotter when he got back from lunch. Then he recognized the handwriting on the envelope. It was identical to the writing on the envelope he had received on the evening of the presidential election. Brad's mouth was dry, and he felt slightly nauseated as he opened the envelope and read the letter it contained.

> Dear Brad,
>
> I hope this letter finds you in good health and enjoying your exciting new job. There is plenty of excitement here on death row, too. My convictions have been reversed. I will soon have new trials, which I hope will end in "Not Guilty" verdicts and freedom. Wouldn't it be wonderful if I could visit you and your lovely bride in our nation's capital? And, speaking of Ginny, how is the love of your life? I hope things are still piping hot between you two.
>
> Your Friend,
> Clarence

Who had smuggled this letter and the letter Clarence had sent him on the night Maureen Gaylord was elected president out of the penitentiary? Was it a guard Little had bribed or his attorney? Brad decided that it wasn't worth his time to find out.

Should he write Little and tell him to stop writing? No, that would just encourage the psychopath. Brad hadn't answered Clarence's first letter, and he decided that he wouldn't answer this one.

Brad thought about the new trials. After mentally reviewing everything he knew about the cases, he concluded that the chance of Little winning his freedom was small. The best that could happen if he got a top-flight attorney was a life sentence. When Brad calmed down, he started to crumple up the letter to use in a game of wastepaper basketball, but he stopped and put it in the lower drawer of his desk instead.

Chapter Six

A cold rain carrying the salty, seaweed scents of the ocean pelted Ali Bashar as he stood at the rail of the freighter.

"America!" Ali said to the stocky, stone-faced man who stood beside him. His companion turned toward Ali for a second, then turned away. His dark, cold eyes showed none of the excitement Ali felt, as if passion for anything but his mission had been leached out of the man in the camp. Ali believed himself to be as dedicated as the others, but he still retained a sense of wonder.

Ali's dark complexion and milk-chocolate-colored eyes were common among the tribal people who grew up in the mountainous section of Pakistan where he had been born. His straight black hair was concealed beneath a knit watch cap, and he wore a heavy pea jacket as protection against weather that Manhattanites would consider uncomfortable but which chilled the blood of someone who had spent the last eight months in the desert. Ali was five feet eight and had been sick frequently when he was a child, so his constitution was frail. When he was young, he had been the butt of many jokes and the object of the cruelty that comes naturally to children. Ali was bright, was especially good with numbers, and had an excellent memory. These traits had helped him to excel in the classroom but often made his life outside of it difficult. His intelligence had finally been rewarded at the al-Qaeda camp in Somalia, but the physical part of the training had been difficult for him.

Ali's time in the camp and his brief stay in Karachi, where he had been smuggled aboard the freighter, were his only experiences in the world outside his village. As the freighter pulled into New York Harbor, he stared wide-eyed at the Statue of Liberty and New York's skyline. Then he looked for the empty space in the skyline where the Twin Towers had stood, and he smiled. He had been shown the destruction of the Towers several times on a television in the camp. He didn't know why he and his three companions were being smuggled into America, but he believed that he would soon be part of something that would make the self-absorbed, godless citizens of the United States forget about September 11.

The freighter was registered in Liberia, but the captain was a Pakistani, as were many in the crew. Ali and the others had fit in, and they all had false papers and cover stories that would hold up under all but the most intense scrutiny. It was dusk when the freighter docked, and the pier was spotlighted when the crew began unloading the cargo. Ali and his companions mingled with the rest of the crew as they shifted crates containing machine parts from the ship to the dock, but they peeled off from the legitimate crew members when a nondescript taupe station wagon glided down the pier and pulled up next to a pallet piled high with wooden crates. They had been told about the station wagon just before they boarded the freighter.

Ali slid into the passenger seat next to the driver, who wore a New York Yankees jacket and baseball cap.

"I'm Steve, and I'm going to take you to a safe house near Washington, D.C.," he said in perfect Urdu. "When we get to the gate, let me do the talking. If the guard asks you a question, I'll tell him you don't speak English and I'll translate."

The man's looks and accent convinced Ali that the driver was an American. This surprised him. He had met Americans sympathetic to the cause at the camp, but they had been blacks who had converted to Islam or young, disaffected Arab Americans. This American had blue eyes to go with the blond hair that crept out from beneath his cap.

English was the second official language of Pakistan, and Ali was conversant in it. His stomach was in a knot when they pulled up to the gate, and he listened carefully when the driver spoke to the uniformed guards. He was expecting the guards to demand his papers and subject him to an interrogation he was not convinced he could withstand, but they let the station wagon through without any trouble. Ali wondered if a bribe had changed hands.

Steve didn't say much after they left the dock. Ali and his companions strained to see the sights as they passed through Manhattan, but they were exhausted, and all but Ali nodded off as soon as they were on the interstate headed south.

"You are American?" Ali asked as soon as he got up the nerve to start a conversation.

Steve nodded.

"You are Muslim?"

The driver nodded again.

"Is that why you help us?"

Steve turned his head toward Ali. When he was talking to the guards, Steve had looked like the star of an American sitcom Ali had been shown in the camp to help with his training; all smiles, joking about trivial matters. Now he looked dangerous.

"The less you know about me, the better off you are, understood?" he asked in a hard, cold tone.

"Of course," Ali answered, backing off immediately. Fear of abuse had been nurtured in Ali since early childhood, and he never did well in physical confrontations.

Ali turned away and closed his eyes, but he didn't fall asleep immediately. To distract himself, he thought of all the possible targets in America's capital. Which one would he destroy in the name of Allah? When he fell asleep, there was a contented smile on his lips.

It was still dark when Ali woke up. He felt dull witted and spent a few moments rubbing sleep from his eyes. There was a sour taste in his mouth. The station wagon was driving down a dirt road in rural Maryland. Steve pulled into the driveway of a ranch-style house and woke up the sleeping men.

"This is where you'll be staying until we're ready to act," he said. "The refrigerator is fully stocked, and there's cable television. I'll make runs with groceries around this time, once a week. If there are problems, tell me then. I'll give you a cell phone number, but it's only for emergencies. Remember, the Americans can listen in on your calls. You'll ask for pizza, and I'll say you have the wrong number. Then I'll come right over.

"This house is pretty isolated. The nearest neighbors are a quarter mile away. You shouldn't get visitors. If you do, tell them you're students, and use the cover story you were given. Any questions?"

Steve showed them around the house and got them set up. There were clothes in the closets in everyone's size and food in the kitchen.

"You'll receive instructions soon," Steve said before he left. "Be patient and trust in Allah. You will make history."

Despite the sleep he had gotten during the drive, Ali was logy when they arrived at the house. His initial elation in the harbor was gone. Before he'd gotten out of the car, he was beset by doubts that depressed him. Things could go wrong. They could fail. The CIA and FBI were not fools. What if they were caught?

Steve's last words elated Ali and erased his doubts. Allah was great, and he would see to their success. Steve closed the door behind him. Ali heard the car start. He looked through the slats in the Venetian blinds in the living room and watched the station wagon drive off. It had a Virginia license plate, and Ali memorized it when it passed beneath a streetlight. There was no reason for him to do it. He was just good with numbers and had an excellent memory, and the license plate number was filed away without much conscious thought.

Chapter Seven

The weather in Portland was unseasonably warm, and Jack Carson kept his window rolled down as he drove to Dunthorpe, eschewing air conditioning for the breeze that drifted off the Willamette River. In the distance, Mount Hood loomed, the setting sun tinting its snowy coat to a lovely rose color, but Jack was too on edge to take in the beauty of his surroundings. Normally, he would have had an aide drive him, but he'd given his staff the night off. He'd convinced himself that he'd done this because they'd been working hard and needed some downtime, but his subconscious was rife with images of Jessica Koshani naked and in bed, something he'd never see if a young staffer was waiting in his car or camping out in some part of Koshani's house.

Carson followed Koshani's directions and turned toward the river onto a narrow street that wound between large homes surrounded by expensively landscaped grounds. The house he was looking for was guarded by a gate that swung open moments after he announced himself through an intercom. Jack drove into a courtyard and parked near the front door of a house that was similar to Italian villas he'd seen during a family trip to Tuscany.

Jessica Koshani was waiting for him at the front door, her jet black hair falling loosely across the shoulders of a yellow blouse that was tucked into tight jeans that emphasized her long legs.

"I'm so glad you could make it," she said when the senator got out of his car.

"This is very nice," he answered.

"We'll go around back to the patio. It looks out on the river. It's wonderful being outdoors at this time of night. Can I get you something cool to drink? I make a mean martini, and I've got a full bar."

"Gin and tonic would be great."

"What brand of gin do you prefer?" she asked as she led him through a large living room toward French doors that opened onto a wide terra-cotta patio.

Koshani left the senator with the view while she went inside to fix his drink. His heart rate was up and his mouth was dry. He tried to calm himself and hoped that the gin would help. Koshani walked out of the house with two drinks. His glass felt cold and damp against his hand. He took a quick sip and the cool lime taste chilled him.

"This is a great spot," Carson said.

"As soon as the weather turns, I'm out here every chance I get." Koshani smiled. "But you're not here to talk about the view."

Carson had noticed a manila envelope lying on a glass end table at Koshani's elbow. She handed it to him. He opened it and took out five checks. Each was to the account of a different business situated in a different state and each was for twenty-five thousand dollars.

"This is very generous," Carson said.

"Senator, you are one of only a few congressmen who are

objective about American aggression in the Middle East. Neither I nor any of the people who have made these contributions have any sympathy for terrorists. They do not represent true Islam, and they have turned the world against every Muslim. We value a man with the courage to say that American policy in the Middle East might be wrong and not all Muslims are psychotic terrorists; a man who knows that most Muslims are men and women like the men and women in America, who only want to provide for their families and would love to live in a world where peace reigns."

Carson blushed as Koshani showered him with praise. "I've always tried to keep an open mind." He smiled. "I like to think my open-mindedness is a product of my scientific training."

Koshani nodded. "There is no doubt that you are one of the most intelligent senators. I often wish there were more scientists in the legislature, people trained to avoid jumping to conclusions unsupported by evidence."

Koshani and the senator continued to talk about politics, world affairs, and many other subjects as the sun set. Koshani stroked his ego and provided him with several more cooling drinks. By the second drink, the senator's thinking had become a bit muddled, and he realized that he was becoming sexually aroused. He chalked up his agitated and confused state to the proverbial one drink too many, not to anything Koshani may have slipped into his gin and tonic. When he finally stood to leave, Carson wobbled a bit and Koshani pressed close to brace him. Carson had no idea how it happened, but moments after he stumbled, he had wrapped his arms around Koshani and they were kissing while her hand stroked him gently but urgently. When he left for home, he was thoroughly exhausted and completely sated by the most explosive sex he had ever experienced.

Part II

Love Hurts

Chapter Eight

The moment Millie Reston woke up, she knew she was beginning one of the best days of her life, and life had been pretty good lately. When Judge Case ordered new trials for Clarence, every television station in the state featured the interview she'd given after court, and she became the hot new attorney in town. The retainer that the parents of a man convicted of murder had paid her to handle his appeal would cover her rent for the next two years; a drug dealer who had exhausted his appeals paid her an outrageous sum to file for habeas corpus relief in federal court; and there were less extravagant retainers that, taken together, amounted to a tidy sum. Millie would never have had the courage to ask for the money she'd quoted these clients if it hadn't been for the self-confidence Clarence's love had fostered.

The penitentiary was for convicted felons. As soon as his convictions were set aside, Clarence was presumed innocent of the charges against him, and he had been transferred to the Multnomah County jail in downtown Portland, a few blocks from her office. In anticipation of the transfer, Millie had sprung for a makeover and had had her hair styled in Portland's top salon.

After she showered and applied her makeup, she put on a new outfit she had purchased especially for today, the first day she and Clarence would be able to touch each other without bullet-proof glass to stop the warmth from passing from Clarence's hand into hers.

Millie hummed as she drove downtown. After parking in a lot near her office, she walked to the Justice Center, a modern sixteen-story, concrete-and-glass building that was separated from the Multnomah County Courthouse by a park. The Justice Center housed several courtrooms, State Parole and Probation, the Central Precinct of the Portland Police Bureau, a branch of the district attorney's office, and the Multnomah County jail.

The jail occupied the fourth through tenth floors in the building, but the reception area was on the second floor. Millie walked through a glass-vaulted lobby filled with police officers, attorneys, defendants, and others having business in this hall of sorrows. When she passed the curving stairs that led to the courtrooms on the third floor, she pushed through a pair of glass doors. A sheriff's deputy was manning the reception desk. He searched Millie's briefcase after checking her ID, then motioned her through the metal detector that stood between the reception area and the jail elevator. As soon as Millie passed through the metal detector without setting off any alarms, the guard walked her to the elevator and keyed her up to the floor where Clarence was being held.

After a short ride, the elevator doors opened, and Millie stepped into a narrow hall with a thick metal door at one end. Next to the door, affixed to a pastel yellow concrete wall, was an intercom. Millie used it to announce her presence. Moments later, a uniformed guard peered at her through a plate of glass in the upper part of the door before speaking into a walkie-talkie. Electronic locks snapped and the guard ushered Millie into a narrow corridor that ran the length of three contact visiting rooms. The interior of each room could be seen from the corridor through a large window.

The guard opened the door to the first room. Then he pointed to a black button affixed to the wall.

"Your client will be brought over in a few minutes. When you need to leave—or if there's any trouble—press the button."

The only furnishings in the concrete room were two orange molded plastic chairs set on either side of a round, Formica-topped table that was bolted to the floor. The guard left, and Millie took the chair that faced a steel door on the side of the room across from the corridor. As Millie stared at the door her heart beat faster. The man she loved would enter through it in minutes. She was trembling and her hand shook when she tried to open the clasp on her attaché case. Just as she started to take out the papers she had brought, the electronic locks on the rear door snapped open and two guards led Clarence into the room. He was dressed in an orange jumpsuit, and the first things Millie noticed were that he had let his hair grow and he was putting on weight. Clarence had always been lean, but now he looked a little lumpy, and she credited the starchy jail food for the extra weight. When Clarence was free, they could both go on a diet and slim down.

Manacles securing Clarence's ankles and wrists restricted his movements, but he shuffled forward with a huge smile on his face. The first guard pulled Clarence's chair away from the table so he could sit down. When he was sitting, the other guard unlocked his chains.

"Buzz when you're done," one of the guards said. Then they left Millie and Clarence alone.

Clarence looked her up and down. "I love your hair. You had it done, didn't you?"

Millie blushed. "I wanted to look good for you."

"Well, you succeeded. You look great, and I'm honored that you went to all this trouble for me. I don't imagine you have much free time. You must be incredibly busy after the publicity you've gotten."

Millie couldn't help grinning. "My business has been amazing. I'm actually turning away cases."

"You deserve your success. It's not every attorney who could have convinced Judge Case to reverse two murder cases as notorious as mine."

Clarence paused and stared into Millie's eyes. Then he reached across the table and took her hand in his. Millie felt an electric charge pass between them.

"Thank you for standing up for me," Clarence said. Then he released her hand and looked down at the tabletop. Millie had the impression that he was gathering his courage to broach something important. When he looked up, he radiated none of the self-confidence she was used to seeing.

"Millie, maybe this is premature but . . . well, when I'm free—and I know you'll help me gain my freedom—would you consider . . ."

Clarence paused. Then he flashed a shy smile. "I'm sorry, but when I'm around you, well, you make me so happy, but you also make me nervous." He took a deep breath and looked Millie in the eye. "I should have a ring with a diamond as big as the moon, but," he said, turning his palms up, "Tiffany won't deliver in here."

Millie couldn't breathe.

"What I'm trying to say is, would you consider marrying me?"

Millie had dreamed about this moment, and now that Clarence had proposed, she was speechless. Clarence stopped smiling. He looked so sad. Then his eyes dropped to the tabletop again.

"I'm sorry. I shouldn't have asked. I . . ."

Millie reached out and covered Clarence's hands with hers.

"Don't be sorry. I'm just so happy I couldn't speak. Of course I'll marry you. I love you."

Clarence looked up, a wide smile on his face. "Thank you, Millie. You've made me the happiest man in the world. I wish I could kiss you but . . ." He nodded at the closed-circuit camera that was fixed to the wall. "But soon, Millie, soon we'll be together, and we'll be able to kiss and . . . and make love."

The blood rushed to Millie's cheeks.

"I hope I haven't shocked you, but I've wanted to hold you for so long."

"I want to be with you, too."

"You will be, as soon as I'm acquitted. Do you know when my first trial will be held?"

"I talked to Monte Pike. He's the chief criminal deputy, and he's prosecuting. We're going to have a scheduling conference soon to work out the logistics; which case to try first, dates, that sort of thing."

"Good. Please tell me as soon as you know."

"I will."

"There is something else I'd like you to do."

"Anything."

Clarence smiled. "This shouldn't be too difficult. Can you get the judge to order the jail to let me wear a suit and tie when I'm in court? There are going to be television cameras all over the place, and I don't want potential jurors seeing me like this," he said, pointing to the jumpsuit.

"I'll do it today. And I'll buy you a beautiful suit and tie. You'll look just like a lawyer."

For the rest of the meeting, Millie and Clarence talked about the wedding and where they would go on their honeymoon. Clarence hinted that he had money that he would use to treat her like a princess, and Millie was afraid that her heart would burst from joy.

Finally Millie had to end the conference because she had to get back to her office to meet a new client. She rang for the guard. As she walked down the corridor away from the visiting room, she kept her eyes on Clarence until the concrete wall blocked her view of her beloved.

Millie arrived at her office with no memory of the trip from the Justice Center. The phrase *walking on air* came to her, and she suddenly knew what it meant. She had accepted the fact that she would go through life alone, but now, through a miracle, she was in love with a man who loved her. She smiled. She couldn't help herself. She would gain freedom for Clarence, and in so doing, she would free herself from a life of loneliness.

Chapter Nine

The Senate of ancient Rome was the inspiration for the United States Senate; the name is derived from *senatus*, which is Latin for "council of elders." The American Senate is often described as the world's greatest deliberative body, and membership in this exclusive club is more prestigious than membership in the House of Representatives. If you are a congressman from California, Texas, or New York, you are one of thirty to fifty people who can make that claim. Only two people from each state can serve in the Senate. The only qualifications for the office are that one must be at least thirty years old, a citizen of the United States for at least the past nine years, and an inhabitant at the time of the election of the state one wishes to represent.

The halls of the Dirksen Building were usually filled with casually dressed vacationers and groups of self-important men and women clothed in power suits on a mission to get this or that done. The constant din was a sharp contrast to the quiet in the halls of the United States Supreme Court, where Brad had just finished a year as a law clerk. At the Court, silence was the norm, visitors were few, and lobbyists were strictly prohibited.

An American flag and the Oregon State flag stood on either side of the main door to Senator Carson's suite of offices on the second floor of the Dirksen Building. Visitors entered a reception area where a young man and a young woman greeted them when they were not dealing with a constant flood of telephone calls. When the Senate was in session, the waiting room was usually filled with vacationing Oregonians who wanted to say hello to the man they had helped to elect and with constituents and lobbyists who wanted something from him.

When a senator moved in, the office was deconstructed, then rearranged for the senator's needs. Walls went up to create offices of various sizes for the staff. A door in the reception area opened into a narrow, crowded corridor that ended at Senator Carson's large corner office. A cubicle occupied by one of the legislative correspondents, who answered the letters the senator received every day, formed a barrier between the corridor and Brad's office.

The offices for legislative assistants were small but looked different, depending on the occupant. All were furnished with bookshelves, gray metal filing cabinets, and desks, but some of the spaces were neat and well organized, while chaos reigned in others. Brad's office was in between these extremes. His desk was neat, but he was starting to use the floor as extra filing space, and it would not be long before it resembled an obstacle course.

Much of the Senate's important work begins in committees, which review legislation and oversee the executive branch. One of Brad's jobs was to help Senator Carson prepare witnesses who were going to testify in front of one of the committees on which he sat. The testimony of these witnesses was received in writing the night before they were going to testify but was embargoed to the press. Brad was preparing a list of questions to ask a witness who was going to testify in favor of an immigration bill the Judiciary Committee was considering when the senator sent for him.

Senator Carson had hired an interior decorator, and his office now had a regal look. A credenza filled with books on various subjects on which the senator had to be educated stood under a window with a view of Union Station. A set of chairs with polished wood arms and burgundy upholstery sat along a wall decorated with photographs, framed newspaper pages, and awards that highlighted important events in the senator's business and political careers. Across the way, a long, comfortable sofa sat kitty-corner to a second, smaller sofa and opposite two high-backed armchairs. A coffee table holding two coffee-table books with photos of Oregon's spectacular scenery stood between the large sofa and the chairs.

A recess with a flat-screen monitor and a computer keyboard occupied another wall. Senator Carson sat in front of the recess behind a large wood desk and listened while Brad briefed him on the witnesses who would testify about the immigration bill. They had been talking for twenty minutes when the senator's secretary buzzed to tell him that Senator Elizabeth Rivera of New Mexico, the chairperson of the Senate Select Committee on Intelligence, was holding on line 3.

Jack Carson was a member of the Select Committee on Intelligence, which oversees the United States intelligence community, including the Office of the Director of National Intelligence, the Central Intelligence Agency, the Defense Intelligence Agency, the Federal Bureau of Investigation, and the National Security Agency, among others. Since 9/11 the importance of this committee had increased, and he made sure that his constituents knew that he was important enough to have been made a member.

"Good morning, Betsy," Carson said as soon as they were connected. "What's up?"

"We're convening a special session of the SSCI in one-half hour. Can you make it?"

"I'll be up," he told Senator Rivera.

When the call ended, Carson buzzed his secretary. "Francis, do I have a meeting at ten thirty?"

"You're scheduled to meet with a delegation of Oregon filbert farmers."

"Shit! Look, I've got an emergency meeting with Intelligence. Can you get Kathy to cover for me?"

"Sure thing."

"Have her mention national security. I hope the filbert growers won't be too pissed off at me for not being able to hear their gripes in person. And send Luke in, will you?"

The senator turned to Brad. "Come with me, Brad. You'll find this interesting."

"Are you sure I can go?" Brad asked. "I don't have a top-secret clearance."

"I'm a U.S. senator, which means I can do pretty much anything I want. You've got a law degree, and I don't. And I want my lawyer with me."

Brad entered the most secure room in the Senate through a pair of unmarked frosted-glass doors and found himself in a waiting area decorated with pictures of men and women who had served as the chair of the SSCI.

"You'll have to leave all of your electronic devices," Lucas Sharp said as he took out his BlackBerry and handed it across a wooden barrier to a stern-looking Capitol Hill policewoman, who placed it in one of many cubbyholes that filled the wall to her left. Brad emptied his pockets and followed the senator and his chief of staff through a door into a corridor with bookshelves on the right and an alcove on the left with a telephone and a small round table surrounded by four chairs.

The door to the hearing room was open. Looked at head-on, it appeared to be a normal wood door, but Brad could see that it was steel and had the thickness of a door to a vault. On his way to the door, Brad walked by a conference room with a regular phone and a secure, encrypted phone.

In the center of the conference room was a long rectangular table furnished with comfortable high-backed leather chairs. A plaque identified each senator's place at the table. The room was swept daily for bugs, and the walls were thick enough to foil anyone trying to hear what went on. No personal electronic devices were allowed, but there was a television at each place with a view of the Senate floor so the senators could see if they were needed for a vote. The television could also show videos of drone strikes in Afghanistan or other top-secret operations. Chairs lined the walls behind the senators, and Lucas told Brad these were for the senators' aides. While Sharp was speaking, Brad noticed a man sitting at the far end of the conference table. Brad recognized him as someone he had seen on TV.

Dr. Emil Ibanescu, the deputy director of national intelligence, was a balding, middle-aged man with a sallow complexion. He was wearing an expensive tailored suit, but his paunchy build made it look lumpy. Ibanescu's parents had emigrated from

Romania when Emil was seven. He had graduated at the top of his public high school class in Brooklyn with a perfect grade-point average. Scholarships had covered his tuition at Harvard, where he earned a PhD in record time. Ibanescu spoke many languages, most of them fluently, and had fast-tracked through the CIA. When the Office of the Director of National Intelligence was formed in 2005 to oversee and direct the National Intelligence Program, Ibanescu was tapped to serve as a deputy director.

"Something must be up if Emil is here," Lucas said. Carson took his seat without comment. Brad and Lucas sat behind him with their backs to the wall, and an aide shut the door.

"Let's get started," Senator Rivera said. "Dr. Ibanescu is here to brief us on a very real threat to our national security. Emil, why don't you take the floor?"

"Thank you, Madam Chairperson." Ibanescu's speech betrayed a faint hint of Eastern Europe. "In the past year, we have received information from multiple sources pointing to the strong possibility that a major terrorist operation is under way in the United States. We are facing two obstacles. First, we know the event is scheduled to take place in the near future, but we have not identified the target. Second, we are convinced that the group that is behind this plot is centered in Pakistan, but the group is not al-Qaeda or any other known terrorist group. This means that monitoring these known terror networks has not provided the information we need to foil the plot."

"It doesn't sound as if you've made much headway here," said Senator Allen McElroy of Alabama.

"That's true. Because this plot is the work of a small unknown group, many of our methods of gathering intelligence have not been particularly useful. However, there is some good news. We have obtained one solid lead in the past few days. InCo, an Oregon company, may be involved in laundering money that is being used to finance part of this operation."

Behind Carson, Lucas Sharp shifted in his chair.

"Our evidence is not conclusive," Ibanescu continued, "but we're putting together an affidavit for a search warrant for the company records. Hopefully we will know more in the next few days. The purpose of this briefing is to let the committee know about this potential event. If it happens, there could be as much damage to the national psyche as there was after 9/11, and we want you to be prepared."

Ibanescu's report continued for twenty minutes more. By the constant movement behind him, Carson could sense that Lucas Sharp was uneasy. Carson looked over his shoulder and Sharp caught his eye. He was very tense.

As soon as the meeting adjourned, Sharp told Brad that he had to speak to the senator in private. Then he pulled his friend into an empty meeting room and shut the door.

"Do you remember talking to a woman named Jessica Koshani two months ago at the Hilton fund-raiser?" Sharp asked as he watched his friend intently.

Carson couldn't stop the heat from rising in his cheeks. Sharp noticed.

"Koshani, yes. She and some of her business associates gave us a sizable contribution."

"Is anything going on between you and Koshani?" Sharp asked.

"Nothing. She's just a supporter," the senator stammered. His answer wasn't convincing.

"I hope to God you're telling me the truth, Jack. Remember the night you met Koshani at the fund-raiser at the Hilton?"

Carson nodded.

"Do you also recall my telling you that she'd been the subject of discussions when I was in the DA's office?"

"Yes."

"And do you remember I told you she was suspected of laundering money through several companies? One of the companies we discussed when I was a prosecutor was InCo."

"Oh, shit."

"Yeah, 'shit.' I don't think it will go over well with your constituents if it's revealed that one of your supporters is also supporting terrorists."

Carson started to sweat. "Emil didn't mention Jessica."

"He didn't mention a lot of stuff. The people running this operation worry about leaks, for which politicians are notorious. So, Jack, how bad is this?"

"It's not bad," Carson answered, fighting hard to keep calm.

"Did you screw her?"

Carson's eyes dropped. "Just one time," he lied. "I had a little too much to drink."

"Fuck!"

"We'll be fine. Don't worry."

"You pay me to worry."

"We'll be fine," Carson repeated, but like a lot of things he said on the campaign trail, he didn't believe one word of what he had just told his best friend.

Chapter Ten

"Jessica, it's me, Jack. I have to talk to you."

"It's two in the morning. What's wrong with you?"

"I'm at the gate. Let me in. I flew all night to get here."

"You know the rules. We meet when I say we meet."

"This isn't about sex. It's urgent and it concerns your future, your life."

Koshani was silent for a moment. Then the gate swung open and Carson ran a hand across his face. He was a mess. Ever since his first night with Jessica Koshani, he had been her slave. He craved her the way an addict craves his drug. He was besotted, and he lived for the infrequent times she permitted him to see her, times she rationed out slowly so that the days between became sheer torture. And now this. Everything he'd worked for could crash and burn.

The senator was terrified that Koshani's house was under surveillance, so he was wearing jeans, a dark jacket, sunglasses, and a baseball cap, and he parked in the shadows so his rental car could not be seen from the gate. The front door opened and he rushed inside. Koshani was wearing a black see-through teddy, and the sight of her near-naked body stopped his breath.

"We're in trouble," he blurted out, praying that the CIA had not bugged the mansion.

"Stop," Koshani commanded, and he obeyed. "We'll talk upstairs in my bedroom."

Koshani turned and Carson's eyes followed her tight, swaying buttocks as she walked up to the second floor. It was difficult for him to think so close to her. Despite the danger, he grew hard.

When they entered the bedroom, Koshani turned and looked at him with contempt.

"Why are you here?" she demanded.

"I shouldn't be. I'm taking a huge risk," he babbled.

"Get to the point."

"Our committee met this afternoon,"

"What committee, Jack? You're an important man," she said, her voice dripping with sarcasm. "You sit on many committees."

"Intelligence. There's concern—real concern—about a terrorist plot. One of your companies was mentioned. The FBI suspects it's being used to launder money for terrorists to finance an operation."

"Nonsense. What company did they mention?"

"InCo, the import-export company. Jessica, if you're questioned, you can't mention me."

"Who does the FBI suspect the company is aiding?" Koshani asked.

"I . . . I can't tell you that. It's classified. I'd be in big trouble if they found out I came here to warn you. I just wanted to make sure you know you might be questioned so you won't be surprised and get me in trouble."

"Why in the world would you think that I'd place your well-being over my own?"

"Look, if it's money you want . . ."

Koshani swept her hand around her beautifully appointed bedroom. "Does it look like I need your money?"

"Please, Jessica."

Koshani studied him the way an entomologist studies a common and uninteresting insect. Then she walked over to a cabinet and took out a DVD, which she inserted in a slot in a DVD player that stood beneath the plasma TV across from her bed. She clicked the remote and a picture appeared.

"This is your last session," Koshani said. Carson blanched and he felt as if he might throw up.

On the screen, a woman in black latex was holding a leash attached to a dog collar worn by a naked man, who was on all fours. The woman's identity was concealed because the camera was behind her. United States Senator Jack Carson's face was clearly visible.

"You are a good boy and you deserve a reward," the woman in the DVD said. "Do you want a reward?"

"Yes," Carson said, his voice hoarse with desire.

"Is that the way I have trained you to answer?" the woman asked angrily.

Carson cowered. Then he said, "Yes, mistress," and kissed the woman's foot.

Koshani clicked the remote and the picture disappeared.

"How would your wife and children react if this recording appeared on the Internet? How many votes do you think you would get after it was shown?"

Carson's hands balled into fists and his face flushed with anger. He took a step toward Koshani, then stopped abruptly. He had been so focused on the television that he had not seen her take the Beretta out of the drawer that held the DVD.

"That's a good boy," Koshani said in a tone that mocked the words that had been said on the screen. She waved the barrel toward the bed.

"Lie down," she ordered. Carson knew what would come next. He'd done it often enough during their sex play.

Koshani used sets of velvet-lined handcuffs to fasten the senator's hands and feet to the four corners of the bed. Then she sat on the bed and caressed Carson's crotch. His penis was limp.

"Has the fun gone out of sex for you?" she asked with false concern. Carson turned his head so he wouldn't have to look at her. She slapped him.

"Look at me when I speak to you," she ordered.

When Carson brought his eyes to hers, there was real fear in them. This was not a game anymore. Koshani jammed the gun barrel under the senator's chin.

"What is the FBI going to do about InCo?"

"I can't tell you. I'd be committing treason," he whined.

"I don't think you fully appreciate your situation, Senator. You are going to answer my questions with complete honesty or the DVD will be released and you will be disgraced. Then, when your humiliation is complete, your wife will be killed in an extremely violent manner, and your children will be kidnapped and sold as sex slaves."

Carson stared openmouthed. Then he gagged. When he was through, Koshani got a tissue and dabbed at his mouth.

"You've ruined my silk sheets, but the sacrifice was worth it if you're clear about what will happen if you disobey me. And don't think you can lie to me, then go to the FBI. I'm a small cog in a big machine. There are people who enjoy violence. They will do what needs to be done to punish you if you go to the authorities.

They have copies of the DVD, and they know where your children go to school. Do you understand?"

Carson nodded. Koshani slapped him again.

"Answer me out loud."

"Yes, I understand," Carson said, utterly defeated.

"Good. Now tell me what the FBI has planned for InCo."

"They're going to serve a subpoena for business records."

"When?"

"Soon. I don't know the exact day."

"What are they looking for?"

"I don't know specifics. They've heard rumors about a major attack in the United States."

"Where is this attack supposed to take place and when is it supposed to happen?"

"They don't know."

Koshani thought for a moment.

"I'm going to send you back to Washington, Jack. You will tell me where the authorities suspect the attack will take place and when they think it will occur. You will also inform me of any actions that are planned against me or anyone else."

"The FBI may not know where the attack will take place. I don't know if I can get the information."

Koshani leaned forward and stared directly into Carson's eyes. "Pray that you can."

Chapter Eleven

Lawrence Cooper's office was in a strip mall in Hyattsville, Maryland, between a liquor store and a nail salon. Cooper rarely had visitors he needed to impress, so the office reception area was furnished with cheap furniture that looked as though it could have been made in a high school shop class. Most of the furniture and furnishings in Cooper's private office weren't much better, but his wife had hung hunting prints on the wall behind his desk in hopes of giving the office a little class.

Cooper had an aversion to exercise and the sun. You would expect him to be fat, but he had allergies to so many foods that he ate like a bird and looked anorexic. His chest was sunken, his shoulders stooped, and his skin had an unhealthy pallor. Initial impressions pegged him as weak, but he was tenacious in business and strong-willed if not strong of limb. Cooper earned a respectable living by fighting his way up the food chain, and very little scared him. Steve Reynolds was an exception.

Reynolds appeared in his office shortly after Cooper's secretary left. Cooper thought his secretary had locked the front door so he was surprised when he looked up and found Reynolds standing in his doorway. Cooper got over his initial surprise quickly, but he didn't pull out the drawer where he kept a loaded .38 Special because his visitor was a neatly shaved white man with a styled haircut who was dressed in an Armani suit. Instead, he furrowed his brow, perplexed by the situation, and asked his visitor what he wanted.

Reynolds sat on a plain wooden chair across from Cooper.

"I want to make you some easy money," he said with a warm smile.

Cooper didn't return the smile. Life had taught him that there was no such thing as easy money. Still, he was intrigued.

"Talk to me," he said as he eased open the drawer that held his protection.

Reynolds raised an eyebrow. "There'll be no need for the gun, Mr. Cooper. Besides, I emptied it last night."

Cooper looked as though he had not understood Reynolds or understood him but couldn't get his head around the idea that he had been burglarized. Reynolds waited patiently while Cooper checked the gun. There were no bullets in the chamber. Cooper's face darkened.

"What the fuck is this?"

Reynolds held up a conciliatory hand. "I apologize, but I don't like getting shot, and I thought our conversation would go better if neither of us was armed."

"You know what?" Cooper said, "We're not going to have a conversation. I don't converse with assholes who break into my office."

Reynolds nodded. "I'm not surprised that you're upset, but hear me out. I'm going to offer you ten thousand dollars in exchange for a favor and another ten once it's performed."

The money caught Cooper's interest. "What kind of favor?"

"I want you to hire four men. You won't have to pay them to earn the money. You'll just have to tell your managers to use them."

Cooper smirked. "What will these gentlemen say when INS asks for their green cards?"

"They'll say they have them. You won't get in trouble with the Immigration people."

"I don't like this."

Reynolds sat up and leaned forward. "You don't have to like it. You just have to do it."

"And if I don't?" Cooper answered belligerently.

"This is not a negotiation," Reynolds said. "Either you do everything I ask of you and make some money or you refuse and your comfortable life will come to an end. And don't even think about going to the police. That would be a huge mistake. Any-time you get set to contact the authorities, think about how easy it was for me to break into your house last night."

"My house?"

"Check the dresser in your bedroom. Look under your winter pajamas. The envelope with the ten thousand dollars is folded inside the flannels with the tartan check."

Chapter Twelve

Transcripts from Clarence Little's trial for the murder of Winona Benford were piled up on the coffee table in Millie's living room. An empty mug was perched on top of the transparent plastic cover that protected one of them. Scattered across the living room floor were more transcripts and the police, forensic, and defense investigation reports in the Winona Benford and Carol Poole cases.

Millie put down the police report she had just finished and rubbed her eyes. Then she picked up the coffee mug and picked her way through the legal debris until she reached her kitchen. It was Monday morning, and Millie had risen with the sun to finish rereading all of the paperwork in the two murder cases, a task she had started on Saturday and was about to finish after two twelve-hour weekend days.

In Clarence's postconviction cases, the issue before Judge Case was whether the state had violated Clarence's legal rights, not whether Clarence had murdered someone. In preparing for the postconviction hearing, Millie had focused more on the legal issues than on the facts. At Clarence's new trials, the issue the juries would decide was whether Clarence had killed the two girls, so Millie was rereading everything from a different angle. The more she read, the more uncomfortable she felt.

The state did not have overwhelming evidence that Clarence had murdered Benford or Poole, but the evidence against him was disturbing. Of course the evidence against Clarence in the *Erickson* case had been very persuasive, and he was totally innocent of that murder. Still . . .

Millie refilled her coffee mug and walked over to the kitchen window. The leaves on the trees that lined her street were starting to turn from green to gold, and the sun looked cold. Fall was visiting Oregon, and months of rainy, dark days would soon follow.

Millie took a sip of coffee and thought about the jar of severed pinkies that had been discovered while Clarence was on death row. The evidence was significant because the pinkies in the jar matched every one of Clarence's alleged victims except Laurie Erickson. It was strong circumstantial evidence that the person who had placed the pinkies in the jar had not killed Erickson. The contents of the jar and other evidence pointing to the real murderer had led the state to concede that Clarence had not killed Christopher Farrington's babysitter.

The discovery of the pinkies had cleared Clarence of one murder, but it raised a disturbing question in Millie's mind.

An attorney could not be compelled to tell the authorities anything a client confided, but a lawyer had a duty to turn over physical evidence that came into his possession if it related to a crime. One police report mentioned that Brad Miller had given the jar with the pinkies to Paul Baylor, a private forensic expert, to make sure they were properly preserved, and a partner in Miller's firm had told the authorities where to find the bodies.

Everyone assumed that Brad Miller had unearthed the jar and the two decomposing bodies that had been buried in the Deschutes National Forest.

If it was Miller who had unearthed the bodies and the jar, who had told him where they were buried? Millie had looked through the file searching for the answer. It was nowhere to be found because there was no record of an interview with Brad Miller. What upset Millie was the possibility that Clarence had told Brad where to find the evidence. That would explain why no one had interviewed Miller, who would have been compelled by law to assert the attorney-client privilege to protect his client.

Had Clarence been lying to her all along when he claimed he was innocent? That was the only conclusion she could draw if Clarence knew where the bodies and fingers were buried. The impressions Millie had formed while representing Clarence convinced her that he was a victim. All of a sudden, she wasn't so certain.

Millie considered other possible explanations. Brad Miller would have asserted the attorney-client privilege if another client revealed the location of the evidence. And he could have asserted his own Fifth Amendment right to be free from self-incrimination if he was afraid he'd committed obstruction of justice because he had moved the jar and uncovered the corpses. Neither of these explanations made a lot of sense.

The easiest way to find out who had told Brad where to find the fingers and the bodies would be to ask him. Millie had mailed Clarence's letter to Miller care of United States Senator Jack Carson. It was seven o'clock in Portland, which made it ten o'clock in Washington, D.C. Millie went on her computer and found the phone number for the senator's office. When the receptionist answered, Millie asked to be put through to Brad.

"Brad Miller."

"Thanks for taking my call, Mr. Miller. I'm Millie Reston, a lawyer in Portland, and I'm representing Clarence Little. I don't know if you've heard, but I won Mr. Little's postconviction cases. His convictions in the *Benford* and *Poole* cases have been set aside."

"I assumed Clarence would get someone to attack the rest of his convictions once it was established that the jurors who convicted in *Benford* and *Poole* could have been influenced by evidence concerning a crime he didn't commit."

"That's what the judge held. You made my job easy by proving Mr. Little didn't kill Laurie Erickson."

"You know it was another lawyer who won the appeal in the Ninth Circuit."

"I know you weren't the attorney of record when Little's conviction in the *Erickson* case was thrown out," Millie said. "But everyone knows that it was you and Dana Cutler who provided the real basis for the reversal."

"That's ancient history. When I moved to Washington, D.C., to clerk at the Court, I lost track of what was happening in Oregon. I haven't been involved in the case for some time, so why have you called me?"

"I've been prepping for Mr. Little's trials, and I had a question about something that happened while you were representing him."

"Okay."

"It's about the jar with the pinkies and the two bodies you found. I'm confused about how you found them."

"I'm afraid I can't discuss that."

"All I want to know is who told you where to find the jar and the bodies."

"I'm sorry, Miss Reston. I can't help you."

"Does that mean you're protecting a confidence of Mr. Little's?"

"I can't comment on that," he said.

"We both represent Mr. Little, so you won't be violating a confidence if you answer my question."

"Look, Miss Reston, I can't even be sure you are who you claim to be. You could be a reporter looking for a story and pretending to be Mr. Little's lawyer. But even if you are who you say you are, I can't help you. I don't even know why you're asking me about this. Clarence is your client. Ask him."

There was dead air for a moment, and Millie thought Brad was going to hang up. Instead, he asked her a question.

"When were you appointed to handle Clarence's postconviction cases?"

"Shortly after the Ninth Circuit reversed in the *Erickson* case."

"That was a month or two before the presidential election, wasn't it?"

"Yes."

"I just received a letter in the mail from your client. It's similar to a letter from Mr. Little that was hand-delivered to me on the evening of the presidential election. Did you have anything to do with those letters?"

"I don't know what you're talking about," Millie answered a little too quickly.

"Do you know who helped him send them to me? They weren't mailed from the penitentiary."

"No, I don't. I'm sorry I bothered you," Millie said, ending the conversation abruptly. She hadn't expected Brad to ask her about the letters, and she was scared to death that he would talk to someone at the prison about them. She was sorry she'd called Brad. She might have put herself in harm's way if he followed up. Even worse, although he had not come out and said it, Miller certainly acted like a man protecting a client's confidences.

Millie went back to the files after she hung up on Brad Miller, but she had trouble concentrating, because she could not help thinking about their conversation. Miller was no longer involved with Clarence's case. Why would he refuse to answer her question? The only reasonable explanation was that Clarence had revealed the locations as part of a confidential communication, which the law forbade Brad to reveal.

That evening, Millie tossed and turned for almost an hour after getting into bed and slept in fits and starts. She was exhausted when she woke up, and had no appetite. She dreaded confronting Clarence about the pinkies, but she had to know if everything she believed she and Clarence had together was built on a lie. She had to know if Clarence was the person who had revealed the location of the two murder victims and the jar full of horrific souvenirs.

Chapter Thirteen

The first time Millie met Clarence Little at the state penitentiary, she had been afraid. But fear had given way to trust and trust to love. Now, once again, seated at the table in the contact visiting room, Millie's stomach was in a knot, her throat was dry, and she dreaded meeting Clarence. Then the door opened and he walked in with a wide smile on his face. He looked so happy to see her that she could not help returning his smile. As he walked toward her, Millie's doubts were nudged aside by the joy she felt whenever they were together. Suddenly her suspicions seemed foolish. How could someone who made her feel this way be a sadistic torturer?

"This is an unexpected surprise," Clarence said as soon as the door closed behind the guard.

Millie remembered why she was visiting Clarence and her smile disappeared.

"What's wrong?" Clarence asked.

They'd come to know each other so well, Millie thought. He could read the slightest shift in her mood. Isn't that what people in love were able to do? Didn't they become one person, one soul?

"I . . . I was going through the transcripts and the police reports to prepare for trial and, well, something is bothering me."

Clarence reached across the table and took her hands in his. As always, his touch was electric and disorienting.

"Tell me. Let me help you," he said.

"It's the pinkies, the ones in the jar, and the bodies in the forest."

"What about them?" Clarence asked.

"How did Brad Miller know where to find them? Who told him where they were?"

Clarence didn't flinch. He looked totally at ease. "Have you asked him?"

"I did but he wouldn't discuss it."

Clarence frowned. "That's strange. And there's nothing in the case file that explains how that evidence was found?"

"No."

Clarence shook his head. He looked puzzled. "Brad isn't involved with the murders of those poor girls anymore. If he knew, what reason would he have to keep that information from you?'

Millie felt sick. Her voice broke a little when she spoke. "He might not tell me if the information was given to him by a client."

Clarence's brow creased and he seemed confused for a moment. Then his eyes widened.

"You think that I told him? How would I know? I had nothing to do with those girls."

Millie felt awful. She had broken the trust that bound Clarence to her. Clarence looked up and locked eyes with Millie's.

"I can't believe this," he said, his voice shaking. "I thought you loved me."

"I do," Millie pleaded, desperate to heal the breach her ridiculous suspicions had created.

Clarence took a deep breath. "You see what they've done?"

"Who?"

"The people who framed me. The prosecutors and detectives. These were horrible crimes. If the police can't solve them legally, they have to find a scapegoat. And I'm it. Why else would they prosecute me after it became clear beyond any doubt that I was framed for Erickson's murder? If I'm not convicted, they'll all look bad."

Millie reached across the table and covered Clarence's hands with hers. She squeezed them. Her suspicions were forgotten.

"They won't convict you. I promise."

Clarence took Millie's hands in his and returned the pressure. "I know you mean well—and you're one hell of a lawyer—but they've stacked the deck against us. They've even made *you* suspect me, and you love me. What do you think they'll do to the jurors? Those people don't know me the way you do. They'll want someone to pay, and I'll be the only one in the room they can blame. If we go to trial, I'm doomed."

"Don't give up hope!"

"I hadn't until now." Clarence looked so sad. "Admit it, Millie. You've had doubts, haven't you? You really thought I was capable of . . . of doing . . . things to those girls."

Clarence swallowed. He looked sick. Guilt overwhelmed Millie.

"I'm so sorry," she said, on the verge of tears.

"It's what they do to you, and it's the reason I'll never get a fair trial."

Millie didn't know what to say. Clarence was quiet for a moment. He appeared to be deep in thought.

"There is a way," he said finally.

"What way?"

He opened his mouth. Then closed it and shook his head. "No, I couldn't ask you to do it."

"Do what, Clarence? I'd do anything for you."

"I can't put you at risk. If it works, we'll be together. But if it doesn't . . ."

"Tell me."

Clarence leaned across the table and dropped his voice to a whisper.

"I've told you before that I have money stashed away, lots of money, enough for us to live on for the rest of our lives."

She nodded. It was one of the many confidences he'd bestowed on her.

"Millie, there are countries that don't have extradition treaties with the United States. If we got to one of those countries, we could get married and live together in peace."

"But how would we . . . ?" Millie started. Then she got it. "Oh, I couldn't . . ."

"It's the only way, and I've been giving it a lot of thought. I'm certain we can pull it off."

"But we'd be fugitives. We'd never be able to come home."

"We'd be together, Millie. That's all that matters to me. Ask yourself what kind of a life you have now. Mine is horrible. It's day after mind-numbing day in a tiny cell, never seeing the sun, grateful for any change in my routine, even a court appearance. I had nothing until I met you. You've given me hope. Without you I would have gone insane. I'd do anything—take any risk—to be with you."

Millie let go of Clarence's hands. She sat back. "I've got to think."

"Of course," he said. "I know this is a lot to spring on you. But listening to the doubt in your voice . . . It tore me up, Millie. To think you might have lost faith in me . . . It made me realize how hopeless my case is if we're depending on a fair result at my trial."

Millie stood up and rang for the guard.

"Are you okay?" Clarence asked.

"I'm confused, Clarence, and I'm scared."

"I'm sorry. Forget what I said. We'll take our chances in court."

She turned her back so she wouldn't have to face him.

"I'll think about what you said," she told him just as the guard appeared.

"Okay. And, Millie, no matter what you decide, I love you."

Millie wandered back to her office building in a daze. When she got upstairs, she closed the door to her office and tried to distract herself by working on another case, but she couldn't concentrate. If she did what Clarence asked her, life as she knew it would be over—but she and Clarence would be together.

"What do I have now?" she asked herself. Until she met Clarence, her life had been dull gray. When she was with Clarence, everything was highlighted in bright colors. True, she was starting to make money and a name for herself, but that could end. One highly publicized loss, and she could be back where she started, a nobody. And even with her professional success, she was still who she was, colorless, boring, and drab. She only felt like a woman when she was with Clarence. He made her feel alive. Could she give up everything for him? If she did what he asked, she would be a fugitive; she would be trapped in the country to which they fled, never able to leave for fear of arrest.

But she would be with Clarence; they would be bound to each other.

Millie tried to imagine what it would be like to wake up every morning in bed with Clarence, sated by a night of lovemaking, warmed by the heat of his body. That life would be so much better than what she had now.

Millie told her secretary that she had a headache, and she left for her apartment. When she was inside, she kept the lights off and sat on her sofa. She looked around. Her apartment was as much a prison as Clarence's cell. What would she be giving up if she left it and went on the run with Clarence? She would live in fear, but fear was an emotion, love was an emotion. Before she met Clarence, her life had been a wasteland, bare of all emotions except depression. This was her chance, maybe the only chance she would ever have, to experience life. But did she have the courage to take it?

Chapter Fourteen

A week before the NFL exhibition season started, Steve drove the members of the cell to FedEx Field, where the Washington Redskins play. Ali Bashar thought the stadium looked like a massive, elongated pottery bowl whose size was accentuated by the empty asphalt parking lots surrounding it. On a game day, bumper-to-bumper traffic would move at a snail's pace down the street leading to those lots, while exuberant fans surged toward the entrances. But there had been no game that day, and FedEx Field was eerily quiet.

Ali had been told to report to Jose Gutierrez, who ran a concession stand for the company that leased it from the Redskins. Gutierrez told Ali what he would have to do and when he would have to show up. Then he'd brought him to the security office, where his picture was taken, an ID card was issued, and his fingerprints were scanned into a computer.

Weeks later, two hours before kickoff, on the morning of the second exhibition game, Steve dropped off Ali and the others in the employee parking lot across the street from the stadium. A bus drove the employees to Gate D, where a security guard compared Ali's features to the face on his ID card before Ali placed his finger on a scanner that matched his prints to the ones on record. A wave of sound hit Ali when he got off the bus, and the din was worse when he was inside the stadium. Rock music blared at a level high enough to cause deafness but was almost drowned out by the noise caused by ninety thousand fans yelling to be heard over the cacophony of sound. All of this noise bounced off the stark gray concrete walls and floor of the concourse that circled the stands. Bordering the concourse were concessions selling hot dogs, bratwurst, hot chocolate, hot pretzels, and cold beer.

Ali went to the vendors' room, which was next to the entry gate. He was wearing his own clothes, but he picked up a shirt provided by the concession. It resembled a referee's shirt but had stripes in the Redskins' burgundy and gold colors. The vendor's room was a big concrete square filled with refrigerators stocked with cold beer and soft drinks and machines that were constantly cooking hot dogs. Mr. Cooper, the owner of the concession, had brought in the hawkers' trays the day before, and Ali stocked his with Coke-filled cups. When he sold all of the cups, he would return for more after handing in the money he had collected.

Halfway through the fourth quarter, the Redskins took the lead over the Indianapolis Colts, and the stands at FedEx Field erupted. As the teams prepared for the kickoff, Ali sold the final soft drinks in his hawker's tray to a father and son wearing Redskins jerseys. When the sale was complete, Ali headed for the concession stand to cash out.

Vendors stood in a long, narrow space behind the bar where

the customers shuffled up to place their orders. Behind the vendors were soft-drink machines, toasters that kept the pretzels hot, and rotating ovens that constantly grilled the meat. As soon as he got to the stand, one of the female vendors smiled at him, and Ali found he was smiling too. Women had always been a sore subject with him. He was a virgin who believed subconsciously that any attempt to have a girlfriend would only result in rejection and disappointment.

"Hi, Ali, how did it go today?" Ann O'Hearn asked cheerfully.

"Good," he said as he lifted the empty tray over his neck and set it on the concrete floor.

Ann was the personification of everyone Ali Bashar had been trained to hate. In the remote mountain village where he had been raised, the teachers in his all-male madrassas had drummed into him that his only concerns in this life were the Koran, Sharia law, and the glorification of jihad. O'Hearn was a blond, blue-eyed female, she was a Catholic and therefore an infidel, and she was not deferential to men. Yet try as he might, he could not hate her. He actually liked her.

"You must be happy," Ali said.

"You mean because the Redskins won?"

"Of course."

O'Hearn laughed and it sounded to Ali like bells pealing.

"I couldn't care less about football. I work here to pay my tuition. I'm into soccer."

"You are?" Ali had answered, surprised that an American girl would be interested in a game most Americans found boring.

"Sure. I've been playing soccer since I was a kid. I'm on my college team now."

"I too play soccer, but we call it football in my country."

"I know that. What position?"

"Goalie," Ali answered.

"Whoa. You'll never catch me in goal. That's the toughest position on the field."

Ali blushed and shrugged. "I enjoy playing in the goal." He did not tell her that none of the other children in the village wanted to play that position. On the rare occasions he was included in the village games, goalie was the only position he was given.

"I don't know how you stand the pressure. And you're always the goat if your team loses."

One of Ali's jobs was to help clean up after the game. He and Ann continued to talk about soccer until their work was done and the crowd had cleared out. Ali rode the bus to the employee lot with Ann. When they got to the lot, Ann smiled and said, "See you at the next game."

Ali smiled too, and it was not a duplicitous smile aimed at creating a false confidence in someone he wished to betray. To his surprise, it was a genuine smile of friendship. Then Ali remembered that Ann had said she'd see him at the next game. As soon as her back was to him, Ali stopped smiling. He did like Ann O'Hearn, and that made him sad, because she would die a horrible death if his mission succeeded, and his mission would succeed because it was blessed by Allah.

Chapter Fifteen

Millie slept in fits and starts the night before the hearing on the motions in Clarence's case. She was up before her alarm went off, exhausted, her stomach in knots. All she could handle for breakfast was tea and toast, but moments after she ate, she rushed into the bathroom, bent over the toilet bowl, and threw up. When she tried to straighten up, she felt light-headed and had to sit on the floor, paralyzed by fear.

Millie squeezed her eyes shut and imagined what Clarence would say if he were sitting beside her on the cold bathroom tiles. He would tell her that there was nothing to worry about, that their plan could not fail. But was it foolproof? Would she bring him down? She had no confidence that she could carry out her part of the plan. She was certain that she would blunder and the plot would unravel.

If Clarence were with her, he would whisper, "Have faith," in that self-assured way that made Millie believe she could do anything when she was with him. But she wasn't with him now, and she was terrified that she would be caught, disbarred, disgraced, and sent to prison.

Millie's head fell into her hands. She took deep breaths, but they didn't help. She couldn't do it. She was too frightened.

Then she thought about what would happen to Clarence if her fear caused her to abandon him. He would die. It was that simple. Her cowardice would kill him. Clarence had explained how the state had stacked the cards against him. He had convinced her that no matter how brilliant she was in court, he would be convicted and sentenced to death. If she didn't execute their plan, the man she loved would die, and it would be her fault.

Millie struggled to her feet and staggered to the sink. She rinsed her mouth and splashed cold water on her face. Then she straightened up, squared her shoulders, and took slow, deep breaths. When her composure returned, Millie went into the bedroom and dressed for court. Then she put the thick, older model cell phone she had found in a pawn shop in her purse. Last night, she had taken out the phone's innards and replaced them. If she could get the cell phone past the metal detector at the courthouse, Clarence would go free, and they would spend the rest of their lives together. If she failed, her life as she knew it would be over.

Clarence had instructed Millie to park on the street as close to the courthouse as possible. After she parked, Millie drew a detailed map of the car's location and wrote a description of her car, including its license plate number, for Clarence had never seen it.

The Multnomah County Courthouse had been the largest courthouse on the West Coast when it was completed in 1914, and the eight-story concrete building took up an entire block in downtown Portland between Southwest Main and Salmon and

Southwest Fourth and Fifth avenues. As Millie drew closer to the courthouse, she paused to see if there were any reporters waiting in ambush. She spotted vans from several local television stations, but none of the faces that had become familiar to her since the reversal in Clarence's case had made her famous. She assumed that the reporters would be waiting outside the courtroom.

Millie entered the courthouse and stood in the shorter security line reserved for attorneys, court personnel, judges, and police officers. As she inched toward the metal detector, doubts assailed her again. She was weak-kneed and light-headed when she finally got to the head of the line. A stack of plastic trays stood on a table in front of the metal detector. Millie took her keys, her change, and the cell phone out of her attaché case, put them in the tray, and passed the tray around the metal detector to a guard. Then she took off her coat and put it and the attaché on the conveyor belt. The guard barely looked at the contents of the tray because her attention was focused on Millie as she walked through the metal detector. Millie went through without setting off the alarm. Then she put on her coat, put the cell phone, change, and keys back in her briefcase, and walked up the stairs at a natural pace, even though she wanted to run.

When Millie reached the second floor, she found the ladies' room. As soon as she locked herself in a stall, she started to shake. She bent forward and rested her elbows on her thighs. It took an effort to keep from crying with relief, but she didn't want to ruin her makeup. She knew Clarence would be so proud of her. She'd done it. She had gotten through security.

When Millie regained her composure, she took the cell phone out of her purse and smacked the casing against the side of the toilet until it cracked. Inside the hollowed-out cell phone was a gun. When Clarence told her about it, Millie had trouble believing it existed, but it did: a .22 Magnum Mini-Revolver that held five bullets but was so small that it fit in her hand and looked like a toy.

Millie slid the revolver inside the crotch of her panties and rearranged her clothing. When she stood up, the metal felt odd and cool against her skin. Millie left the stall. No one else was in the restroom. She took a few steps to get used to walking with the gun in her underwear. When she was comfortable, Millie left the ladies' room and walked down to the ground floor and around to the back of the courthouse to an alcove near the door that opened onto Fifth Avenue. Inside the alcove was an elevator that went up to the courthouse jail where prisoners with court appearances were held.

Millie checked her watch. Clarence's court appearance was scheduled for 9:00. At 8:30 Millie pressed a button on the intercom attached to the wall. A disembodied voice asked her business, and she told the jailer she was Clarence Little's attorney. Moments later, the elevator took her up to the jail. She waited in a narrow hall for a guard to escort her into a room similar to the noncontact visiting room at the prison. Glass separated her from Clarence. At Clarence's insistence, Millie had gotten a judge to order that Clarence be allowed to wear a suit and tie to court appearances.

"You look more like a lawyer than I do," Millie joked to ease the tension that threatened to paralyze her.

Clarence smiled. "And you look beautiful."

"Thank you," Millie answered nervously.

"Is everything okay?"

"Yes."

As they spoke, Millie hiked up her dress. She took the miniature gun out of her panties and palmed it.

Millie and Clarence engaged in small talk while they anxiously waited for a jailer to end the meeting so Clarence could be escorted to court. Millie felt faint when the jailer unlocked the door behind Clarence and led him out. She opened her door and waited. Two guards handcuffed Clarence and walked him to the elevator. They made no objection when Millie asked to ride down to the fifth floor with her client. The elevator door opened and Clarence stepped to the rear. Millie pressed against him and passed him the gun. One guard stood facing the door. The other stood next to Clarence but slightly in front of him. As soon as the elevator door closed, Clarence raised his hands and shot the nearest guard in the back of the head.

The tiny gun made a popping sound that would not have attracted much attention in a large room but sounded hard and horribly loud in the confined space. Millie gasped as the jailer slid down the wall. The other guard turned. Clarence pressed the gun between his eyes and squeezed the trigger. There was no room to fall and the guard lurched against Millie. She screamed.

"What have you done?" Millie asked.

"The key," Clarence commanded. "Quick, Millie. We only have a few moments."

Millie had seen the guard put the handcuff keys in his front pocket after he handcuffed Clarence. The guard was pressed against her. She fought back a strong urge to throw up as she groped in his pocket. Blood was flowing from the wound between his eyes and she had to contort her body to keep it from getting on her dress.

"Good girl," Clarence said when Millie unlocked his cuffs. The elevator shuddered to a stop on the fifth floor. Clarence found the button that kept the elevator door shut and jammed it in. Millie stared at the dead men.

"You said no one would get hurt," she said, her voice breaking.

"It was us or them, Millie, and I chose us. It was the only way we could be together. Now we have to move fast. Where is your car?"

Millie was horrified by what she'd just seen, and she didn't trust herself to speak. So she took the map with the location and the license plate number out of her attaché case and held it out to Clarence with a trembling hand.

"Did you put my change of clothes in the trunk?" Clarence asked. Millie nodded.

"Give me your car keys."

Millie handed Clarence the keys, and he put the keys and the gun in his pocket. He looked sad. "Here comes the hard part. Come to me."

Millie turned her back to Clarence. She was shaking.

"We'll be together soon," he said.

"Will it hurt?"

"No, dearest. I'll be gentle. It will be quick, and you'll just pass out. I have to do this so they don't suspect you helped me."

Millie closed her eyes and felt Clarence's arm encircle her throat. She was frightened. Then Clarence kissed her ear and said, "I love you, Millie."

She tried to smile, but she was too tense. Then she remembered that they were going to be together forever. She imagined palm trees, a warm, gentle breeze, a pearl white beach, and a sea so blue that the scene looked like a picture postcard. Then the choke hold tightened and she panicked.

Millie tried to speak but her larynx was being crushed. She clawed at her true love's arms, but the hold didn't ease. Fear flashed through her. *Have I made a terrible mistake?* Millie thought, moments before she died.

Chapter Sixteen

Every day on death row was mind-numbingly similar. The lack of intellectual stimulation had been torture for a man with Clarence Little's IQ, so Clarence had distracted himself for large parts of each day with mental reenactments of the slow torture and ultimate death of his playthings. Clarence never thought of the women he killed as victims. Victims were human beings. He thought of Winona Bedford, Carol Poole, and the other women as toys he used to act out his sexual fantasies.

Clarence had felt intense pleasure and an explosive sexual release whenever his playthings screamed or pleaded for mercy or died. Strangely he did not experience sexual pleasure while he was strangling Millie Reston. Maybe that was because he found her repulsive. He actually wondered if putting Millie down wasn't a humanitarian act. The poor simpleton had no life and had been so easy to manipulate. He didn't even have to waste a bullet on her. He shook his head in wonder. She was really like a cow in a slaughterhouse, following instructions without a thought as she was led to the abattoir.

Clarence marveled at the fact that she was so blinded by love that she hadn't thought about how she was going to explain the gun. Millie had to have known that Clarence would be searched thoroughly before he was brought to court. She was the only person who could have smuggled the gun into the courthouse. She would have been asked to take a lie detector test, which she would have failed. If she had refused to take the test, her refusal would have confirmed the suspicions of the police. And Millie was weak. Eventually she would have cracked. Then she would have been arrested, disbarred, and put in prison. Clarence honestly believed that putting an end to Millie's pathetic existence had been one of the few good deeds he had ever performed.

Clarence opened the elevator door and stepped out into the alcove on the fifth floor. Then he peeked into the back hall. There were a few people in it, but he didn't think he would attract attention in a business suit, carrying Millie's attaché case.

Next to the alcove was a little-used set of stairs. Clarence didn't meet anyone on the way down, but he discovered that the stairs were blocked off below the second floor. He nudged open the door to the second floor. His luck held. There were very few people in the corridor. Clarence walked to the end of the rear hallway and turned right into the corridor that ran parallel to Salmon Street. Then he turned right again and headed down the marble stairs to the courthouse lobby. He was in luck again. Most people took the elevator, so there were few people using the stairs. They were either engaged in conversation or focused on their own problems, and no one gave him a second look.

The front door came into view. Clarence headed for it, keeping his head down so it would be difficult to see his face. Seconds later, Clarence Little was breathing fresh air for the first time in a long time.

Millie's car was exactly where the map said it would be. Clarence slid behind the wheel and breathed a sigh of relief. He wasn't home free, but he was damn close. He left the parking spot and headed for the I–5 bridge that crossed the Columbia River into Washington.

Clarence assumed there would soon be an APB out for Millie's vehicle. Just before he reached the bridge, he drove off I–5 into the Jantzen Beach shopping center and parked in the middle of a crowded row in the center of the large lot. Until someone discovered that the car was abandoned, the police would believe he was driving it.

Two large SUVs flanked Millie's vehicle and shielded him from view. He took the clothes Millie had bought for him out of the trunk. They were on a wire hanger, and there was $1,000 in cash in a wallet in one of the pockets. He changed into jeans, a flannel shirt, and a leather jacket before donning a Seattle Mariners baseball cap. He pulled the bill down before wandering around the parking lot until he found a car to steal. He used the wire hanger to break in and was back on the road to Seattle twenty minutes after he'd turned off the highway.

It took a little under three hours to drive from Portland to Seattle. Once he was in the city, Clarence planned to ditch the stolen car and get a room in a cheap motel. Then he would withdraw the money he kept in several Seattle banks in accounts he had set up under aliases. He hadn't lied to Millie about the money. He was well off financially. There had been an inheritance, and his engineering firm had done well. He also had several passports under different names in a safe-deposit box. He would lie low until the initial furor died down. Then it was off to South America to visit a plastic surgeon who asked no questions if you could pay his fee. And then . . . ? Then there would be a world of possibilities. His priority after he was sure he was safe would be to buy an isolated house. In it he would construct a secret room where he could entertain. Spanish was a more melodious language than English, and Clarence wondered if the screams of Latin women would sound different from the screams of his American pets. He smiled as he contemplated answering that question.

Chapter Seventeen

Keith Evans had been born and raised in Nebraska and probably would have spent his life there if it hadn't been for a lucky break. He was a twenty-eight-year-old detective on the Omaha police force when he arrested a serial killer who had run circles around an FBI task force. The agent-in-charge had been so impressed by the deductions that had led the young detective to discover the killer's identity that he convinced Keith to apply to become an FBI agent.

Keith saw a whole new world opening up to him when he started the course at Quantico, but he never duplicated the Sherlockian performance that had led him to the FBI. His subsequent successes were achieved with old-fashioned police work that involved long hours at the office or in the field and large blocks of time away from his wife. Four years after he became an agent, Keith's wife filed for divorce, and he found himself living alone in a sterile apartment in Maryland.

One morning, Keith looked in the mirror and found a forty-year-old man staring back. He was still six two, but he had to wear reading glasses, there were gray hairs among the blond, and ten extra pounds surrounded his midsection. Evans's career had been stagnating until he became the public face of the D.C. Ripper task force and played a part in bringing down President Christopher Farrington. His involvement in another case involving U.S. Supreme Court Justice Felicia Moss had given his career another boost. But his personal life was still bleak. There had been a few women since his divorce, but none of them had put up with his all-too-frequent absences any better than his ex-wife. He didn't blame the women for the failed relationships. He couldn't discuss his work, he had to break dates on a regular basis, and the things he experienced led him to be emotionally cold at times.

Half an hour ago, Keith had read a bulletin that affected two of the few people he counted as friends. He felt uneasy about having to break the bad news but not as uneasy as he felt sitting beside his partner, Special Agent Maggie Sparks.

Maggie was a slim, athletic woman in her early thirties. Her DNA was a hodgepodge inherited from Cherokee, Spanish, Romanian, and Danish ancestors that conspired to create a very attractive woman with glossy black hair, high cheekbones, and a dark complexion. The only blemish on her beauty was a faint scar on her cheek, the product of a gunfight during the Farrington investigation. Maggie still maintained a wry sense of humor and a positive outlook on life despite the horrors she encountered on the job, and Keith always felt his spirits rise when he was with her.

Keith's attraction to Maggie had grown over the years, but he had never gotten up the nerve to ask her out because he wasn't certain how Maggie felt about him and he was terrified that any overtures he made to her would destroy their working relationship.

"How do you think they'll take the news?" Maggie asked as they climbed the steps to Brad and Ginny's apartment.

"I don't know. I never talked that much to Brad about Clarence Little. We went over the similarities in his case and the Ripper case, but he never talked about how he got along with the guy."

Keith was breathing a little unevenly when he got to the third-floor landing. If Maggie was experiencing any physical stress, Keith couldn't see it.

"This is it," he said, stopping at the second apartment. He knocked, and the door opened a few seconds later, revealing a smiling Brad Miller clad in sweatpants and a New York Jets T-shirt.

"Hey, guys, come in," Brad said, stepping aside to let the agents into his apartment.

"Thanks," Keith said.

"Hi, Keith, Maggie," Ginny said. She was also wearing sweats and a T-shirt, only her team of choice was the Kansas City Chiefs.

Brad took a closer look at Keith and Maggie, and he stopped smiling.

"What's up?" he asked cautiously.

"Something happened in Oregon we thought you'd want to know about," Keith said. "Clarence Little was in Portland for a court appearance. He killed two guards and his female attorney in the jail elevator while they were going from the jail to the courtroom."

"He killed Millie Reston?" Brad asked, shocked.

"Did you know her?" Maggie asked.

"Not really, but she called me a little while ago to talk about Clarence's case. That's the only time I talked to her."

"How did he kill the guards?" Ginny asked.

"The authorities in Portland reviewed tapes of Reston's visits to the jail, and they think she may have fallen for Little. They're pretty certain Reston smuggled a gun into the courthouse."

"The poor sap," Brad said.

"Is there anything you can tell me that might help catch Little, any favorite places, friends, relatives?" Keith asked.

Everyone looked at Brad, who flushed and couldn't meet anyone's eye.

"I can't remember anything like that, but something happened that I never told you, Ginny."

"About Clarence Little?" she asked.

Brad nodded. "He sent me two letters."

"What kind of letters?" Ginny pressed.

"They were creepy, but there weren't any threats in them. I didn't tell you about them because I didn't want to worry you."

"When did you get them?" Maggie asked.

"The first one was slipped under the door of our apartment in Portland on the evening of the presidential election. I found it when we came back from the election-night parties. The second one was sent to my office in the Senate right after Clarence's cases were sent back for new trials."

"Do you have them?" Keith asked.

"I threw out the first one. I figured Clarence was just playing one of his mind games, and I didn't want to buy into it. He was on death row, anyway, and I didn't think of him as a threat. I kept the second one. It's in my desk at the office. I can give it to you."

"I'll have someone from the lab pick it up," Keith said.

"Neither letter was mailed from the prison. The first one wasn't mailed at all, and the second was sent from Portland. They contained some personal details that Clarence shouldn't have known about. Not anything secret. Anyone who knows us would have known about them. The first one mentioned Ginny, and I never discussed anything about my personal life with Clarence. So I figured he had an accomplice. For what it's worth, I think Millie Reston helped him. I confronted her about the letters when she called, and she was very evasive and sounded nervous."

"I'll give this information to the people who are looking for Little," Keith said. "Someone will get in touch with you."

"Why did you hurry over to tell us about the escape? Do you think we're in danger?" Ginny asked.

"I have no idea," Keith said. He looked at Brad. "Would Little have any reason to hurt you?"

"Ginny and I talked about this when we learned his cases had been reversed. Clarence and I got along pretty well but—as Ginny pointed out—a psychotic serial killer doesn't think like a normal human being. I'm not that worried, though. Clarence has no logical reason to want to hurt me. He'll be trying to hide or get out of the country. I doubt he'll come all the way to D.C. to get to me or Ginny."

Chapter Eighteen

It was general knowledge among the members of Senator Carson's staff that Brad had represented Clarence Little. The morning after Little's escape made the front page of every newspaper and led every television newscast in the D.C. area, the escaped serial killer became a constant topic of conversation in the senator's office.

Bonnie Berliner was the legislative correspondent with the cubicle outside Brad's office. An attractive brunette with a cheerful manner and a bright smile, she had just graduated from Oregon State with honors and a degree in government. Her father was a big contributor to Carson's campaign, but she probably would have been hired on merit. Bonnie was answering e-mails about health care issues when Brad walked by. She swiveled away from her monitor.

"Mr. Sharp wants to see you," Bonnie said.

"About what?"

"He didn't say."

"Okay. I'll just get rid of my stuff."

Brad expected Bonnie to go back to her computer. Instead, she looked him over.

"Are you okay?"

"Why wouldn't I be?"

"You know, Little."

Brad had been reassuring every workmate he had passed, starting with the receptionists, and he had his patter down pat.

"Mr. Little and I got on fine. Anyway, he's probably in Mexico by now."

Bonnie shuddered. "I was in school when he was torturing those women. I don't see how you can be so cool."

"Every law enforcement officer in the country is after Clarence. He's probably spending every waking minute figuring out how to stay out of prison. And there are three thousand miles between us. I'm sure he hasn't given me a thought."

Brad hung up his coat, grabbed a steno pad for notes, and headed down the hall to Lucas Sharp's office, which was next to the boss's. The chief of staff had the second biggest office, but it was nowhere near the size of Carson's corner suite. The walls were of the same movable metal as Brad's, and a picture window closed off by blinds faced the hall. One quarter of the office was taken up by a round conference table and the chairs that surrounded it. A flat-screen TV was affixed to the wall behind the table. Sharp's desktop was invisible because of the legislative bills, magazines, newspapers, and files that covered it.

When Brad walked in, Sharp motioned him toward a chair on the other side of the desk.

"Have reporters tried to interview you about Little?" Sharp asked.

"The phone was ringing off the hook, so we unplugged it. There were reporters in front of our apartment, but I escaped through the service entrance in the basement."

"Good. Stick with no comment. The senator doesn't need this distraction with the race heating up."

"I don't know anything, so not commenting won't be a problem."

"You know I was a deputy district attorney when Clarence killed his first three victims."

"No, I didn't know that."

Sharp shook his head. "Little is one sick puppy. I was called to the second crime scene. This was before we knew the killings were connected. I still get the occasional nightmare, even though it's been years since I saw the body."

"I've seen the autopsy photos and those kids in the forest. That was enough for me."

"Yeah, well, if you even dream you're in danger, you tell me and I'll get you protection."

"Thanks, but I'm sure I won't need it."

Brad had assured everyone that he didn't feel he was in danger, but he found himself scanning crowds for a glimpse of the serial killer, and he made sure he walked home during daylight. By the end of the first week, news of the escape had slipped from the front page to the interior of the newspapers because there were no new developments. By the second week, Ginny had stopped obsessing about Little, and Brad thought about his ex-client less and less.

Friday morning, the senator's secretary buzzed Brad and told him to come to Senator Carson's office. Brad put on his jacket, straightened his tie, and walked down the hall. When he got to the office, his boss was bent over the draft of a bill, scribbling notes on a legal pad. Brad stood in the doorway and waited. After a few moments, Carson looked up and waved Brad toward a chair. While Brad crossed the room and sat down, Carson took off his glasses, shut his eyes, and massaged his eyelids. Brad waited patiently as the senator replaced his glasses. Carson's tie was undone, and the sleeves of his dress shirt had been rolled back. His hair looked as if he'd been running his fingers through it, and he seemed tired. When he spoke, he sounded subdued.

"I'm getting good reports about your work, Brad."

"It's pretty interesting, so it's not hard to get engaged."

"Yeah, it's definitely interesting, although not always in a good way." He pointed at the papers spread across his desk. "Senator Dumont is driving everyone nuts with his half-assed immigration bill."

Brad permitted himself a smile. Dumont, who was from a state bordering Mexico, was in a tight reelection campaign. His bill was loaded with proposals for electrified fences and border guard "shoot to kill" exceptions he knew would never become law but would make him sound more anti–illegal alien than his challenger.

"So, I hear you've had a little excitement in your life," Carson said. Brad looked puzzled. Then he realized that the senator was alluding to Clarence Little's escape.

"I haven't been involved with Clarence Little for almost two years."

"Are you worried he'll come after you? I can arrange for protection."

"Thanks, but I don't think I'll need it. Clarence is probably in another country by now. And," he said ruefully, "even if he's still in the U.S., he wouldn't have any reason to be mad at me, since my efforts on his behalf helped get the *Erickson* case reversed and gave him the opportunity to escape."

Carson smiled. "When you put it that way, I guess you are safe. But I didn't ask you in here to talk about Clarence Little. I called you in here because you've shown an ability to deal with delicate situations."

Brad frowned. After the Farrington affair and his adventures at the Supreme Court, he wanted nothing to do with "delicate situations."

"The Senate Select Committee on Intelligence is meeting on Monday. Jessica Koshani, a constituent, has been subpoenaed to testify. She's flying in tonight on a private jet. I want you to pick her up at Dulles. Don't go to the main terminal. Private planes land at their own area. Park in front and go to the waiting room. She'll meet you there. Then you'll take her to a house I own in Georgetown." Carson gave Brad the address and tossed a key to him. "I've rented a car for you. It's in the parking lot."

Carson tossed Brad another key and told him where to find the car.

"Miss Koshani will be landing a little after seven. Get her settled in, then drive her to the hearing on Monday morning. We convene at nine thirty, so you'll get her around eight thirty. Take her in the back way so no one sees her. After the hearing, you'll drive her to the airport. Think you can handle that?"

"Sure."

"Good."

Carson looked down at the immigration bill, and it was clear that their business was complete.

• • •

Through the window in the waiting room, Brad watched the Learjet carrying Jessica Koshani taxi to a stop. Moments later, steps were lowered to the tarmac, and an elegantly dressed woman walked down them. Brad was madly in love with Ginny, but that didn't mean he didn't notice attractive women. Even though she was dressed simply in black pants and a light tan jacket over a white silk man-tailored shirt, and her only jewelry was a pearl necklace and two gold rings, this woman would have stood out in a room full of fashion models.

"Miss Koshani?" Brad asked, trying not to stare. The woman nodded. Brad knew Koshani had just flown to D.C. from Oregon, but she showed none of the fatigue most cross-country travelers manifested.

"I'm Brad Miller. The senator sent me."

"Those are my bags," she said dismissively, pointing to two large suitcases that a flight attendant had carried from the plane.

Brad hefted the bags and carried them to a black Mercedes. He opened the back door for Koshani and waited until she was settled before putting the bags in the trunk. When he got behind the wheel, he couldn't help taking a quick peek at his passenger in the rearview mirror. Koshani was stunning. Brad felt a little guilty about getting sexually aroused, and he reminded himself that he was married to a fantastic woman. Then he remembered President Jimmy Carter's interview in *Playboy*, in which he said that God forgave men for committing adultery in their hearts, and he smiled. If a little unacted-upon lust was good enough for a president, it was good enough for him.

"You are on the senator's staff?" Koshani asked, shortly after they connected with the highway.

"Yes."

"What do you do for him?"

"I've got a law degree, so most of my work has to do with analyzing bills from a legal perspective."

"You know I am testifying before the Intelligence Committee?"

"I'm driving you on Monday."

"What do you think the senators will ask me?"

Brad was surprised that Koshani would pump him for information. All he knew about the inquiry was what he'd learned when Koshani's name had come up, and he wasn't going to divulge what he'd heard.

"I don't have any idea," he said. "The senator is pretty tight-lipped about security matters."

Koshani asked a few more questions. When it became obvious that she would learn nothing from Brad, she stopped, and they rode the rest of the way in silence.

Part III

Strange Interlude

Chapter Nineteen

The city of Georgetown was founded in 1751 and was a major port and commercial center in colonial times. It was assimilated into the District of Columbia in 1871 and was Washington's fashion and cultural center until the capital grew and new Victorian homes and Gilded Age mansions were built closer to the centers of government. The area went into a steady decline until members of the Roosevelt administration moved there in the 1930s, and it became one of Washington's most fashionable residential areas again after Georgetown resident John F. Kennedy became the thirty-fifth president of the United States.

Many of the homes in Georgetown's tree-lined residential area are two-hundred-year-old row houses with beautiful gardens. The three-story house where Jessica Koshani was staying stood back from the street on a small tree-shaded lot. Brad had gotten a quick look around when he brought Koshani's bags in from the car. The downstairs living room was furnished with elegant French Provincial furniture. The theme continued upstairs. There was a grandfather clock in the second-floor hallway and a four-poster bed in the bedroom where he had left Koshani's valises. Brad thought the house was pretty classy.

There hadn't been any lights on when Brad dropped off Koshani on Friday night, and there were no lights that he could see Monday morning. As he walked up the path to the front door, it dawned on him that he had been to the senator's home in Virginia for a staff picnic shortly after he started. The house had been built at the turn of the twentieth century on several acres of farmland and was within reasonable commuting distance of the Capitol. Brad wondered why the senator also owned a second house in town. Of course, Senator Carson was rich, and he might have bought it as an investment or for out-of-town guests or just because he wanted to.

Brad rang the doorbell and waited. After a reasonable amount of time, he rang the bell again. When there was still no answer, he started to worry. Senator Carson had given him the phone number for the house in case he had to talk to Koshani for some reason, and Brad had programmed it into his cell phone. He let the number ring ten times before cutting the connection.

What to do? Brad hesitated, then grabbed the doorknob and twisted. The door opened an inch. Brad was surprised, and he held the door so that the only view of the interior was through a narrow slit. He dreaded the idea of entering the house uninvited and bumping into Koshani. How embarrassing would that be? But it was getting late.

"Miss Koshani, it's Brad Miller, your driver," he shouted.

When there was no response, Brad shouted a little louder before opening the door the whole way and stepping into the vestibule. He was about to call Koshani's name again when he saw someone sitting in the middle of the living room. The curtains were drawn, and there was very little light, so he had to squint into the shadows that cloaked the room. He still couldn't make out much.

"Miss Koshani?"

There was no answer and no movement. Brad's heart beat faster. There was a sickening smell in the air and Brad was certain he knew what was causing it. He wanted to run out of the house, but he held his breath to keep from inhaling and forced himself to inch forward. Jessica Koshani was tied to a high-backed chair. She was naked, she was covered in blood, and there was a gag in her mouth. Hideous things had been done to her.

Brad knew he shouldn't enter a crime scene, and he started to back out of the house when a thought stopped him. Brad leaned forward and squinted at the dead woman. What he saw made his stomach roll. He definitely wanted to run now, but he needed to know if he was right. Brad forced himself to approach Koshani's corpse. She had been horribly mutilated. What terrified Brad was the fact that he had seen photographs of other women who had been defiled in a similar manner.

There was one more thing Brad had to see before he could leave. Koshani's arms were secured behind her back. He circled the body, stepping around and over pools of blood that covered sections of the rug. When he was behind Koshani, Brad forced himself to look at her hands. Clarence Little had hacked off a pinkie from each of his victims to keep as a souvenir. Jessica Koshani's right hand had only four fingers.

Brad staggered out of the house into the light, feeling dizzy and sick to his stomach. He collapsed on the front stoop and took slow, deep breaths. As soon as he regained his composure, he took out his cell phone and punched in the senator's number. The phone rang several times before a recording told him to leave a message. Brad called the office.

"I need to talk to the senator right away," Brad told the receptionist. "It's an emergency."

"He's not here, Brad."

"Did he go to the Intelligence Committee hearing?"

"I don't know. I haven't seen him this morning."

"What about Mr. Sharp? Is he in?"

"He's not here, either."

Brad thought for a minute. "Okay, if you see them, have them call my cell immediately. Something has come up they need to know about right away."

Brad hung up and called 911. While he waited for the police, he called Ginny.

"Hi, honey," Ginny said. "What's up?"

"We might have a problem," Brad said. "I'm at the house where Jessica Koshani is staying."

"Who is Jessica Koshani?"

"The woman I picked up at the airport on Friday for the senator. She was staying at a house Carson owns."

"And you're telling me this because . . . ?"

"She was murdered, and Clarence Little may have killed her. It's his MO down to the missing pinkie."

"Why would Clarence Little kill this Koshani woman?" Ginny asked, incredulously.

Brad felt sick again. "It could be me, Ginny. Clarence might have done it to get at me. If he's here and he followed me to the airport, he would know where Koshani was staying, and he might have guessed that I'd drive her again or at least learn how she died."

"Where exactly are you now?"

"Outside the house."

"Have you called the police?"

"Yes, right before I called you."

"That's good, but I don't like you being out there all alone. If Little killed Koshani, he could still be around."

Brad was so distraught that he hadn't thought of that possibility. His heartbeat sped up and he cast anxious glances around the neighborhood.

"I don't see anything suspicious, but I'm worried about you. Can you call Dana and ask her to escort you home?"

"You think that's necessary?"

"Probably not, but I'll feel better knowing you're protected. Right now I'm still upset and not thinking straight. We'll decide what to do tonight after I've had time to calm down. The big thing now is that I want to be sure you're safe."

Brad stayed at the crime scene, answering questions. Then he was taken to police headquarters, where he gave a statement. He didn't get into the office until a little after two. As soon as he walked in the door, the receptionist told him that Lucas Sharp had just arrived and wanted to talk to him.

"Does he know about the murder?" Brad asked.

"Two detectives were here to talk to the senator. They left when they found out he wasn't in, but they told me why they needed to talk to him, and I told Mr. Sharp."

As Brad walked down the hall to Lucas Sharp's office, the staff members gave him odd looks, then turned away quickly. Gossip moved swiftly through the halls of Congress.

"How are you doing?" Sharp asked with great concern as soon as Brad walked in.

"I'm much better now, but I was pretty rocky for a while."

"Sit down. Do you want water or something stronger?"

"Water would be good," Brad said as he lowered himself onto one of the chairs on the other side of Sharp's desk. Lucas walked over to a small refrigerator and brought Brad a bottle of water.

"What are the police saying?" Sharp asked.

"Nothing to me," Brad said after he took a few sips. "It's probably too soon for them to draw any conclusions, anyway. The forensic people weren't done when they took me downtown. I told them about Clarence Little, and they're contacting the authorities in Oregon."

"What does Little have to do with Koshani's murder?"

"I only got a quick look at the body . . ." Brad paused and swallowed as his body reacted to the gruesome memory of what he'd seen in Senator Carson's living room. "She looked like Clarence's other victims, and the killer took her pinkie."

"Good God! Why would Little be here in D.C.?"

"I have no idea. Does the senator know about Miss Koshani?"

"I haven't had a chance to tell him. He's at his cabin in Oregon. It's very remote and there's no cell phone service or Internet."

"Why is he in Oregon? Koshani was supposed to testify today."

Sharp hesitated. Then he looked directly at Brad and stared hard enough and long enough to make Brad nervous.

"I'm going to tell you something in confidence," Sharp said. "You've got to promise me this will stay between us."

"Of course."

"We received campaign contributions from friends of Koshani's, large contributions. That's not a problem, but Koshani could be. You were at the committee meeting when InCo was mentioned. That's one of Koshani's companies. If one of her companies helps finance a terrorist attack and Jack's name is linked to hers . . . Well, I don't have to spell out what the consequences could be. We thought it would be best if Jack was someplace where the press couldn't get at him in case someone leaked what went on at the hearing."

"I can see why you're worried, but you've got to tell the senator."

"I will. I just hope no one digs into the reason Koshani was in Washington. Now why don't you head home? I don't want you being hounded by the press, and you can use some downtime after what you just went through."

Sharp arranged for one of the interns to drive Brad home. Even though it was midday and the sun was shining, Brad looked up and down his street before he got out of the car. The stairwell that led to his apartment was suddenly as dark and foreboding as the stairs in a haunted house. Every sound made him startle, and his imagination turned every shadow into Clarence Little.

Brad didn't relax until he had locked himself in and toured his apartment, clutching the biggest knife he could find. As soon as he was certain he was alone, he fixed himself a stiff drink and sank down on the couch.

Brad heard a key turn in the lock a little after six. He grabbed the knife and stood up. When he heard Ginny's and Dana's voices, he put the knife on the end table. Ginny rushed to Brad and hugged him.

"That had to be horrible. Are you okay?" Ginny asked.

"Now that I know you're safe, I'm fine."

Brad turned to Dana. "Thanks for playing bodyguard."

"Anytime."

"I'm really worried," Brad said.

"Yeah, well, you should be," Dana answered. "I made a call to one of my friends at the D.C. police, a detective in Homicide. He told me some of the preliminary findings. There were signs of a struggle on the landing outside the second-floor guest room. It looks like she tried to fight off her assailant."

"Did any of the neighbors see or hear anything?" Ginny asked.

"No," Dana said, "but it's looking a lot like Clarence Little is involved. Portland sent the autopsy and crime-scene photos in Little's cases. The MO is very similar. The major difference is that Koshani was tortured and killed where she was staying. In the Oregon cases, Little abducted his victims, then tortured them for days before dumping them far from the place where he held them."

Something occurred to Brad. "Clarence hasn't had a victim in years. I can't believe he wouldn't take time to . . ."

Brad could not finish his thought. He felt ill just thinking about the suffering Koshani and Little's other victims had endured.

"You're right," Ginny said. "He'd have all that sexual energy pent up inside him. He'd want to enjoy himself. So why the quick kill?"

"The only thing I can think of is that he was sending a message to me, telling me that he's here," Brad answered. "I just don't get why. I know he's not normal, but I helped him out. And he's escaped from death row. You'd think he'd want to go underground. Why risk everything to threaten me?"

"Is it possible that Koshani was his target all along and the murder had nothing to do with you?" Ginny asked.

"She does live in Oregon," Brad said. "Clarence could have met her there."

"There's another possible explanation for the quick kill," Dana said. "The MO is almost identical to the MO in the Little cases, but unlike the Oregon cases, many of the torture wounds were postmortem."

"They were made after she died?" Ginny asked.

Dana nodded. "The medical examiner is guessing that she died unexpectedly while she was being beaten."

"That would explain why she wasn't abducted and why the torture wasn't drawn out," Brad said.

"Exactly," Dana said.

"Ginny told me that you met Koshani at the airport and were picking her up on Senator Carson's orders this morning."

Brad nodded.

"What was Koshani's connection to the senator?"

"She was going to testify before the Senate Select Committee on Intelligence."

"About what?"

"I don't think I can tell you that without the senator's permission. Everything that goes on in their sessions is secret."

"This could have a bearing on why she was killed and whether you're involved or just a bystander."

"I know, but I can't discuss what I heard in the committee session."

Dana looked frustrated, but she knew better than to press Brad.

"I guess we'll just have to proceed on the theory that Little might be a threat to you and Ginny until we know otherwise."

Chapter Twenty

Ali met the three other members of his cell for the first time a few days before they were smuggled out of Pakistan. It soon became apparent that they were slow-witted. Nothing he had learned about them in the intervening months had changed his opinion. As soon as Steve Reynolds showed them how to work the cable television in the safe house, his companions had no trouble passing the time. Porn occupied a good part of each day, but action movies with a lot of explosions and car chases were a close second.

Ali found pornography offensive and the action movies mindless. He got out of the house on Sundays when the Redskins had a home game. If he went outside, he couldn't go far for fear of being seen. Ali prayed and read the Koran, but he was going stir crazy. So it was a great relief when Steve Reynolds phoned one Thursday morning and told him they were going for a ride.

Ali heard the horn and was out of the house before it honked a second time. Reynolds was driving a white van decorated with a plumbing company logo. The American said very little during the ride, and Ali knew better than to start a conversation.

At the camp in Somalia, Ali's intelligence had been recognized and appreciated, and he had been trained to construct bombs. None of the material he needed to build a bomb was in the house. He hoped that this trip was connected to the final phase of his mission.

As they drove, Ali had an unsettling thought. By killing unbelievers, he was serving the one true religion and guaranteeing an eternity in paradise. But carrying out his mission would mean that Ann O'Hearn would die. This was troubling, but it could not be helped. Maybe Ann would be spared. Allah was merciful. Then again, Ann was a heretic. Ali forced himself to stop thinking about Ann because it confused him.

An hour and a half after leaving the house, they were driving through farmland in western Maryland when Reynolds turned off a two-lane rural highway onto a narrow dirt road. Two miles farther on, he drove through a gap in a weathered slat fence and onto a gravel drive that led to a farmhouse. Next to the house was a barn covered in peeling red paint. Two horses and some sheep were grazing in a pasture behind the barn.

"We're going to meet some people," Reynolds said when he stopped the van. "They have the detonators and our explosives. I'm going to tell them that you don't speak English. I'll do all of the talking."

Three men walked out of the house as soon as Reynolds parked in the yard. The man in the lead was shorter than the other two, clean shaven and slender with wheat-colored hair and narrow blue eyes that lasered in on the van as he walked toward it. He was wearing jeans and a faded Baltimore Ravens T-shirt.

The other two men resembled Baltimore Ravens. They were

huge and bearded and looked like men who enjoyed violence. They made Ali very nervous.

Reynolds hopped down from the van and nodded at the slender man. “Hey, Bob, it was good to hear from you. I was starting to worry.”

“I said I’d get the stuff.”

“Yes, you did. So where is it?”

“First things first,” Bob said. He motioned toward Reynolds and Ali, and one of the behemoths walked toward them. Before he’d gotten halfway across the yard, Reynolds reached behind his back and pulled out a matte black Glock.

“Let’s do this the way we did it the first time we met. You show me yours, then I’ll show you mine.”

Bob’s features darkened, and the two giants tensed.

“You think we’re cops?” Bob asked.

“Except for what I’ve been told by some criminals, I don’t know shit about you, and criminals are notoriously untrustworthy.”

Bob turned to his bodyguards. “Business is business,” he said. “Let them frisk you.”

Reynolds turned to Ali. “Pat them down to make sure they’re not wired,” he said in Urdu.

“Speak fucking English,” Bob barked.

“He doesn’t speak English. I just told him to pat you down.”

Bob looked at Ali with distaste and spat in the dirt. Then he raised his hands. Ali went over the men very professionally, the way he’d been trained to do it in the camp.

“Satisfied?” Bob asked.

Reynolds nodded. He put away his gun and raised his hands. One of the giants patted them down. Ali thought he was excessively rough.

"Now that that's out of the way," Reynolds said, "show us what you got."

Bob nodded, and one of his bodyguards went into the barn.

"You have the money?" Bob asked while they waited.

"Every penny. Where did you get the stuff?"

"A coal mine in West Virginia."

The bodyguard came out of the barn carrying a cardboard box. His eyes were glued to it, and he walked slowly. Warnings on the sides of the box identified the contents as dynamite. The man set the box down in the dirt and returned to the barn.

Reynolds knelt down beside the box and opened it. Ali looked over his shoulder. Inside were stacks of yellow tubes made out of heavy paper and surrounded by clear plastic to prevent leakage.

The man who had returned to the barn came out carrying a cardboard carton. He set it down next to the dynamite. Reynolds opened that box. Inside were several two-inch-long aluminum tubes with the diameter of a pencil. Reynolds looked up at Bob.

"I want to test one of the blasting caps and one of the dynamite sticks," he said.

"Be my guest."

Reynolds's hand hovered over the detonators. Then it dipped down and plucked out one of the tubes. After examining it, he selected a stick of dynamite. Then he turned to Ali.

"Let's see what you've learned," he said in Urdu as he handed over the blasting cap and the stick of dynamite.

Ali's chest puffed with pride. As he went to the van, he vowed to show Steve how much he appreciated the American's trust.

Ali returned with a shovel and a length of lamp cord. He took one wire from the blasting cap and attached it to one portion of the two-part wire in the cord. Then he attached a second part of the cap to the other part of the lamp-cord wire and stuck the detonator into the dynamite. When he finished, he looked at Steve. Reynolds nodded his approval.

Ali walked far away from everyone into the field at the side of the barn. Steve followed. Bob and his bodyguards stayed near the entrance to the barn. Ali stopped when he found a spot in the yard where the dirt was soft. He dug down deep and buried the blasting cap and the dynamite. Then he carried the other end of the lamp cord to the van and popped the hood. Steve followed. Ali attached the ends of the exposed lamp-cord wire to the positive and negative terminals of the car battery. There was an explosion. A geyser of dirt flew into the air. In the pasture behind the barn, the horses panicked and the sheep froze.

"Have your boys get the rest of the goods and put it in the van," Reynolds told Bob.

Bob turned to his bodyguards and pointed at the open boxes. "Seal that shit up and bring out the rest of the boxes."

The bodyguards picked up the open boxes and returned to the barn.

Steve turned to Ali. "Good job," he said in Urdu. "Now bring me the gym bag and the duct tape."

Moments after Ali handed him the bag and the tape he'd taken from the van, Bob's men reemerged from the barn carrying the first two boxes, which had been resealed with duct tape, and several other boxes containing dynamite and blasting caps. While Bob checked the money in the gym bag, Steve opened each box to make sure of the contents, then resealed the boxes with the duct tape.

"What you boys fixing to do with this shit?" Bob asked with a grin, knowing damn well that Reynolds wasn't going to tell him.

Reynolds let his eyes flick across the Baltimore Ravens logo on Bob's T-shirt and grinned.

"That's for me to know and you to find out, Bob, but you're going to be pleasantly surprised when the time comes."

When they got back to the house, Reynolds parked the van next to the side door.

"Have the others help you unload the van, and bring everything into the basement," Reynolds told Ali.

When the three other members of the cell came out of the house, Reynolds opened the back of the van. Stacked in the back were four trays identical to the ones the men carried around their necks when they sold food and drinks in the stands during the Redskins games. Reynolds told the men to bring the trays to the basement after they brought down the blasting caps and the dynamite.

When everyone was downstairs, Reynolds ignored the explosives and put one of the trays on a table. The men were silent, very tense, and totally focused on the tray. Reynolds removed the top and revealed a hidden compartment lined with ball bearings, which were glued to the bottom of the tray. Next to the ball bearings was a space large enough for two sticks of dynamite and a detonator. A nine-volt battery was already in place.

After Reynolds explained to Ali how to attach the dynamite, detonators, and battery so that the tray would be primed to explode, he slid aside two panels on opposite sides of the outside of the tray revealing two red buttons.

"Each of you must push both buttons at the same time to set

off the explosives," he told the four men. "This way, no tray will explode accidentally."

Reynolds's features hardened into a mask of hate. "During the game, you'll carry your tray into the stands and inflict horror on the infidels. Remember, this game will be televised to American troops in their bases around the world. They will see the cost of their unholy crusade. We will bring their war home. We will make them suffer."

Chapter Twenty-one

After days of being raped and beaten, Dana was numb to almost all sensation. She no longer smelled the dank odor of mold on the basement walls or the stench from the foul water that pooled against them. She didn't shiver when the chill air stroked her naked, battered body. She was dead to the pain caused by each thrust of the meth cook who was inside her.

There were, however, sensations she was capable of experiencing. There was the tactile pleasure she got from holding the smooth, cool rounded glass of the broken beer bottle the meth cook had foolishly discarded in his haste to satisfy his sexual desires. There was the joy she felt when she drove its jagged edge into the meth cook's face and watched blood erupt from his eye socket. And there was the rage that gave her the strength to slash his face and throat until he was dead.

As the biker fell toward Dana, his lacerated head on a collision course with her face, she shot up in bed and screamed. It took a few seconds for her to realize that she had been dreaming. Dana fell back on the bed. Her breathing was ragged, and she was soaked with sweat. If Jake had been home, he would have comforted her until her night terrors smoothed out, but Jake was in Afghanistan, and she had to deal with her personal demons alone, in the dark.

During her yearlong stay in the mental hospital, Dana had learned how to deal with the horror of her captivity and the insane violence that had characterized her revenge against the men who had imprisoned her. She doubted that she would ever shake loose the graphic memories of her days in captivity, but those memories no longer had the power to paralyze her.

The nightmares had come less frequently by the time she was released from the hospital. For a while, she thought there might be a time when she was completely free of them, but they kept coming. At first, the nightmares had terrified her, because dreaming about the rapes was like being raped again. After a while, the nightmares made her furious, because the bikers were stealing a part of her life each night and she could not kill them again. Now the night terrors depressed her. They robbed her of sleep and left her exhausted.

Dana walked into the kitchen. She was tempted to unscrew the cap from the bottle of scotch Jake kept in their liquor cabinet, but she knew better than to go there. Instead, she filled a glass with ice-cold water and carried it into the living room. She sank down on the couch, closed her eyes, and held the glass to her forehead. The cold felt good.

Dana's flashbacks and nightmares were usually triggered by stress. So what had triggered her dream? Was it her fear that something would happen to Jake? She loved Jake. For a long time, she could not tolerate even the thought of a man touching her. Jake had understood that, and he had been there for her anyway. It had taken her a long time to open up to him and admit that she loved him, because love made you vulnerable. Jake's assignments were usually in places where violent death was common, and Dana suffered until he was home again and safe.

And then there was her business, which was not going well. All of the notoriety she had gotten from the articles in *Exposed* about the incidents involving President Christopher Farrington and Supreme Court Justice Felicia Moss had worked to her disadvantage. She was too well known to go undercover, and she heard that some potential clients worried about the fees someone as famous as Dana would charge.

The loss of income bothered Dana. She could not tolerate the idea that she wouldn't be carrying her own weight in her relationship with Jake. For a good part of that relationship, Dana had lived in her own small apartment and stayed in Jake's spacious house when she chose to. Jake had given her space after she was released from the hospital, and she had not let go of her apartment and moved in with Jake until she was able to admit to herself that she loved him. Although it wasn't necessary, she insisted on splitting all of the expenses, and she worried that she might not be able to do that if the money from her private-investigation business dried up.

Dana forced herself to think about Brad and Ginny to take her mind off subjects that were making her anxious. Dana had been a policewoman, and she was used to danger. Brad and Ginny were ordinary citizens who had become involved in nation-shaking scandals due to forces beyond their control. What she admired most about her friends was their normalcy. They both came from loving families and had been raised in middle-class comfort. Until the Farrington affair, their biggest problems had been grades, dating, what college or law school would admit them, and what job choice they should make.

Dana's mother had walked out on the family when Dana was a sophomore in high school, and her father had died of a stroke while working on a carburetor in the garage he owned. Money was always tight in Dana's family, and she'd worked in high school and paid her way through community college by waitressing. She thought she'd found her niche when she joined the police force, but she'd left the force after being kidnapped and tortured while working undercover.

Dana was exhausted, but she doubted she could get to sleep right away, so she turned the television to CNN. Two talking heads were discussing a story that she gathered had led off the evening news programs. From late afternoon until eleven, Dana had been working surveillance for an insurance company and had not watched any TV. The newscasters paused while they replayed a clip of a press conference that had been held by United States Senator Jack Carson.

"Senator," one of the reporters shouted, "didn't you think about coming back to Washington when you heard about the murder in your town house?"

"Our cabin is in a remote area in the mountains, and I go there to decompress. Cell phones don't work up there, we don't have a television or radio, and I'm miles from a store that carries newspapers. So I had no idea that Miss Koshani had been killed." Carson broke eye contact with the camera. "I guess I picked the wrong time to go on vacation," he said with an embarrassed smile.

"Why was the murder victim staying in your town house?"

"We're getting into areas of national security here, so I can't respond to that question. And now, if you'll excuse me."

When the clip of the press conference ended, Dana was frowning. Something didn't feel right. Brad had told her that Koshani was going to be a witness before a committee on which Carson sat. He put her up at his town house. Why would he leave before she testified? Then she shrugged. Whatever the reason, it was none of her business.

Dana had gotten back to bed at three thirty. The phone rang at seven. Dana struggled out of a deep sleep and managed to find the receiver after the third ring.

"Cutler?" a familiar voice said.

Shit! Dana thought.

"Cutler, wake up," Patrick Gorman barked.

Dana struggled into a sitting position. "You called at a great time, boss. I ran into Elvis last night pumping gas at a Shell station in Bethesda, and he said he'd tell me how he was abducted by aliens if I slept with him. This could be a big scoop. You want me to wake him up?"

"Have a little respect for the fine newspaper stories that make it possible for me to pay your exorbitant fees," Gorman answered, trying his best to sound like a gruff, old-time editor from a responsible newspaper. Patrick Gorman was the publisher of *Exposed*, D.C.'s most outrageous supermarket tabloid, and he couldn't care less that he made his money by printing stories that only the most gullible readers would believe. He had also made a few pennies by running exclusives based on Dana's inside knowledge of President Christopher Farrington's involvement in a serial murder case and the attempts by an ex-CIA bigwig to rig the result in a case before the United States Supreme Court.

"If you didn't know I was screwing Elvis, why did you wake me up?"

"Have you heard that Senator Jack Carson has surfaced?"

"Yeah," Dana said as she rubbed her eyes.

"He says he was exhausted and went on vacation in a remote mountain cabin in Oregon to, open quote, 'recharge my batteries,' close quote."

"And you're calling me because . . . ?"

"I don't believe a word of it, so I want you to fly to Oregon and check out his story."

A few days in Oregon's spectacular mountains, all expenses paid, sounded like a great cure for the blues.

"My usual rates?" she asked.

"Yeah, and I'll have the corporate jet fly you there. I'm probably not the only newspaper editor with this idea. When can you leave?"

"When can you fuel the jet?"

Chapter Twenty-two

A quick check of property records was all it took to locate the senator's cabin. It was a few hours east of Portland and several miles up in the mountains on back roads, so Dana called ahead and rented a Range Rover with all-wheel drive. It was waiting for her when the jet touched down just before sunrise.

Dana was wearing jeans, hiking boots, a flannel shirt, a cable-knit sweater, and a parka, because snow and freezing temperatures were expected in the mountains. She was also carrying a selection of concealed weapons, even though she wasn't expecting trouble. Ever since her kidnapping, Dana never went anywhere unarmed, and her precautions had paid off on several occasions.

Dana threw her duffel bag in the backseat of the Rover, set the GPS, and drove out of Portland toward the wilderness. The sun was up by the time she left the airport, and the sky was clear even though the temperature was hovering around 32 degrees. The ride down the interstate was boring, and she had time to think about Jake and how much she missed him.

The scenery was spectacular once Dana got off the interstate, and it proved enough of a distraction to take her mind off of her troubles. Suddenly Dana was surrounded by a forest still bright green because of all the Douglas firs scattered among the leafless deciduous trees. Runoff from the mountains created unexpected waterfalls. Every once in a while, the road would curve and Dana would be treated to a brief glimpse of a towering snowcapped mountain through a break in the foothills. Then, as suddenly as it appeared, the mountain would vanish at the next turn in the road, like the object of a spectacular magic trick.

The elevation increased as she drove through the pass that took her over the Cascades, and a light rain turned to snow. In no time, the state highway looked as though it had been dusted with powdered sugar. Dana drove through a one-street town with a café, a general store, and a garage with a sign announcing that this was the last place to gas up for fifty miles. Fifteen minutes later, the GPS told her to make a left onto a narrow road that curved up into the mountains. The road was paved for a few miles, but the snow was falling fast and there were only a few spots where the asphalt could be seen beneath the accumulating flakes.

Trees towered over the road on both sides, and the canopy and thick storm clouds made midday seem like dusk. Dana was glad she wasn't claustrophobic. A slight dip signaled the end of the pavement and the beginning of a one-lane dirt road. The temperature was dropping as the elevation increased, and the thermometer on the dash put the weather outside in the high twenties. The Rover skidded twice, but Dana got it under control before any damage was done. The snow in the forest covered the bases of the tree trunks, and it was clear that it had been snowing at this altitude for a while.

The GPS spoke again seven miles after Dana turned off the highway. She had to squint through the windshield to see the road because the pelting snow was fighting the wipers to a draw. If it weren't for the GPS telling her to turn, Dana would have missed the slight gap through the trees on her right. A quarter mile later, a log cabin appeared.

The trees had been cut back on either side of a wide driveway that led uphill to the house. Dana was not expecting problems, but one of the adages she lived by was "Better safe than sorry," so she parked the Rover in front of the driveway in the direction of the highway so she wouldn't have to turn if she was forced to make a fast getaway.

Dana got out of the car and cursed when she stepped into a pile of snow. A frigid wind raked her cheeks. She threw up the hood of her parka and focused on the cabin. The driveway looked pristine. Dana thought of several reasons why there might not be footprints or tire tracks on it. Carson might have parked on the road, as she had, or the new snow might have covered the tracks. Still, shouldn't there be some furrows in the snow?

The senator was telling the truth when he said there was no reception, but Dana could still use her cell phone to photograph the driveway. When she was through, she trudged up to the covered porch in front of the cabin. Dana stamped her boots to shake off the snow that had accumulated on them. Before trying the door, she looked through the front window into a large living room with a high stone fireplace. There were no lights on inside, and the light from the sun was starting to fade, so Dana couldn't make out any fine details. She walked to the door. It was locked. Dana took out a set of tools and picked the lock.

As soon as she was inside, Dana sniffed the air. A musty odor pervaded the living room, the type of smell caused by dust and disuse. There were no cooking aromas, no scent left by burning logs.

Dana found a light switch and flipped it on. The living room had a homey atmosphere. An Afghan had been flung over the back of a sofa that faced the fireplace, and a blanket graced the back of a chair. Throw rugs covered the wood-plank floor. There were no mounted animal heads, not surprising, given the senator's dot-com, high-tech background, but there were original oils depicting forest and mountain scenes.

Dana walked over to the fireplace. It looked as though it hadn't been used in a while. She turned slowly, surveying the room. A thermostat was attached to a wall by the stairs that led to the second floor. The senator might have used the heater instead of the fireplace, but the air in the cabin was very cold. Dana could see her breath when she exhaled. How long did it take for warmth to dissipate in weather like this?

Dana inspected the kitchen. The refrigerator was bare except for a half-full bottle of ketchup and a few cans of soda. The freezer section was stocked with two cartons of Rocky Road ice cream and a bag of frozen peas. She walked over to the sink. There were no dirty dishes in it or clean dishes in the dishwasher. She looked under the sink. There was no trash in the garbage can. It looked as though a housekeeper had done a thorough cleaning. In fact, the whole downstairs looked as though it had undergone a thorough cleaning. The senator could have cleaned up before he left, but it was hard to imagine that a cleaning crew had come up in this snow between the time the senator left and the time Dana arrived without leaving tire tracks.

Dana went upstairs. The master bedroom and its bathroom

did not look as if they had been used. Neither did any of the guest rooms. Dana decided she had seen enough. She took pictures of every part of the house. Then she locked the door behind her and returned to the Rover. On the way down to the highway, Dana thought about what she had seen. She decided that either United States Senator Jack Carson had a compulsive cleaning disorder or he had not been in the cabin lately.

During her drive from the cabin to Isolation Creek, the one-street town she'd driven through, Dana caught a weather report on the radio and learned that the pass had been hit by heavy snows. Dana filled her tank at the garage on the outskirts of town and asked the attendant to help her put on chains for the trip back to Portland. While they worked, Dana turned the conversation to Senator Carson. The attendant knew the senator from his previous visits to the cabin but said he hadn't seen him recently.

Dana drove into town and parked in front of the grocery store. She asked the proprietor questions about Carson while she paid for the candy bars that would fortify her during the return trip to Portland. He hadn't seen Senator Carson since the summer, and neither had any other shopkeeper to whom she talked. There was a café with Internet access at the far end of town. While she waited for her cheeseburger, fries, and black coffee to arrive, Dana set up her laptop and e-mailed the photos she'd taken at the cabin to *Exposed*. Then she called Patrick Gorman.

"Did you get the photos?" Dana asked.

"I did."

"I'm in a café in Isolation Creek, the nearest town to the cabin. Most of the people I talked to know the senator. He shops in town when he's at the cabin. No one has seen him in months. I'd bet every penny you have that no one has been in that cabin for a while."

"Where do you think he was?" Gorman asked.

"Beats me, but it wasn't here. What do you want me to do?"

Gorman was quiet for a moment. "Send me your report, and I'll have one of my intrepid reporters write the story."

"Do you want me to fly back to D.C.?"

"Not yet. If the senator were in Oregon, he'd have left a trail. Check into a hotel in Portland and do some sleuthing. See what you can turn up."

"Will do."

The waitress carried Dana's food to her table, and Dana rang off. She typed her report between bites, then e-mailed it. By the time she finished, the sun had begun its descent, but the snow had stopped. Dana paid the check, slipped on her gloves, and trudged toward her Range Rover. When she had the motor going and the heater cranked up, she headed west.

Chapter Twenty-three

Dana was exhausted after the tiring drive through the storm-plagued mountains, and she slept late the next morning. After a big breakfast, she headed back to the Portland airport in a driving rain to try to find out if Senator Carson had flown in or out on a private or commercial flight when he claimed he had been in Oregon. After striking out, when she inquired at the commercial carriers, she drove over to the airfield for private planes, where the manager told Dana that information about arrivals and departures was confidential.

Dana left the office, discouraged by her lack of progress. As she headed for her car, a heavyset, bearded man in mechanic's overalls walked toward her. As he passed, he turned slightly and spoke to her.

"Coffee People on the terminal concourse, twenty minutes."

Dana didn't turn her head, and she knew better than to ask him to explain himself. Instead, she parked at the terminal, got a cup of black coffee at Coffee People and found a table in the middle of the food court. Ten minutes after she sat down, she saw the mechanic scanning the crowd. He spotted Dana and walked to her table, looking around nervously the whole way.

"A friend of mine at United told me you're asking around about Senator Carson," he said as soon as he was seated across from Dana.

"That's right. My name's Dana Cutler, and you are . . . ?"

"That's not important. You're with *Exposed*, right? Not some legit paper like the *New York Times*?"

Dana's initial reaction to the insult was to tense, but there was really no easy way to defend the legitimacy of a paper whose most recent headline was I GAVE BIRTH TO SADDAM HUSSEIN'S LOVE CHILD, so she just nodded.

"Good, because I read that the *Times* don't pay for information."

"What kind of information are we talking about?"

"You want to know if Senator Carson was in Oregon when that lady was killed in his town house. I can answer your question for a hundred bucks."

"I'll give you fifty."

"My price is nonnegotiable, lady. One hundred dollars, or you can keep guessing."

Dana didn't want to waste time arguing, so she laid five twenties on the table and covered them with her hand. It was Pat Gorman's money, anyway.

"Was Senator Jack Carson in Oregon on the Sunday Jessica Koshani was killed?" she asked.

"I saw him get off his private jet Sunday afternoon."

"How do you know it was Carson?"

"He flies commercial when he's looking for votes, but I've worked on his plane enough to know what he looks like."

"And you definitely saw him?"

"Yeah, but just a snatch. What attracted my attention was the hoodie. He was wearing nice slacks, but he was also wearing a gray sweatshirt with a hood."

"Do you remember anything else?"

"There was a black guy with him, and a town car was waiting on the tarmac. The black guy hustled him inside. It drove off right away."

"If he was wearing a hood, how did you see him?"

"The hood fell back when he was walking down the steps. I was with the refueling crew, and I was near enough to look him in the eye. And that's what I know."

"Do you have any idea where the car went?"

"Nope."

"What time did the plane land?"

"That I can tell you. It touched down a little after five P.M."

"Can you describe the black man who helped Carson out of the plane?"

The man thought for a second. Then he nodded.

"He had a shaved head, and he sort of looked like a football player. Not a lineman, a cornerback."

Dana couldn't think of anything more to ask, so she slid the money across the table. The mechanic palmed the bills and slipped them into his pocket.

"It's been a pleasure doing business with you," he said. Then he looked around the food court and left. While he walked away, Dana debated whether to believe his story and decided that he was probably telling the truth. Jack Carson had been in Oregon, but not at his cabin. So where had he been?

• • •

Dana drove from the airport to the senator's Portland office, then to his campaign headquarters. None of the staff in either place admitted seeing Carson during the period he claimed he was in Oregon.

An old friend from Gorman's college days covered politics for the *Oregonian.* Dana treated him to dinner and learned a lot about Gorman's college carousing but nothing about the senator that she could use for her story. Frustrated, she returned to her hotel, watched an in-room movie, and went to sleep.

The next morning, Dana's cell phone rang just as she was getting ready to take a shower.

"What's up, Pat?" Dana asked.

"Turn on CNN."

As Dana switched on the TV, Gorman told her that *Exposed* had put out a special edition with a headline that read WHERE WAS SENATOR CARSON HIDING? with a subhead that read NO PROOF SENATOR WAS IN CABIN and a story based on her investigation. When she found CNN, she saw Jack Carson standing behind a podium with his wife by his side. Neither was smiling.

"I have always believed in the adage that honesty is the best policy, but I stand here today to tell you that I was not honest with my wife, my constituents, or the American people when I stood here a few days ago and said that I had been at my mountain cabin in Oregon during the days I was missing."

"Your story flushed him out," Gorman said. "Good work."

On the screen, Carson's eyes dropped. When they returned to the camera, he looked tormented.

"I was in Oregon, but I am ashamed to say that what I did there dishonored my wife and our marriage."

Carson took a deep breath. "None of this is Martha's fault. I take full responsibility. Martha has been a wonderful wife and a full partner in my political life, and there is no excuse for what I did."

The senator looked down again and paused before resuming.

"Over the years, the American people have heard the sordid tale of one politician after another who has soiled his marriage with an unseemly affair. I am thoroughly ashamed to say that I have become a tired cliché. Some months ago, I spent one night with a woman. I have no excuses to make. The fault is mine alone, and I regretted my betrayal of my marriage vows immediately after I committed this unpardonable sin. I also made it a point to stay away from the innocent partner in my terrible mistake after that single night.

"The woman in question assumed that there was more to it than I did, and I can't blame her. She called me repeatedly. I did not answer her calls. The day before I disappeared, she left a message with Lucas Sharp, my chief of staff, saying that she would go to the press if I continued to ignore her. Mr. Sharp was not aware that I had strayed, and he confronted me. We decided that the best way to end the confusion was for me to fly to Oregon and talk to this woman. And that is what I did.

"The two of us had a heart-to-heart. I explained that I loved my wife and regretted what I had done. She was very understanding. When I returned to Washington, I confessed my infidelity to Martha. She has forgiven me. I would not have blamed her if she didn't, but our marriage has always been strong, and I truly believe we will weather this storm. Thank you."

"Who is the woman?" a reporter shouted as the senator turned to leave. Carson turned back to the microphone.

"In the past, the women who have been named in these situations have been smeared and held up to ridicule. This is my fault and I have promised this woman that I would not reveal her identity. I stand by that promise. The relationship lasted one night, and it was over by the next day. I see no reason other than prurient interest for the press to drag her through the mud. Thank you again."

The senator left the podium, and the talking heads started to dissect him like hyenas tearing at fallen prey. Dana switched off the set.

"The plot thickens," Gorman said.

"It's an old and tired plot that's been done to death, Pat. If you tried to sell the story to a book publisher, no self-respecting editor would buy it."

"You forget that I have no self-respect, Miss Cutler. If I did, I'd have sold *Exposed* years ago."

Dana sighed. "What do you want me to do, as if I can't guess?"

"I want you to get me an interview with Carson's paramour."

Dana went back to the senator's Portland office and his campaign headquarters, but no one would talk to her. Next she called up the reporter from the *Oregonian*. He said he didn't know any more than she did. He was also honest enough to admit that he wasn't going to share any information he dug up if there was any risk that Dana might scoop him.

After a thoroughly depressing day, Dana returned to her hotel and ordered room service. She had just tipped the waiter when her room phone rang. Dana was intrigued. She'd given everyone she talked to her cell phone number, and that was the number Gorman would call.

"Yes?" she answered.

"Dana Cutler?" the caller asked. Dana didn't recognize the voice, and it sounded as though the caller was disguising it.

"Speaking."

"Dorothy Crispin."

"What?"

"The girl the senator screwed. She's a law student, and she has an apartment at 1276 Southwest Spruce Terrace."

"How do you . . . ?" Dana started, but the line was dead.

Dana hung up the phone and sat back in her chair. She'd just gotten a real break, *if* Dorothy Crispin was Carson's lover, but who had given her the information, and why?

Dana checked her watch. It was eight thirty, not too late. She pulled on her trainers, checked her guns to make sure they were loaded, and left her hotel room.

Dorothy Crispin lived in John's Landing, a section of the city near the Willamette River where town houses and apartments filled in the gaps between older homes. Spruce Terrace wound its way from Corbett Avenue up a hill until it dead-ended in a cluster of garden apartments. The entrance to Crispin's apartment was at the end of a short alley. Dana rang her bell and waited. She could see lights through a side window, and she rang again when no one answered. This time she heard footsteps, and a timid voice asked her to identify herself.

"Dana Cutler, Miss Crispin. I'd like to talk to you."

"About what?"

"We both know the answer to that. It was only a matter of time before someone figured out that you're Senator Carson's mystery woman. Fortunately for you, I'm not out to humiliate you. I just want to talk, and I promise to present your story in a dignified manner."

"Please, I don't want to discuss Senator Carson."

"You're not going to have a choice when someone else digs up your name. The next time someone knocks on your door, they'll have a cameraman and a lighting crew, and they won't be anywhere near as nice I intend to be. Talking to me will give you a chance to shape the way this story plays."

Dana gave Crispin time to think. A minute later, locks snapped, and the door opened. Dana found herself facing a brunette with shoulder-length hair, bright blue eyes, and a turned-up nose who managed to look cute even though she wasn't wearing makeup and was dressed in a University of Oregon sweatshirt, sweat socks, and a pair of plain gray sweatpants. Dana stepped inside. Crispin checked outside for more intruders, then shut the door.

The living room had a picture window with a panoramic view of the river and the lights of downtown Portland. It was furnished with tasteful, inexpensive furniture. Framed reproductions of famous Impressionist paintings hung on the walls. The only clutter was caused by thick textbooks that were stacked on a glass-top coffee table next to an open laptop.

"What year?" Dana asked as she pointed at the books.

"My second. Look, is there any way you can give me a break? I won't be able to go to class if this comes out. And I can kiss any chance of getting a decent job good-bye."

"What did you think would happen if the senator divorced his wife for you?" Dana asked, choosing to make her tone kind instead of cruel.

Crispin looked down at the hardwood floor. "I wasn't thinking."

"Look, Dorothy, I'm not here to ruin you. You and Carson both made a mistake. That's the way he's playing it, and he's painted you as the victim. He's a lot older than you. He's a rich and powerful man. Everyone is going to see you as the wronged party. Tell me that's an accurate picture of the way this happened, and I'll make sure that's the first impression everyone has."

Crispin looked conflicted. "Who did you say you're with?"

Dana handed her a business card.

"Oh, shit. *Exposed* is one of those supermarket rags."

Dana laughed. "You hit the nail right on the head. But we've also won a Pulitzer and been nominated for a second for some pretty serious journalism. We used to be a joke, but we're starting to be taken seriously."

Crispin ran a hand across her forehead. She looked like a martyr on the way to her crucifixion. Then she sighed.

"Let's get this over with." She pointed at the sofa. "Do you want some coffee or tea?"

Dana smiled. "Thanks. Coffee would be great. If you feel like a stiff shot of whiskey I promise your beverage of choice won't make it into the story."

Crispin smiled ruefully. "Tempting, but I'm going to do this sober."

"What do you want to know?" Crispin asked when she returned with two cups of coffee.

"Why don't you tell me what happened between you and the senator?"

"I feel so stupid. I met him at a campaign event, and we talked for a while. He seemed interested in what I had to say about legislation for funding Portland's light rail. When he found out I was a law student, he hinted at a possible internship. Before he moved on, he gave me his card and told me to call. And I did. I mean, a job in D.C. It sounded so exciting, and I haven't traveled a lot."

"What happened?"

"He said he was going to be in Portland in two weeks. He told me that he had very little free time and suggested that we get together for a late dinner."

"Weren't you suspicious?"

"No, he made it sound like a job interview."

"But it wasn't?"

"No, no, it was at first. We met at Jake's. He had a booth in the back. It was a place where we couldn't be seen while we were eating. Over dinner he was a perfect gentleman, but he did feed me drinks."

Crispin blushed. "I should have seen what was coming when he started telling me that I was a breath of fresh air and hinted at a job after I graduated. Then he said he was enjoying our conversation so much that we should continue our talk in his hotel room."

"Carson lives in Portland. There's no reason for him to stay in a hotel."

"I didn't know where he lived. I was also pretty naive. And maybe I wanted something to happen. My grades are decent, but I'm not near the top of my class. A job in the Senate would open a lot of doors."

"So you went into this with open eyes?"

"Half open." Crispin shrugged.

"What happened next?"

Crispin blushed. "We . . . we slept together. When we were done, Jack said all the right things, and I went home."

"What did he say specifically?"

"You know, the sex was great, I was great, he'd had a great time and wanted to see me again." Crispin shrugged. "It was what I wanted to hear."

"Did you ask about the job?" Dana said.

"Oh, definitely. He said he or someone from the office would be in touch."

"And?"

For the first time, Crispin looked angry instead of embarrassed. "No one ever called, so I called Washington, which got me nowhere. Finally I called Lucas Sharp, his chief of staff. I told him I would go public if the senator kept ignoring me."

"When was this?"

"The Friday before that woman was killed in his town house."

"What happened then?"

"Jack called me and said he was going to fly out. He got here on Sunday around five P.M. We had a heart-to-heart. He told me he loved his wife and regretted what he'd done."

"Did you buy what he said?"

"He sounded sincere, like he really felt bad about cheating on his wife. He convinced me that he was sorry he'd given in to temptation."

"Weren't you angry that he'd used you?"

"I couldn't get too upset. I tried to use him, too, you know, for the job."

Something about Crispin bothered Dana but she wasn't sure what it was.

"What happened with the job?" she asked.

"Uh, well, we knew that wouldn't work. He told me he was going to publicly confess what he'd done to his wife. It would be uncomfortable for both of us to be in the same office."

"So the senator got here on Sunday?"

"Yes. He came here straight from the airport. He said he didn't want anyone to know he was in Portland, so he couldn't risk being seen in a hotel."

"The senator was gone several days. Was he with you all that time?"

"Yeah, he stayed with me."

"Did you sleep together?"

"No! I felt like I'd been played before, so I made it clear that wasn't going to happen. He was okay with it. I think he really did regret cheating on his wife."

"Did Senator Carson know about the murder at his town house?"

"It was on the news."

"Then why didn't he fly back to D.C.?"

"I don't know," she said. "I didn't ask him."

"It seems unusual. The murder involved him directly."

"You'll have to ask Jack. I can't tell you what he was thinking."

"Too bad about the job," Dana said.

"That's the least of my worries. Now that this is going public, I'm probably going to be the next Monica Lewinsky."

"Not necessarily. I'll do my best to protect you."

"Will you have to print my name?"

"I'm afraid so, but I'll humanize you and make you as sympathetic as I can. Why don't you tell me a little about yourself? For instance, where did you grow up?"

"You're not going to talk to my parents, are you?"

"They'll learn about this anyway."

"No, I'm not dragging them into this."

"Look . . ."

Crispin shook her head vigorously. "Absolutely not. And I think I've talked enough."

Dana pressed her case for a few moments, then got up when it was clear that the interview was over.

"Thanks for talking to me," Dana said. "You have my card. If you want to tell me anything more, or if you just want to talk, call me anytime."

Crispin showed Dana out. The door closed behind her. Dana stood in the passageway. A chill wind was blowing in from the river and she turned up her coat collar. She knew she should be ecstatic. She'd scooped every news source in the country. But something wasn't right. She just couldn't figure out what it was.

Chapter Twenty-four

Dana Cutler's exclusive interview with Dorothy Crispin ran in *Exposed* and created the anticipated uproar. Dana had spent the time before the issue hit the stands trying to interview students and professors at the law school, but the professors wouldn't discuss a student, and the two students who admitted that they knew Crispin knew her only from class. After the story broke, no one would give her the time of day.

Pat Gorman told Dana that he had other plans for the corporate jet, so Dana was scheduled to fly out of Portland on an early-morning commercial flight three days after the story broke. While she was getting ready for bed, Dana watched the news. The picture on the screen showed TV crews standing around the area in front of Dorothy Crispin's apartment complex. Then bright lights from a portable TV camera illuminated the breezeway in front of Crispin's apartment while a bright-eyed reporter excitedly explained that she was standing at the front door of the young woman who had been seduced by United States Senator Jack Carson. Two establishing shots had given anyone who was interested in finding it a pretty good idea of the location of

Crispin's apartment. Dana felt a twinge of guilt about being responsible for the siege, but she didn't worry enough to keep her from falling asleep.

Dorothy Crispin was beginning to question whether putting up with the reporters was worth the money she was being paid. It was a lot of money, and she knew the scrutiny wouldn't last long. Another juicy scandal would draw the hyenas away, and she would soon become a footnote in history. But she had been forced to drop her classes, and it would mean graduating a semester later than she'd planned. Of course, the cost of all of her subsequent semesters was covered, which meant no more student loans.

Dorothy peeked through her living room curtains just before she went into her bedroom. She could see a cigarette glowing near a van with a Channel 8 logo. She sighed. Didn't these idiots ever give up? She'd politely declined all interviews at first. Now she just unplugged her phone and didn't answer the door.

Dorothy washed up and changed for bed. She took a sleeping pill and was soon in such a deep sleep that she didn't hear the latch on the patio door ease open. Twenty minutes later, a slap to her cheek roused her. She felt groggier than she normally did when she awoke after taking a pill. That was because of the mild anesthetic that she'd been given.

The first thing Crispin saw when her eyes opened was a man standing in front of the chair to which she was duct-taped. Adrenaline overcame most of the effects of the pill and the anesthetic, and she almost toppled over in her frenzy to escape. The man watched her but didn't say anything.

Crispin tried to speak, but she had been outfitted with a ball gag. Her eyes darted away from the man and focused on her surroundings. She was in her bedroom, naked. Her arms had been pulled behind her, and her knees and lower legs had been secured to the chair legs, leaving her completely vulnerable. On the end of the bed were a hammer, pliers, pruning shears, and a lighter.

Dana Cutler sat up in bed. She looked at the clock. It was one thirty in the morning, and something she'd dreamed had shocked her out of a deep sleep. What was it? There was an image on the edge of her conscious mind, but it was as elusive as a ghost.

Dana squeezed her eyes shut. In the dream, she'd been talking to Jake, and they had both been sad. Jake had taken her hand and said that they had to have a heart-to-heart talk and then . . .

That was it! She had to talk to Crispin, but her plane left for D.C. at 6:45. Screw it! Dana ran to her closet and threw on some clothes. Crispin was not going to like being roused at two in the morning, but if Dana was right, that was going to be the least of the law student's problems.

All of the TV trucks were gone when Dana drove into the apartment complex. In front of Crispin's front door, she raised her hand to knock but stopped when she heard a noise to her left. It sounded like someone sliding down the steep hill that started at the end of the breezeway and dropped down to the street below. Dana walked to the top of the hill. A man was inching his way down.

"Hey!" Dana shouted as she started down the hill.

The man looked up, but his face was in shadow. Then he pulled something out of his pocket. Dana saw a muzzle flash and saw dirt fly up inches from her. She scrambled back up the hill and dived for cover. Dana drew her gun from the holster at the small of her back while the man slid the rest of the way to the street. When she looked over the side, he was streaking toward a car. She fired and the bullet ricocheted off the sidewalk. The man wrenched open the door and lunged into the driver's seat. Dana's next shot hit the trunk seconds before the engine roared to life and the car skidded down the street.

Dana was sitting in her rented Rover in front of Dorothy Crispin's apartment complex, resting her head against the back of the seat, when someone rapped on the passenger window. She opened her eyes and saw Monte Pike holding up two cardboard cups with Starbucks logos.

The first time Dana met Pike, during her investigation in the case involving Supreme Court justice Felicia Moss, she'd had a hard time believing he was the chief criminal deputy in the Multnomah County district attorney's office. As usual, Pike's hair was disheveled, his clothes appeared to have been selected by a blind man, and he looked more like a junior high student than a brilliant graduate of Harvard Law.

It was cold. Dana reached across and opened the passenger door. Pike slid onto the passenger seat and gave her the coffee.

"Thanks," Dana said as she pried off the lid and took a sip.

The first officers on the scene had taken Dana's statement. Then they had asked her to wait while they checked on Dorothy Crispin. Dana had warned them about what they would see inside the apartment, but she got the impression the men hadn't taken her seriously. Moments after the officers walked into the apartment, one of them staggered out and threw up over the side of the hill. Dana had taken no satisfaction in that. Now, forty-five minutes later, the Rover was blocked in by a morgue wagon, a van from the Oregon State Crime Lab, the car in which two homicide detectives had arrived, and vans from three television stations.

Pike cocked his head in the direction of the detectives who were conferring with a forensic expert near the front door of Crispin's apartment.

"Detective Pierson says you came here to talk to Crispin at two in the morning. That's an odd time for an interview."

"I've got a flight back to D.C. at six forty-five, which I guess I won't make. This was the only time I could talk to Crispin before I left."

"What was so urgent?"

"When I was asking her about her meeting with Carson she said, 'We had a heart-to-heart. He told me he loved his wife and regretted what he'd done.' Those were the exact words Senator Carson used in his press conference. A lot of what she said sounded like she was reading from a script. I wanted to confront her."

"But you didn't get the chance."

"No. I was about to knock when I heard someone scrambling down the hill. I called out to him, and he shot at me. I returned fire, but I didn't hit him. I got his car, though."

"Did you get a license, make?"

"No, it was dark, and I spent a lot of time ducking. When I was sure I was safe, I went in through the patio to see if Crispin was okay. She wasn't."

Monte Pike would have been suspicious of any other witness who was this calm after seeing how Dorothy Crispin had been defiled, but Pike knew a little about Dana's history.

"Can you describe the man who shot at you?"

"No. It was dark. I dived for cover when he fired at me. When I fired back, he was down the hill and his back was all I saw."

"If I tell you something, will you promise me I won't read it in *Exposed*?"

Dana nodded.

"The killer took Crispin's pinkie."

Dana had not spent much time with Crispin's corpse after determining that she was dead, so this revelation came as a complete surprise.

"Clarence Little?" she said.

"Do you think the man you saw was Little?"

"I have no idea. I've never seen him in person, and I was intent on staying alive, so I wasn't trying to see who was shooting at me. Do you have any idea why Little would want to murder Crispin?"

"None whatsoever."

"When can I go home, Monte?"

"Tomorrow, unless some concrete reason to keep you here pops up, but I can't think what that might be."

"I'll tell the people at *Exposed* I'll be delayed. They'll want me to write this story anyway."

"But nothing about Little unless I clear it," Pike reminded Dana.

Dana got back to her hotel at five thirty in the morning and banged out her story. She was out on her feet, but she called Brad at his office before getting into bed. Thanks to the three-hour time difference, she caught him at his desk.

"Good morning, Brad. I'm calling from Portland, Oregon."

"Are you still investigating the senator for *Exposed*?"

"Yes."

"That's what I thought. Wait a minute, isn't it early there?"

"Yeah, I've been up all night at a crime scene. Dorothy Crispin was murdered."

"Why are you telling me?" Brad asked.

"The information I'm going to give you is not public knowledge. I promised I wouldn't tell anyone about a certain aspect of the case until I got permission. If I tell you, I'll be breaking that promise, so you can't tell anyone."

"Sure. What gives?"

"Crispin was tortured, and the killer cut off her pinkie and took it with him."

"What?"

"I got to Crispin's apartment just as the killer was leaving."

"You saw Little?"

"I was too far away to see the killer's face, so I can't say it was him, but I can say that the killer followed Little's MO."

"So let me get this straight. Little escapes in Oregon. Rather than head for some country without an extradition treaty, he flies to D.C. and kills Koshani. Then he flies back to Oregon, where everyone is looking for him, and murders Carson's lover. Does any of what I just said make any sense to you?"

"Not one bit," Dana answered.

Chapter Twenty-five

The phone in Dana's hotel room rang at four in the afternoon. She was going stir crazy, and she hoped that Monte Pike was calling to tell her she could head for the airport. Pike was calling, but he had something else in mind.

"Meet me at the Peet's coffee shop on Broadway and Washington," he said. "I've got something for you."

"Why don't you come to my hotel? It's closer to the courthouse."

"I don't want anyone to see us talking. I'm sitting at a table for two near the back door, and I've got a cup of coffee waiting for you. Don't let it get cold."

Fifteen minutes later, Dana was sitting opposite Monte Pike, who was hunched forward and speaking low enough to avoid being overheard.

"You were right to be suspicious of Dorothy Crispin. One of the guys from Vice thinks he recognized her picture. Crispin may have been a high-priced call girl."

Dana frowned. "So she wasn't a law student?"

"Oh no, she was enrolled as a second-year student, and she

was definitely working toward her degree, but she may also have turned tricks on occasion—expensive tricks, from what I'm told—for a high-end escort service."

"What's expensive?"

"Four figures."

Dana whistled.

"What those figures were depended on what the client wanted."

"This puts Senator Carson's relationship with Crispin in a whole new light."

"True, but that's not all, as they say in those obnoxious TV infomercials. There's more. Guess who ran the escort service?"

"How would I know? I don't live here."

Pike grinned from ear to ear. "I could make you guess—and you'd get it eventually if I threw in a few hints—but I'm not going to torture you. There's good reason to believe that the service was owned by the late Jessica Koshani."

Dana recoiled and almost spilled her drink. "Holy shit!"

"I thought you'd appreciate that tidbit."

Dana frowned. "I notice you used a lot of 'may have beens' and 'good reasons to believe.' Aren't you sure about what you just told me?"

"Proving Crispin was a hooker or that Koshani was involved with the escort service won't be easy. Koshani was well insulated. In fact, my conclusion about her connection is an educated guess. My office was looking at Koshani for some time, and we were never able to nail her."

"Is there any evidence that Carson used Koshani's escorts?" Dana asked.

"No, but there have been rumors circulating for some time that Carson used prostitutes and had kinky tastes."

"Like?"

"S and M, bondage—but this is all rumor on rumor."

Dana sat back. "You've certainly given me a lot to think about."

"Glad to be of service."

Dana cocked her head to one side and studied the DA. "Why are you being so nice?"

Pike grinned. "I owe you one from the *Woodruff* case. I figure we're even now."

It was Dana's turn to smile. She looked Pike in the eye and said, "I don't know what you're talking about."

Dana parked the Rover in front of a branch of U.S. Bank a little after six. The bank was at one end of a strip mall next to a beauty parlor. A stairway between the beauty parlor and a hardware store led up to a second-floor landing. EXECUTIVE ESCORTS was etched into a plaque next to a frosted-glass door two offices down from the stairwell. Dana walked into the small waiting room at the front of the office, and a chubby middle-aged woman with mousy brown hair looked up. She had a phone plastered to her ear and she seemed surprised to see a visitor.

"Eight o'clock at the Heathman Hotel," she said as she held up a finger to indicate that Dana should wait. There were two chairs on either side of a cheap end table, but Dana decided to stand. There were none of the usual waiting-room magazines on the table. From the woman's reaction and the lack of reading material, Dana guessed that the office received few visitors.

The woman responded to a question Dana could not hear. Then she said, "Yes. Yes," and hung up.

"Can I help you?" the woman asked after making several notations on an index card.

"Are you the manager?" Dana asked with a smile.

"No, that's Mrs. Cronin."

"Is she in?"

"Yeah."

Dana waited a bit. Then asked, "Can I see her?"

The woman frowned as if this type of situation was highly unusual.

"My name is Dana Cutler." Dana offered to make the woman's task easier. The woman thought for a moment. Then she got up and walked through the only other door in the office.

A minute later, the door opened and an attractive woman in a business suit walked out followed by the woman Dana had just talked to. The first woman gave Dana the briefest of glances before leaving.

"You can go in," the other woman said.

Dana walked into an office that wasn't much bigger than the reception area. An anorexic woman with peroxide-blond hair and cheap jewelry was sitting behind a scarred wooden desk counting a wad of bills. The woman's nose was a little too perfect, her breasts were a little too large, and the skin on her face was a little too tight. A cigarette smoldered in an ashtray next to a telephone and a stack of index cards.

A man was slumped nonchalantly in a chair next to the desk. Well-defined biceps stretched the fabric of a black T-shirt that wrapped tightly around his barrel chest. The man studied Dana while the blonde put the bills in a green metal cash box and closed the lid. Dana guessed that the well-dressed woman who had just left had given Cronin the money and that the muscle-bound man was Cronin's bodyguard.

"Mrs. Cronin?" Dana asked.

"What can I do for you?" the woman answered in a tone that let Dana know that doing anything for her was the last thing on the blonde's to-do list.

"You can tell me how well you knew Jessica Koshani and Dorothy Crispin."

The bodybuilder sat up, and Cronin brought the cigarette to her lips. While she inhaled, Cronin stared at Dana hard enough and long enough to make Dana feel threatened.

"What makes you think I know either of these people?" Cronin asked.

"You should. Jessica Koshani ran this escort service until she was murdered, and Dorothy Crispin turned tricks for Koshani until she was killed last night."

Cronin didn't give Dana anything, and Dana bet she was a terror at a poker table.

"I'm afraid you've been misinformed," Cronin said.

"I don't think so."

"I don't care what you think. This meeting is over."

"I'm with *Exposed*, Mrs. Cronin, and I'm going to be writing a story about this escort service and the dead women's connection to it."

The man stood slowly, unwinding like a cat stretching after a comfortable nap.

"You fucking deaf?" he asked.

Dana ignored him and talked to Cronin. "Talking to me now will let you give our readers your side of the story."

Cronin looked at the man and nodded toward Dana. "Jeff."

Jeff stepped around the desk and reached for Dana's arm. Just before his fingers touched her, Dana's elbow shot into Jeff's nose with enough force to break it. Blood sprayed out of both nostrils. Dana hit Jeff in the crotch. He started to crumple, but Dana grabbed a clump of the bodyguard's hair and yanked his head up before grinding the barrel of a snub-nosed pistol into his temple.

"I'm off my meds, Mrs. Cronin, so I advise you to call off your dog before I start hallucinating that he's someone who could actually hurt me."

Suddenly Cronin didn't look so tough. She showed Dana the palms of both hands.

"Let him go, please. We don't want any trouble."

Dana backed out of the office and hurried to her car. She didn't think Jeff would come looking for trouble, but she didn't wait around in case he had a gun in the office. She was frustrated by her failure to get any information from Cronin, and it looked as though her investigation was at a dead end. Then, halfway back to the hotel, Dana got a brainstorm.

The woman standing in the corridor outside Dana's room was breathtaking. Her figure was all curves, her hair was silky blond, her eyes were bright green, and her lips were pouty and a marvelous shade of red. If Dana were a lesbian, as she had implied when she'd ordered her "escort," she would have started panting as soon as she opened the door to her hotel room.

"Mrs. Gorman?" the woman asked with a warm smile. This was a natural mistake, as Dana had used her employer's credit card to pay, after explaining to the woman who answered the phone that she was on a business trip without Patrick, her hubby, and was interested in hiring a female escort who wouldn't mind being a companion for a lady.

"Come in," Dana responded, flashing her own smile. The woman gave the room the once over. Then she did the same with Dana.

"What's your name?" Dana asked.

"Cindy."

"Any last name?"

"Crawford."

"Like the model?" Dana asked with a raised eyebrow.

"Exactly."

"What a charming coincidence."

The woman laughed. "It's a pleasure to meet you," she said. "I understand you want me to keep you company at dinner."

"We can cut the euphemisms, Cindy. Didn't the service tell you that you were meeting a married woman with tastes her husband wouldn't understand?"

Cindy laughed again. It was a great laugh, and it made Dana really regret that she was heterosexual.

"I'm an Executive employee who is employed frequently in these situations," she answered. Then she looked at the bed. "Are we going to dinner?"

"I was thinking more of room service," Dana said.

"Sounds good to me."

Dana was beginning to enjoy hiring a high-class call girl. Cindy was so agreeable. Not like Jake, who always argued about where to go for dinner or what show to watch on TV.

Dana handed Cindy the room-service menu. "What would you like?" she asked.

"I'll just have a salad."

"Oh, come on. That won't fill you up, and we're going to be talking awhile. I don't want you to be hungry."

"Talking?" Cindy said, suddenly suspicious.

"I guess it's time to come clean. I'm afraid I got you up here under false pretenses. I'm a reporter, and I want to talk to you about Dorothy Crispin."

Cindy's facade dropped and she looked stricken. "That's the girl who was murdered."

Dana nodded. "She worked for Executive Escorts. Did you know her?"

"Look, I'm not paid to talk to reporters."

"I did pay for several hours of your time."

"I'll make sure you get your money back."

Dana took out her phone and snapped a picture.

"Why did you do that?" Cindy asked anxiously.

"I thought some of my friends at the DA's office might like to see what a high-priced call girl looks like. They can probably figure out your real name, maybe even ask you out on a date to a real live grand jury."

"Shit. Give me that phone."

Cindy took a step forward. Dana tossed the phone behind her onto the bed to free both hands.

"I hope you're not thinking of resorting to force, Cindy, because I have a history of very violent behavior. Make one aggressive move and I will break your nose and jaw and make you look so unattractive that no one will want to date you for some time."

The escort hesitated.

"That's better, and you can trust me to delete your picture after we chat." Then she smiled. "I'm also serious about dinner."

"I'm not hungry."

"Suit yourself. So, Cindy, did you know Dorothy Crispin or Jessica Koshani?"

"I'm not talking about Koshani."

"Why not? She's dead. She can't hurt you."

"The people she was fronting for can," Cindy said.

"Who are they?"

"Look, I'll tell you what I know about Dorothy, but I'm not going to discuss anything else. I don't want to end up dead. If what I know about Dorothy isn't good enough, it's too bad. You can do your worst. It's nowhere near what these people can do."

Dana studied Cindy for a moment. She looked frightened, and Dana was pretty sure she wasn't faking. Dana asked Cindy what she knew about Crispin.

"There's another girl. We work together if the customer wants a threesome. One time she got sick. She was in a bad way. There was no way she could date. So she called Dorothy and she did it with me. That's the only time I met her."

"What was your impression?"

"She was smart, nice." Cindy shrugged. "We really didn't talk much. This guy kept us busy."

"Give me the name of the woman who hooked you up with Dorothy Crispin, and I'll delete the photo and forget we ever met."

Cindy hesitated.

"I'm just going to talk to her, Cindy. I might not even use her name," Dana lied.

"Elsie Teller. She lives in a condo in the Pearl."

"Condos in the Pearl are pricey. She must do okay."

"She has family money."

"Then why work as an escort?"

"Elsie likes to live on the edge."

"And you?"

Cindy blushed and broke eye contact. "I'm not smart like Elsie or Dorothy." She ran her hands down her body. "This is all I've got to work with." She looked up and embarrassment was replaced by determination. "And I do okay with what I've got."

Elsie Teller lived in the Pearl, a former warehouse district that had been redeveloped into an upscale section of Portland populated by people with enough money to afford the restaurants, art galleries, and six- to seven-figure condominiums that had sprung up overnight. When the door to Teller's apartment opened, Dana was expecting to see another glamorous version of Cindy Crawford, but Teller looked like hell. She was barefoot and dressed in a faded Stanford sweatshirt and a pair of equally faded jeans. Her hair looked as though she'd run a comb through it haphazardly without looking in the mirror, she wasn't wearing makeup, and there were dark circles under red-rimmed eyes.

Teller stood aside and ushered Dana into the living room of a spacious corner apartment. While she waited for Teller to close the door behind her, the investigator admired Teller's breathtaking view of the city. Then she studied the apartment. The modern decor looked like something conceived after much thought by an interior decorator who had been told that money was no object. Either the escort business paid really well, or Cindy had hit the nail on the head when she said that Teller's family was wealthy. Colorful abstract oils hung on stark white walls, glass-topped coffee and end tables stood before or next to furniture upholstered in soft pastels. It wasn't Dana's taste, but she knew enough to know that the apartment was decorated in very good taste.

"Francine said you wanted to talk about Dotty," Teller said.

Dana guessed that Francine was Cindy's real name and deduced that Teller was too upset to care about call girl protocol.

"I do. I met Dotty. We talked for some time. She seemed like a good person." Dana paused. "I also discovered her body."

Tears welled up in Teller's eyes, and she wiped them on the sleeve of her sweatshirt.

"Was it bad? Did she suffer?"

"Do you want me to be honest?"

"Please."

"You'll get this from the papers eventually. There's no way to sugarcoat it. She would have suffered."

Teller threw her head back and wailed. Dana helped her to a sofa and held her while she bawled. It took a lot to touch Dana, but Teller was doing it. She wished there was some way she could absorb Teller's pain.

"I'm sorry," Teller said when she could finally speak.

"No need to apologize."

Teller stood up. "I'll be right back."

Dana watched her disappear around a corner. When she came back, she looked as though she had splashed water on her face, and there was a telltale trace of white powder under her nose.

"You two were close?" Dana asked when Teller settled back on the sofa.

"I loved her," Teller answered defiantly.

"I'm so sorry."

Teller seemed to have run out of words. She looked around for a moment. Then her eyes came to rest on the wet bar.

"Can I get you something to drink?" she asked, fighting her sorrow by morphing into the role of host.

"I'm fine, but feel free," Dana answered.

Teller opened a liquor cabinet and poured a healthy glass of very good scotch.

"Why are you here?" she asked when she was seated.

"Have you followed the news stories about Senator Carson's disappearance and reappearance?"

"That pathetic pig!" Teller answered vehemently.

"You know Carson?"

"Dotty did. She used to tell me what she did with him."

"Let me get this straight," Dana said. "Dorothy Crispin knew Senator Carson in a professional capacity?"

Teller laughed harshly. "Jesus, you can say that again. He hired her to fuck him, only that's not what they did, according to Dotty."

"I've heard that Carson had odd sexual needs."

"If I tell you things, I want a promise that my name won't be mentioned and you'll try to keep Dotty's name out of it. It would kill her folks if they learned she was hooking and she was a lesbian."

"I'll try to keep Dotty's identity hidden, but I won't promise I won't write about the senator's sexual habits."

"'Sexual habits.'" Teller laughed harshly. "The senator begged to be treated like a slave, a dog. He was into leashes, obedience training." Teller shook her head and laughed again. "Can you believe, the same guy that's deciding our nation's fate likes being told to roll over and sit up and beg?"

Dana listened to a detailed description of Dorothy Crispin's sessions with the senator. She felt queasy by the time Teller finished.

"Is there any way you can prove anything you've told me?" Dana asked.

"There might be. Dotty never met a date at her apartment.

Executive Escorts owns a condo a few blocks from here where we meet tricks who have special needs. There are hidden cameras in all the rooms."

"For blackmail?" Dana asked.

"No, Executive doesn't go in for that. It makes too much money playing it straight. If it ever got out that we were blackmailing our clients, no one would use us."

"Then why the record?"

"Protection. If a john doesn't want to pay or gets angry and threatens to go to the cops, one look at the way he looks in a hood and dog collar is usually enough to dampen his enthusiasm."

"And there's a record of Senator Carson's sessions with Dorothy?"

"Definitely, only I don't know where it is. The equipment was voice-activated. As soon as anyone entered the apartment, the camera and sound equipment would turn on, but Dorothy had no idea where it was. Neither did I. On the occasions I used the place, I always left with the customer. I'm sure someone got the tape or DVD or whatever they use, but I never saw it, and I don't know where they're kept."

"If you never saw the equipment, how do you know it was there?"

"We were told about it. We were also instructed to make sure the john was facing in a certain direction in each room so his face would show up on camera."

"I would love to get my hands on the recording of Carson's session."

"I can't help you."

"And there's no other way you can think of to prove he had a professional relationship with Dorothy?"

"I'm not testifying or talking to the cops, if that's what you mean."

"Without the tape or DVD, your tale of what Dorothy told you would be inadmissible hearsay."

"A professional call girl wouldn't make much of a witness, anyway," Teller said with another humorless laugh.

Dana talked with Teller a little longer. Then she told her again how sorry she was about Crispin. Teller nodded. Dana guessed that she was too choked up to speak.

Chapter Twenty-six

The next morning, Dana called Brad at work.

"I've found a link between Jessica Koshani and Dorothy Crispin," Dana said as soon as Brad took her call. "Koshani is rumored to be the owner of Executive Escorts, an upscale call-girl service. Dorothy Crispin was a law student, but she was also a prostitute who turned tricks for Executive."

"Can you prove this?" Brad asked.

"Right now I don't have anything that would fly in a court of law or anything *Exposed* can print without getting hit with a huge libel suit, but multiple sources have told me that your boss was one of Crispin's customers and that he had some pretty kinky fetishes, S and M, bondage."

"That's something I'd rather not know," Brad said.

"I was also told that Executive secretly recorded their customers' sex acts as protection in case one of them tried to do something that would threaten the business. If Koshani had that type of leverage on your boss, there's no telling what she could force him to do. Blackmail is a pretty good motive for murder."

“That’s a stretch, Dana. And wasn’t Carson with Dorothy Crispin when Koshani was killed?”

“The medical examiner knows she was killed sometime on Sunday between noon and the early evening, but she can’t pin down an exact time.”

“I know for a fact that Carson didn’t kill Crispin. He was in D.C. Clarence Little is a much better bet for both murders. He’s an engineer, and he made pretty good money. He could afford an upscale escort service. Maybe Crispin was the call girl Executive provided. Maybe there was something Koshani recorded in one of his sessions that could be used to convict him of murder.”

“Good thinking, but I still can’t exclude the possibility that your boss was involved in Koshani’s murder. Do you think you can find a connection between Carson and Koshani? Maybe she gave him campaign contributions personally or through her businesses.”

“Can’t you get that information from public records?”

“I might, but you may be able to dig around in your office computers for records of back-door contributions.”

“I won’t do it, Dana,” Brad said firmly. “Senator Carson is my boss, and I’m not going to betray his trust to help you get dirt on him for an article for *Exposed*. I’m surprised you asked me.”

Dana didn’t respond right away. When she did, she sounded contrite.

“Forget I asked. You’re right. I’ll try to get the information some other way.”

“You know I appreciate all you’ve done for me and Ginny . . .”

“Don’t apologize. Working as a vice cop and digging up dirt for Pat Gorman has given me an odd view of humanity. Sometimes I forget that there are people who aren’t sleazy and try to act ethically.”

Brad laughed. "I'm no saint, Dana."

"You come close, Brad. And you better not change. Say hi to Ginny for me."

Brad hung up just as his intercom buzzed and the senator's secretary told him that his boss was ready to discuss the testimony of a witness who was going to appear before the Judiciary Committee in the morning. Brad wondered if there was any way he was going to get through the meeting without imagining United States Senator Jack Carson bound, gagged, and naked.

Dana Cutler parked in the shadows up the street from Jessica Koshani's house. She wasn't worried about being seen in Koshani's upscale neighborhood. There were no lights on in any of the houses at two in the morning, and the mansions stood well back from the street, surrounded by walls. As soon as Dana got out of the Rover, a frigid wind forced her to pull her watch cap tight over her ears and hunch her shoulders. According to the readout on her dashboard, the air temperature was 39, but that didn't take the wind-chill factor into account.

Dana jogged down the street. She didn't see any lights in Koshani's house. When she was a few feet from the gate that guarded the property, she noticed a keypad. Bummer. She eyeballed the wall on either side of the gate to gauge whether she could scale it. When she turned her attention to the gate for the same reason, Dana noticed that it was slightly ajar. She breathed a sigh of relief. Dana bet that Portland police officers had been through the house at the request of the D.C. police and had forgotten to close the gate. Dana pushed the gate inward, slipped through the opening, and hurried toward the front door hoping that it, too, was unlocked. It wasn't.

Dana circled around the back of the villa to a large covered patio. On the other side of a brown winter lawn was the Willamette River, coal black except for the patches of water that reflected lights from homes on the shore. Dana was about to try one of the French doors when she noticed that a pane of glass had been knocked out of the next door. Dana frowned. Would the police break in this way?

Dana reached through the door and opened it. When she walked inside, she found herself in a large living room that looked as though it had been searched. She turned in a slow circle, looking through the debris that littered the expensive Persian rug for DVDs that might star Jack Carson. There was a home theater in the room next to the living room. A bookcase next to the television had been filled with movies that were now scattered across the floor, their cases open with many of the disks beside them. Dana sighed and started going through them anyway, hoping that whoever had come before her had missed something. Twenty minutes later, she decided that the disk wasn't mixed in with the movie collection.

A search of the downstairs did not turn up more DVDs, and Dana headed upstairs to find the bedroom, the most likely place to find porn. She was afraid to turn on any lights, so she'd brought a heavy police flashlight that could double as a weapon.

The bedroom was dominated by a king-size bed covered by black satin sheets. The first thing that looked interesting was a large flat-screen television that was attached to the wall opposite the bed. Under the TV was a DVD player. Dana turned in place looking for the DVDs and found a cabinet near the bed. She did a knee bend. The cabinet door was open. She played the flashlight beam across the area and around the interior. It was empty. Dana stood up. If the DVD of Carson's sessions with Dorothy Crispin had been in this cabinet, it was gone now. But who had it? She'd searched enough places when she was with D.C. Vice and Narcotics to know that the police would have no compunctions about trashing the home of a low-level dealer. Members of the upper classes were usually treated more diplomatically. She couldn't discount a police search, but someone else may have gone through the house looking for the incriminating DVD.

As Dana descended the stairs, she noticed a small oil painting in an ornate gold frame. She didn't know much about art, but she recognized the work as Impressionist. She checked the signature. It was a Cezanne. She looked at the living room walls and picked out a Warhol. A thought occurred to Dana. If these paintings were the real thing, they were very valuable. A woman who owned a ritzy villa was also going to own expensive jewelry. Factor in the woman's ties to criminal activity, and you didn't have to be Sherlock Holmes to deduce that she would have a top-of-the-line alarm system.

Dana walked to the front door. The keypad for the alarm was attached to the wall next to the door, but it hadn't gone off. A green light shone above the numbers on the pad. Koshani would have set the alarm when she flew to D.C. The police would have been able to get the alarm code if they searched at the behest of the D.C. police, but they would have reset the alarm when they left unless the alarm wasn't on when they arrived. The only conclusion Dana could draw was that the person who had searched the house had the alarm code and the code for the front gate.

How had that person learned the code? The answer that Dana

came up with made her queasy. She remembered the torture she'd endured during her kidnapping. If the meth cooks who'd held her had asked for the code to her alarm, she would have given it to them to stop the pain. Jessica Koshani had been tortured methodically. She would have given up her alarm code without much resistance.

Dana left the house empty-handed and drove back to her hotel to pack for her flight to D.C. During the drive, she mulled over what she knew. A few things bothered her, and one of the most troubling questions involved the identity of the person who had taken the DVDs. Did it make sense that Little had them? With every cop in the country looking for him, would he have risked capture to travel to D.C. to get an alarm code from Jessica Koshani? Dana had a hard time believing that Clarence Little was jumping back and forth across the country when he had so much to lose if he was captured. So if Little didn't break into Koshani's house, who did?

Part IV

Jihad

Chapter Twenty-seven

Very few people know the exact moment of their death. When Ali Bashar woke up Sunday morning, he knew precisely when he would give up the life of the body for a new life in paradise with Allah. Ali and the other members of his cell had spent the week before their martyrdom in seclusion and prayer. They had immersed themselves in spiritual contemplation free of the corrupting influence of television and music. Ali welcomed the silence as he purified himself for his holy mission.

The Sunday Night Football game paired the undefeated Washington Redskins with the New York Giants, their undefeated division rivals. It was being telecast nationally and was also being beamed to American troops in the Middle East. During the first quarter, when the game clock at FedEx Field clicked down from 7:01 to 7:00, Ali and the other members of his cell would detonate their trays in four widely spaced areas of the stadium. The stands would be packed and the devastation would be monumental. Ali's only regret was that his body would be atomized by the explosion before he could see the massive destruction wrought moments later by the remote-controlled detonation of the four explosive-laden ambulances that would be strategically placed at several points below the stadium.

As soon as he was awake, Ali showered and dressed in clean clothes. Then he prayed and reflected on what he was about to accomplish and how joyful he would be when he met Allah. He had heard that some martyrs ingested drugs or alcohol to steel themselves, but he was repulsed by the idea of meeting Allah while drugged or intoxicated. Far from fearing death, Ali had never been happier. He could only imagine the terror he would create. The Americans cursed terrorists as if being one was a bad thing, but the Koran commanded a good Muslim to bring terror to the enemy. "Against them make ready your strength to the utmost of your power, including steeds of war, to strike terror into (the hearts of) the enemies, of Allah and your enemies. . . ." With his last breath, Ali would bring horror and devastation to the enemies of Islam that would be remembered for a thousand years.

At three o'clock, Steve's van arrived. The other members of the cell joined Ali outside. There was a refreshing chill in the air and the sun was shining. Ali took a deep breath and smiled. God had made his last day a good day.

Steve opened the rear door of the van and they piled in. There was total silence during the trip to FedEx Field. When Steve dropped everyone off in the employee parking lot, there was no pep talk. None was needed.

Steve had picked up the members of the cell early so they would be the first to arrive at the stadium. Ali willed himself to be calm as he approached the vendors' room. Jose welcomed Ali with a smile, and Ali smiled back. Ali's tray had been brought to the room the day before by Mr. Cooper, and Ali had no trouble finding it because it had a notch in the lid. By arriving first, he had made sure that no one else would take it. Other hawkers came in. He knew a few, but he did not initiate any conversations. When someone spoke to Ali, he was calm and sounded normal when he responded. Then Ann O'Hearn arrived, and his calm deserted him.

Before Ann's arrival, the events of the day had the quality of a vivid dream, and Ali felt he was watching someone who looked like him go through the steps that would lead to his death and the death of thousands. The moment he saw Ann, Ali had a vision of her golden hair in flames, her eyes wide with horror, and her mouth filled with screams of pain. The barrier his mind had erected between his deed and reality was stripped away. Ali felt light-headed and his stomach rolled.

"Hi, Ali," Ann said with a wide, welcoming smile.

"Hi, Ann," he said. It took all of his will to force his smile. "How was your week?"

Ann rattled on about her classes and a movie she'd seen with a friend, but little of what she said registered. Then, mercifully, Ann was distracted by something one of the other vendors said, and he was able to escape.

Game time approached and Ali stocked his tray. As he waited to go into the stands, the tension grew, and his cool demeanor began to evaporate. Then it was time to leave. In order to reach his post, Ali had to go in front of Jose's concession stand. As he passed by Ann, he stopped. She didn't have any customers at the moment. He knew he should pass her by and say nothing. He knew he should not compromise the mission. But some part of him cared enough for her to make him lean in and say, "I need to speak to you."

Ann glanced quickly at Jose. He was occupied with a customer. She leaned toward Ali.

"Go home," he whispered.

"What?" Ann answered, unsure she had heard Ali correctly.

"Say you are sick. Go home."

Ann laughed. "I can't go home, Ali. That's crazy. We're mobbed. And why should I? I'm not sick."

Ali didn't know what to say. There was no way he could explain. Then he was seized by guilt. He was endangering a plan that had taken years to develop. Worse, he was betraying Allah by showing compassion for an infidel, a woman. What was he thinking?

Ali shook his head. "It's nothing," he said, forcing a smile. "I'm being foolish."

Ali turned his back on Ann and left the concession stand. Behind him, Ann shook her head in confusion. Then she returned to the counter. Ali hefted the tray and walked into the stands.

Ali stood on a set of concrete steps surrounded by a sea of screaming fans. The Giants had scored first, but the Redskins were marching toward the Giants' end zone. Every few seconds, the stands erupted with cheers or moans, and the huge clock on the scoreboard ticked down.

8:01, 8:00, 7:59.

The sky had grown dark, and lights illuminated the field. Ali looked up and felt a breeze caress his face. He smiled as he imagined the sky opening and Allah reaching down for him from paradise, arms spread wide in a welcoming embrace. In less than a minute, he would be enfolded in that embrace, and the infidels' cries of joy would turn to screams of fear and horror as shrapnel from the exploding tray ripped through them just before the stands crumbled and they fell into a pit of fire.

7:45, 7:44.

The Redskins broke the huddle. The quarterback dropped back. A Giants linebacker broke through and hurtled toward him. Just before he was hit, the quarterback hurled a desperation pass. The receiver was covered by two defenders. They all jumped for the ball, and the Redskin snagged it out of the air before crashing to the ground. The fans went wild. Ali slid aside the slim panels that hid the red buttons. All eyes were on the field, and no one noticed.

"Allah," Ali prayed, "purify my soul so I am fit to see you, and bless my mission with high casualties among the Americans."

7:30, 7:29.

Ali placed his fingers on the buttons and repeated his prayer. As he did, he noticed movement at the bottom of the stairs. Two large men were walking toward him. One was wearing a Redskins jersey, and the other wore a jacket emblazoned with the Redskins logo. They looked like typical fans, but they were not acting like typical fans. At the most exciting moment in the game, their eyes were not on the players. They were staring at him.

7:15, 7:14.

Ali made a half turn and saw a man and a woman walking down the steps. Their eyes were also on him. He glanced at the scoreboard.

7:10, 7:09.

One of the men below him had a gun and shouted, "FBI!"

Ali closed his eyes, shouted *"Allahu akbar"*—God is great—and pressed the buttons.

Nothing happened. "FBI! Don't move!" Ali's eyes snapped open, and he pressed the buttons again. The man and woman above him were shouting "FBI!" Ali tried the buttons separately, then together again. Then he was grabbed from behind. He turned, yanked his body away from his attacker, and his feet slipped out from under him. Everything happened in slow motion. The people in the rows at his side were standing and pressing away from him. The tray was flying through the air. Then his head connected with the edge of a concrete step and he slid downhill backward like a boy on a sled, dazed. Ali's head cracked against a second step, and he found himself upside down staring at the scoreboard. It read 6:52.

Someone rolled him on his stomach. He felt handcuffs snap around his wrists as his mind filled with confusion. There had been no explosions. Death had not been visited on the infidels. Then a black hood was thrown over his head and he couldn't see.

What had gone wrong? he wondered as he was lifted by several hands and hustled up the steps. Why was he alive? Why was he not with Allah? Why were the infidels alive?

His captors were running with him now. He heard the occasional shout of "FBI!" and guessed that he was on the concourse and being carried past gawking fans. Then he heard a door open. The agents stopped identifying themselves, and he was carried down a flight of stairs. The only thing he heard for a few minutes was heavy breathing. Then the agents stopped and he was laid on the ground. He wanted to speak, but he sensed that he was better off saying nothing. Moments later, the choice was made for him. Someone rolled up his sleeve, and Ali felt a needle slip into a vein. Moments after that, everything went dark.

Chapter Twenty-eight

Keith Evans's team had followed Ali Bashar from the concession into the stands and had kept him under surveillance until they got the signal to move. The takedown had gone off without a hitch and had ended in a staging area under the stadium, a stretch of asphalt shaded by the overhanging stands and blocked off by a high chain-link fence. While Maggie Sparks and another agent hustled Bashar into the back of a black van, Keith leaned over, rested his hands on his knees, and took deep breaths. Maggie slammed the van's door shut, and it drove out through a break in the fence behind three other black vans, each with its own prisoner. Then she walked over to her partner and flashed a tolerant smile.

"Someone needs to spend more time in the gym." She took hold of his elbow and he straightened up, embarrassed. "Come on, old man."

Keith was too winded to make a witty retort. Maggie laid a calming hand on Keith's back, and he suddenly felt better and followed her to a group of agents who were listening to Harold Johnson, a tall, balding, middle-aged black man with a rugby player's physique.

"Good work, people," Johnson said. "We got the lot without any casualties. Now we do the boring stuff. The Redskins are going to set us up in offices and suites around the complex as soon as the game ends. Their security people will round up the prisoners' coworkers so we can talk to them. None of these people are considered suspects at the present time, so go easy. They're going to be shaken up when they learn that someone they worked alongside was planning to kill them and everyone else in the stadium."

Maggie and Keith got comfortable in the skybox the Redskins had made available for them. It had a buffet, a bar, and rows of seats that looked out at the field through a huge floor-to-ceiling picture window. The Redskins had won on a last-second field goal, and the jubilant fans who occupied the suite had left a mess when they celebrated. The janitors had cleaned up the debris, and the buffet had been restocked for the agents. Keith was washing down a sandwich of cold cuts with a Coke, and Maggie was eating a salad and drinking a bottle of Evian water when the door to the luxury suite opened and a security guard stuck his head in.

"I've got eight people from the hot dog concession out here," he said. "How do you want to handle this?"

"Is the person in charge of the concession here?" Keith said.

"Yeah, that's Jose Gutierrez."

"Okay, let's start with him."

Moments later, the guard ushered in a heavyset man in his forties with long black hair and a dark pockmarked face. The man's eyes ricocheted around the room, and he was obviously nervous.

"My name is Keith Evans, Mr. Gutierrez, and this is my partner, Maggie Sparks. We're with the FBI, and we want to thank you for taking the time to talk to us."

Keith gestured toward the food. "Are you hungry? Can I get you something to eat?"

Gutierrez shook his head. "No, thanks, but you can tell me what's going on here."

"Ali Bashar works at your stand, right?" Keith asked.

"Yeah, where is he?"

"Mr. Bashar is under arrest. He and several other men were planning to set off suicide bombs in the stands. Fortunately, we were able to thwart their plot."

"You're shitting me? Ali was going to blow the place up?"

Keith nodded.

"I can't believe it."

"Why don't you sit with us and we'll talk about it."

Gutierrez took the seat Keith indicated.

"What can you tell us about Mr. Bashar?" Keith asked.

Gutierrez started to say something. Then he stopped and thought for a moment before shaking his head.

"Now that I think about it, not much. He was a good worker, always on time. He never complained. That's about it."

"Did he ever talk about his personal life? You know, what he did when he wasn't working at the games?"

"Not that I remember." Gutierrez shrugged. "He wasn't around much. He sold hot dogs and drinks in the stands, so that's where he was on game day, and we've only had a few home games. He told me he was a student once, but we never talked about personal stuff."

"Did he say where he was studying?"

Gutierrez's brow furrowed. "No, just that he was a student."

"Do you have a copy of Ali's job application?" Keith asked.

"No. Mr. Cooper does the hiring. I just got a call saying Ali was going to show up for an exhibition game and to give him a job hawking. Mr. Cooper owns the concession. He owns a couple. You should talk to him. I can give you his business address and phone number."

"That would be great."

"Is Ali crazy?" Gutierrez asked.

"He's a jihadist, an Islamic radical like the people who brought down the Twin Towers."

"Holy Mother." Gutierrez shook his head. "He never said anything like that. I mean I thought he was a Muslim with that name, but he never talked crazy shit."

"He wouldn't have."

"Yeah, I guess not."

"Mr. Gutierrez, was Mr. Bashar friendly with anyone in the concession stand? Is there someone he talked to more than the other workers?"

Gutierrez thought for a moment. Then he nodded. "Yeah, Ann, Ann O'Hearn. They seemed friendly." Suddenly Gutierrez looked concerned. "But she's no terrorist. She's in college. This is her second year here."

"We don't suspect anyone in your concession of being a terrorist," Keith assured him. "We just want to learn as much about Mr. Bashar as we can. Ann isn't in trouble."

Gutierrez exhaled. "That's good. She's a nice kid."

"Is she waiting in the hall?"

"Yeah."

"Okay. You've been very helpful. Can you get us that address and phone number for Mr. Cooper before we go?"

"Sure thing."

Keith gave Gutierrez his card. "Give me a call if you think of anything else."

Maggie escorted Gutierrez into the hall and asked him to point out Ann O'Hearn.

"Ann, they want to talk to you," Gutierrez said.

Maggie walked up to the girl and smiled to allay her fears. "Hi, Miss O'Hearn. I'm Maggie Sparks," the agent said as she led the nervous girl into the skybox.

"The first thing you need to know," Maggie said when they were seated, "is that you aren't suspected of any criminal activity. We want to talk to you to get more information about a man who worked with you in the concession stand, Ali Bashar."

"Why do you want to know about Ali? What did he do?"

"We'll talk about that in a minute. Mr. Gutierrez told us that you were friendly with Mr. Bashar."

"Yeah. I mean I only saw him at work, and we've only had a few games, but he was always nice."

"What did you two talk about?" Maggie asked.

Ann took a moment to think. "He told me he played soccer. I'm on my college team. Once, after a game, we talked about soccer."

Maggie nodded to encourage her to continue.

"He said he was going to school too, that he was a student."

"Did he say where he went to school?"

"No, I got the impression he wasn't going yet, that he planned to go, but I'm not completely sure about that."

Ann looked troubled. "Can you tell me why you're asking about Ali?"

"I can see that you liked Mr. Bashar, so this may upset you.

Ali Bashar was part of a cell of Islamic radicals who tried to blow up FedEx Field today."

Ann lost color and looked as though she might faint. Maggie laid a hand on her shoulder.

"Are you okay? Do you want some water?"

Ann shook her head. She seemed dazed. "He tried to warn me," she managed, her voice barely above a whisper.

"Warn you how?" Maggie pressed.

"Just before he took his tray into the stands, he told me he had to talk to me, that it was important. Then he told me to say I was sick and to go home."

"What did you say?"

"I told him I wasn't sick and we were very busy. If I left, Jose would have been shorthanded. I asked him why I should go home."

"What did he say to that?"

"He looked like he wanted to tell me something. Instead he said he was being foolish and that it was nothing. Then he left, and I was too busy to think about what he'd said anymore."

"It sounds like Mr. Bashar likes you. Did he ever ask you out or say anything inappropriate?"

"No. I told you, we barely talked because he hawked in the stands. I'd only see him before the stand opened or when we were cleaning up. He seemed shy. The day we talked about soccer, I got the impression that talking to me took a big effort."

"Can you think of anything else that might help us understand Mr. Bashar?" Maggie asked.

"Not really." Ann shook her head. "This is a lot to take in. You're saying he was going to kill everyone?"

Maggie nodded.

"My God. He was so nice. I can't believe it."

"He just appeared to be nice, Miss O'Hearn."

"No, he was nice to me. He . . . he tried to save me. God, I feel sick."

Maggie questioned Ann O'Hearn for a few more minutes before getting her address, e-mail, and phone number. Then she told Ann she could go home. Mr. Gutierrez was waiting outside the door with Lawrence Cooper's phone number and business address. Maggie thanked him and called the next witness into the skybox.

An hour later, Keith ushered the last witness into the hall. No one knew much about Ali Bashar. He was quiet, worked hard, and didn't cause any trouble. No one except Ann had talked with him about anything except work.

Keith closed the door and settled into a seat beside Maggie. "What do you think?" he asked.

"We have to talk to Cooper to find out how Bashar got his job."

"I'm betting Cooper placed all four of the bombers, which is interesting."

Maggie nodded. "Do you think Bashar liked Ann O'Hearn?"

"He must have if he tried to get her to go home."

"Let's tell Harold. Maybe he can use it when they interrogate Bashar."

Chapter Twenty-nine

All of the concessions where the suicide bombers worked were owned by Lawrence Cooper, and the managers had been told by him to let the suicide bombers work at each one. Harold Johnson told Keith and Maggie to pick up Cooper and bring him in for questioning.

Cooper lived in a ranch-style house at the end of a cul-de-sac in a development in Rockville, Maryland, that had been built in the late fifties. It was dark when Keith parked in the driveway. He noticed that the lawn was mowed and the house looked as though it had been given a fresh coat of paint in the not too distant past. The agents walked up a narrow slate path to the front door and rang the bell. There was no answer. Keith rang again, then knocked and called Cooper's name. When there was still no answer, Maggie walked around back while Keith tried to see around the curtains that had been lowered to cover the picture window that looked out on the lawn. The living room was dark, but Keith made out a pale glow that he took for lights that were on in some other part of the house.

Maggie returned to the front yard. "The side door opens into the kitchen. It isn't locked. What do you think?"

"I don't like this."

"Let's have a look."

Keith followed Maggie around the side of the house. They drew their guns, and Maggie eased the door open. They were immediately hit by the nauseating smell that hung over every scene of violent death they had ever entered.

"Mr. Cooper," Maggie called, not expecting an answer.

Keith nodded and the agents crept into the kitchen. The lights were on, and there were pots soaking in the sink and half a loaf of bread and a knife with a serrated blade on a cutting board.

Keith and Maggie entered the dining room cautiously. They saw half-finished meals at place settings where two chairs had toppled over when their occupants leaped up from them. Neither the man nor the woman had made it very far. Mr. Cooper had been shot in the head and had toppled to the floor. A woman who Keith assumed was Mrs. Cooper had made it halfway to the living room when a shot to the back had brought her down and a second shot to the back of the head had finished her off.

Maggie knelt beside Mr. Cooper and studied the entry hole in the center of his forehead.

"One shot, dead center. That's not easy," she said.

"Tying up loose ends," Keith said wearily as he took out his cell phone and dialed Harold Johnson's number.

"The bombers didn't do this," Maggie said as soon as Keith finished the call.

"Their handler, the guy who told Cooper to place Bashar and the others?"

"That's a good guess."

"Let's check Cooper's bank records to see if he deposited a large sum of money recently."

"He could have been a dupe. I mean, Bashar and the others were probably smuggled in, so they couldn't have gotten jobs legally. Cooper might have thought he was getting a group of illegals jobs without knowing what they were planning to do."

Keith looked at Cooper's corpse. "We may never know the answer to that one."

Chapter Thirty

One of Imran Afridi's companies owned a home on the beach in Southern California. Another owned a palazzo near Lake Como in Italy and an apartment in Tokyo. But Afridi had watched the Redskins play the Giants on a big-screen television in the den of his mansion in northern Virginia because he wanted to be close to the terror and chaos that would follow the demolition of FedEx Field.

Afridi knew that the networks used many cameras during a football game so they could film the action from many angles. He hoped some of them would still be filming as FedEx Field crumbled to dust beneath the feet of the infidels. Lying naked between silk sheets in his bedroom was a fifteen-year-old girl who had been provided to him by a Russian who specialized in such things. Afridi planned to ravish her as soon as the full extent of the devastation at the football stadium was clear. Violent sex was his preferred way to release tension.

Afridi waited with a combination of elation and nerves as the game clock counted down the minutes. He tensed when the scoreboard clock showed seven and a half minutes left in the first quarter. He leaned forward expectantly when the clock showed 7:00. Then nothing happened, and the clock ticked down to 6:59.

One of the announcers commented on disturbances in several sections in the stands. Another commentator said that it looked as though some of the vendors were being arrested. Then Washington's tight end caught a pass in the end zone, and the incidents in the stands were forgotten by everyone except Imran Afridi.

Afridi waited five minutes more, to see if the ambulances would explode, before grabbing a disposable cell phone and calling Steve Reynolds.

"We will meet in one hour! You know the place," Afridi shouted into the phone before disconnecting and repeatedly slamming the phone against his coffee table until it was smashed to pieces. Then he stormed upstairs to visit his fury on the naked girl who was bound and gagged in his bedroom.

Half an hour later, Imran stuffed a bonus into the purse of the severely battered girl and had his driver take her to a private clinic that had dealt with the objects of his sexual attentions in the past. He was calm now that his needs had been satisfied, and he was able to think clearly about the debacle at the football stadium. There had to be a traitor, but who was it?

The Chesapeake and Ohio Company was chartered in 1825 to construct a canal connecting tidewater on the Potomac River in Washington, D.C., with the headwaters of the Ohio River in western Pennsylvania. The canal would open a trade route for ships between the eastern seaboard and the trans-Allegheny West. The endeavor did not go smoothly, and the canal was not completed until 1850. In 1938, the 185-mile-long C&O Canal was sold to the United States government, and the C&O Canal National Historical Park was established by Congress in 1971.

Afridi parked in Georgetown and followed a walking path alongside the canal until he arrived at a stone bridge that crossed it. He was wearing jeans, running shoes, and a hooded sweatshirt that hung over a black Glock. A sheath holding a hunting knife was attached to his belt on the side opposite the holstered gun. Afridi was no stranger to violence and had used the knife and the gun on different occasions.

Five minutes after Afridi settled into the shadows beneath the bridge, Steve Reynolds materialized out of the darkness. The American was dressed in black. The bill of his baseball cap left his face in shadow. Afridi was certain that Reynolds had been hiding, watching him, when he arrived.

"This isn't smart," Reynolds said. "The last thing we want is to be seen together."

"Don't tell me what is smart. Tell me what happened," Afridi demanded. "I have been planning this . . . this event for years. Everything was in place. Why is that stadium still standing?"

"The detonators failed."

"How do you know that?"

"I tried to detonate the explosives in the ambulances. Nothing happened, and I never heard any explosions in the stands, just the normal noise you hear during a game. When I was certain that the plan had failed, I drove to the safe house to sanitize it. When I was through, I set charges using the detonators we bought. They didn't explode, so I torched the house. Then I took a close look at one of the detonators. It was defective."

Afridi looked furious. "You told me your seller was reliable."

"He's an arms dealer, Imran, a criminal. I checked him out the best I could. Everyone I talked to said he wasn't law enforcement, but he could also have been FBI or CIA or ATF. Anyone can be bought or scared into cooperating."

"And if he did not betray us?"

"Ali Bashar is the only member of the cell with the skill to sabotage the detonators. He was trained to use explosives in the camp, and he's smart."

"Why would he betray us?"

"I have no idea."

Afridi thought for a minute. Then he looked directly at Reynolds. "Did you test the detonators before you bought them?"

Reynolds glared back, and Afridi saw the American's hand drift toward his side. "Are you accusing me of something, Imran? Let's get this shit into the open."

"Did you test the detonators?" Afridi repeated. His voice was steady and his tone was as cold as ice.

Reynolds started to answer Imran angrily, but he stopped and his brow furrowed.

"Ali tested a stick of dynamite and a detonator, and they worked. The box with the detonators and the box with the dynamite were open. While we got the money out of the van, the seller had his men go into a barn where the rest of the explosives were being kept. They also brought the open boxes into the barn to reseal them. A switch could have been made while the boxes were out of sight."

"You idiot," Afridi snapped.

"Calling me names isn't going to solve anything, Imran. And if you calm down, you'll see that we have a bigger problem. It's the reason I think this meeting is a mistake. I'm going to find the man who sold us the detonators, and you can be certain that he'll tell me if he's responsible for this clusterfuck by the time I'm finished with him. But whether it's him or Ali or someone else behind the switch, one thing is obvious. Someone got to the seller or Ali, and that person knew what we planned to do, where we planned to do it, and when. And they may know that you and I are involved in this, which could mean we're under surveillance. So we should not meet or communicate unless it's absolutely necessary. And we should both try to figure out who the mole is in this operation."

"Do you think Ali Bashar is in custody?"

"I'd bet on it," Reynolds said.

"Can he tell the FBI about you?"

"Yeah, but he'd have no idea where I live or who I am. He just knows me as Steve."

Afridi was quiet. The men could hear the water flowing softly beside them.

"You're right. We should have no further contact unless it's absolutely necessary."

Reynolds nodded. Then he folded into the darkness and disappeared.

Afridi had brought another disposable cell phone with him, and he punched in an overseas number as soon as he was in his car.

"What happened?" Rafik Nasrallah asked.

"It was the detonators. They were all faulty."

"How could that happen?"

"We were betrayed."

"By who?"

"I'm not certain, but I have my suspicions. We may have made a mistake with Reynolds."

"You think he was deep cover?"

"It's possible, but there is another possibility. Koshani knew about the operation. She was tortured before she was killed."

"I thought that escaped serial killer murdered her."

"Perhaps that is what the CIA wants us to think. Koshani was blackmailing Senator Carson for information on what the CIA knew about the operation. What if he went to them, and they had him arrange for the Intelligence Committee to subpoena her? They could have been waiting for her and tortured the information about FedEx Field out of her."

"Is there something I can do?"

"Send Mustapha. If he thinks he needs help, tell him to choose some men to come with him. The traitor is Ali Bashar, Senator Carson, or Steve Reynolds. We can't get at Bashar but we can get to Carson and Reynolds."

"It's done." Nasrallah paused. When he spoke, he sounded subdued. "I've been sick with disappointment. How are you handling this failure?"

"I have been too angry to process what happened. Everything was in place. Every contingency was accounted for. Then this."

Afridi choked up. Nasrallah waited for his friend to gather himself.

"Be strong," Nasrallah said. "You will find who did this and make him pay. Then we will regroup. Allah's vengeance will come. It will just take more time. Do not despair. Allah has great patience."

Chapter Thirty-one

When Ali Bashar came to, he was lying on a cot in a narrow, windowless concrete cell wearing an orange jumpsuit. Shining down on him was a caged lightbulb. The light hurt Ali's eyes. He closed them and forced himself to sit up. The effort made him dizzy. He rested for a moment, then struggled to his feet. His knees buckled, but he managed to stay upright.

Ali looked around. His only furnishings were the cot and a squat toilet. There was a thick metal door in one wall with a spy hole in the middle and a slot at the bottom. Ali tried to open the door even though he assumed his efforts would be futile. They were. He was sealed in. Ali sank down on his cot and tried to clear his head.

In the camp, Ali had been told how to act if he was captured. Ali's instructors had told him that he would be tortured, and he had been briefly subjected to waterboarding and other cruelties so he would know what to expect. The consequences of capture were an added incentive to carry out his mission.

Ali's imagination started to work on him. His life was filled with incidents in his village when he was singled out for teasing or beatings by older and bigger children. Ali was always too frightened to fight back, and he endured humiliation and pain daily. It was his fervent hope that he would find the peace in paradise he had never found on earth, and now his hope of meeting Allah had been dashed. Fear ate at Ali and robbed him of his strength and his will. He waited for his torturers to come. But no one came.

There were no clocks in Ali's cell, and no one fed him. The ceiling light was always on, and every time he tried to sleep, loud music blasted into his cell through an invisible loudspeaker. Once he had slipped into unconsciousness despite the noise, and a guard had slapped him awake and threatened worse if he caught him dozing off again.

Other than these intrusions, silence was Ali's constant companion, with one exception. Every so often someone would scream. The screams would go on and on, and they were horrible. Ali would get sick to his stomach as he imagined what you would have to do to people to make them scream like that.

Ali had been clean-shaven when he was arrested. By feeling his stubble, he estimated that he had been a captive for two to three days. He hoped that he would be brave when his time came to be taken for interrogation, but his bowels loosened and he grew faint when the locks in his door finally snapped open.

The guards were big and moved with athletic grace. Ali knew that there was no point in resisting. They pulled Ali to his feet without a word, shackled his hands and ankles, and placed a hood over his head. Ali's legs felt like jelly. If the guards had not held him up, he would have melted onto the floor.

When the hood was removed, Ali found himself in a bare concrete-block room. The guards sat him on a chair with a headrest. Then they secured his head to the headrest, tied his arms and legs to the chair's arms and legs, and put a strap around his chest. When they stepped away, Ali could not move.

Seated in front of Ali behind a metal desk was a slender man dressed in a suit and tie. He had on old-fashioned tortoiseshell glasses with thick lenses and his black hair was slicked back. He looked like an attorney.

"How has your stay been so far, Ali?" he asked.

Ali found the question odd. It was a question a friend would ask a guest. Ali had been told that he should not answer questions and should resist any attempts by his captors to seduce him with kindness, so he remained mute.

"Do you know where you are?" the man asked. "No? I'll tell you. You have disappeared into hell. But there are different levels in hell, and you will have a chance to save yourself from being cast down into the depths. Answer my questions, and you will save yourself from pain and receive the most comfortable quarters available to our prisoners. You will have access to the Koran, books, and television. You will be allowed to exercise. Your food will be decent. If you resist, there will be terrible consequences."

The man gave Ali time to think about what he had said. While they sat in silence, Ali's interrogator stared at Ali. Ali was afraid to close his eyes and his head was secured in place so he couldn't look away. The stare was ice cold and unfeeling. Ali could see no sign of pity and no hope of mercy. Suddenly, the man graced Ali with a gentle smile.

"Before we have a serious talk I want to tell you a little about myself. I have no family. I did have a family—a wife, a son who was eight, and a daughter who was eleven. I loved them very much. On September 11, 2001, they visited my brother, who worked in the World Trade Center."

Ali's stomach clenched.

"You can probably guess what happened." The smile disappeared and all the darkness that had been hidden behind it was suddenly revealed. "When they died, most of my emotions died with them. But a desire remained for revenge against their murderers and anyone like them."

The man paused to give Ali time to think.

"Do you know how I know your name?" the man continued. "Your fellow prisoners told me. Like you, they did not answer any of my questions the first few times I asked them. After a fairly short time, they were only too glad to tell me anything I wanted to know.

"I have been given a list of things we want to know, and I will ask you these questions to elicit this information. But I am different from other interrogators. Other interrogators hope that pain will force the person they are interrogating to answer their questions. I hope you resist so I can keep torturing you. The longer you hold out, the longer I can inflict pain. I will enjoy making you scream, and I am expert at it, Ali. I have a lot of practice."

Ali struggled to maintain his dignity. He wanted to beg and grovel. He wanted to do anything to avoid pain.

"There may be a chance for you, Ali," the man said. "We have learned a few things that lead us to believe you may be different from the other members of your cell."

Ali saw a glimmer of hope. The man nodded, and one of the guards wheeled a cart that held a television set with a DVR in front of Ali. The interrogator picked up a remote control.

"Someone you know, who cares about you, has something she wants to say. Listen carefully."

The man pressed the PLAY button, and Ann O'Hearn appeared on the screen. Her hands were clasped in her lap, her shoulders were hunched forward, and she looked very nervous.

"Ali? I . . . I can't believe you wanted to kill all those people. You seemed so nice. I can't begin to understand why you would want to take your own life and hurt so many innocent people who have never done anything wrong to you. There were children at the game, Ali."

Ann paused. Ali felt shame and hated himself for feeling shame. What he'd tried to do was just. The people in the stands were unbelievers, infidels, enemies of Islam.

Ann took a breath. "I know there is good in you, Ali. If there wasn't, you wouldn't have tried to warn me, to tell me to go home. I care about you, Ali, and you must care about me, because you tried to save my life. I've asked the FBI to help you like you tried to help me. I don't want them to hurt you. Please, Ali, do what they ask. If you got to know the people who came to the game the way you got to know me, you wouldn't have been able to go through with . . . with what you planned. I believe that deep down you are good. I . . ."

Ann looked away from the camera.

"Please do what they ask. I don't want you to be hurt."

The screen went blank. The man stood up.

"I'm going to give you time to think, Ali. I hope Miss O'Hearn is right about you. When I come back, I will ask you questions. If you answer them, it will go well for you. If you refuse to answer my questions, you will be stripped naked, and I will go to work. If that happens, you will suffer in ways you cannot imagine."

The man left the room, and the guards faded into its corners, silent and out of sight. Ali was terrified. His village, the camp in

Somalia, even the safe house where he had spent the past months seemed like dreams. These concrete walls were his reality. Terror was his new companion.

Ali was having trouble breathing and he was sweating. Hunger made it hard for him to think. The man's family had died at the hands of al-Qaeda; his wife, his children, his brother. There would be no mercy, and he knew he would talk eventually. Even brave men broke at some point.

Ali thought about Ann. Why had he tried to save her? Would he have warned her if he truly believed in his mission? If he had died, there would have been no remorse, no guilt. He would have been with Allah in paradise. But he had not died, and he had to face the consequences of failure, and the consequences were captivity and unspeakable pain that would end only when he did what his captors asked. Why endure any pain when he was certain he would give in? Would Allah forgive his cowardice? Would he be barred from paradise if he gave the enemy what they wanted?

Ali felt tears form. He was weak, he was a coward. While he was in his cell, he had heard his companions scream. They had resisted. But for how long? The man said they had given him Ali's name, he said they had answered all his questions. Had they held out to save face, knowing they would give their tormentors everything eventually? Had any not broken?

Ali didn't want to be hurt. He did not want to be burned, to have his bones broken, and to be drowned over and over and over. When the man returned, Ali was sobbing. When he stopped crying he begged for mercy and agreed to answer every question.

Chapter Thirty-two

"My name is Alan," the interrogator said as soon as Ali agreed to cooperate. Of course, Alan was not his real name, but that didn't matter. He had given Ali a name so he would appear to be less threatening.

Alan ordered the guards to remove Ali's restraints. He wasn't worried about being attacked. He was very adept at self-defense, and the guards were younger and faster and even better than he was.

Moments after Ali's restraints were removed, the door to the interrogation room opened and a cart with a meal composed of food and drink from the area where Ali had grown up was rolled in.

"If you're wondering how we knew the location of your village, one of the other prisoners told us."

Alan gave Ali this tidbit of information to make him unsure of what the FBI did and did not know. While Ali ate, Alan emphasized the importance of complete cooperation and the consequences to Ali if Alan discovered that he was lying.

When Ali was finished eating, Alan threw him some softballs.

He asked Ali what it was like growing up in the mountains of Pakistan. Alan listened to Ali's answers attentively. At first, Ali answered reluctantly. His shame at being broken was obvious, but it was easy to talk about the village and his family and his school. As he and Alan bonded, he began talking freely. Alan asked him how he was recruited. After that, it was an easy transition to a discussion about the camp, his trip to America, and the mission.

"Your friends told me that you were the only one trained to use explosives," Alan said.

Ali looked wary, but he nodded.

"The people at the camp must have valued your intelligence."

Ali blushed.

"I also understand that Steve took you along when he picked up the dynamite and the blasting caps."

"Yes."

"Tell me about that."

Ali recounted the journey. Alan asked him to describe the van and the logo. He asked for a description of the men who had given Steve the explosives.

"Did they say how they got them?" Alan asked.

"They said something about a mine in West Virginia."

"Did they tell you the name of the mine?"

"No. Steve asked where they got the dynamite, and Bob said it came from a coal mine in West Virginia."

Alan smiled. "A coal mine. Thank you. Now, we've talked about Steve a lot, and you've given me a very good description. Did he ever mention his last name?"

"No, never. He never said anything about himself."

"So you don't know where he lives or works?"

"No," Ali answered. Then he hesitated. Alan could see that he had remembered something useful that he was reluctant to give away.

"You know we're going to give you a lie detector test so we can be certain that you're being completely truthful. Don't hold anything back, Ali. You're doing very well, and I've come to like you. I do believe Ann O'Hearn. I do believe you're different from the others. Don't prove me wrong. I don't want to think about what will happen to you if I find out you've been playing me for a fool."

Ali licked his lips. He looked down. "There is one thing," he said, the shame of betrayal evident in his voice. "Steve picked us up from the freighter in a station wagon. He drove us to the safe house. I saw the license plate number of his car when he drove off."

"Do you remember the number?" Alan asked as if it was of no importance.

Ali repeated the number from memory. Alan wrote it down.

Half an hour later, Alan stood up.

"We've been talking for a while, and you must be tired. We'll wrap this up. You'll be returned to your cell while we check on the information you gave us. If it checks out, you'll be transferred to much better accommodations."

The moment he was alone, Alan pulled out his cell phone and dialed Harold Johnson.

"We may have caught a break, Harold. Ali Bashar has a knack for remembering numbers, and he memorized the license plate of a Volvo station wagon that was driven by the American who called himself Steve."

"I'll get someone on this right away," Johnson said as soon as he wrote down the number.

Alan hung up. He was exhausted, but he allowed himself a tired smile. He was an expert on breaking men, and he had succeeded once again without spilling a drop of blood. The story about 9/11 and the screams Ali had heard were psychological ploys to unnerve his subjects. The screams had been duped from horror movies, and Alan's wife and children lived in a pleasant suburb in Maryland. He wished he could be with them, but he would be bunking here tonight. In the morning, Ali would be given a polygraph examination. If he passed, Alan would milk him for more information, although he suspected that Ali had told him everything of importance.

Alan stretched. There was a room on another floor in the facility with a comfortable bed. He'd get a bite to eat before sacking out. Tomorrow he would work on the last member of the cell.

Alan was in a deep sleep when the light in his room went on and a guard told him to wake up. It took him a second to get oriented. His mouth felt gummy and everything was out of focus. He sat up and put on his glasses.

"What happened?" he asked.

"Bashar killed himself. You better come with me."

Alan put on his pants, shirt, and shoes and took the elevator to the basement where the cells were. Another guard was posted in front of the open door to Ali's cell. He stepped aside to let Alan in. The scene that confronted him was straight out of a slasher film. Ali was sprawled in a pool of blood, and spatter patterns resembling a Jackson Pollock painting decorated the walls and floor of the cell. There was even blood on the ceiling.

Mark Dobson, one of the doctors at the facility, was kneeling beside the body.

"The radial artery?" Alan asked. The artery was at the base of the thumb. He'd seen something like this once before.

Dobson nodded. "He chewed through both of them."

Dobson pointed at the spatter pattern on the walls, floor, and ceiling. "He probably got light-headed from blood loss toward the end and staggered around waving his arms. It's a shitty way to go. I figure it probably took him fifteen to twenty minutes to bleed out."

They talked a little longer. Then Alan went upstairs to phone Harold Johnson with the news. He wasn't going to lose any sleep over Ali's suicide. Bashar was a terrorist and deserved to die.

Chapter Thirty-three

Imran Afridi knocked on the door of the motel room, and Mustapha Haddad opened it. Mustapha was not someone you would notice in a crowd. He was slim, of average height, and neither handsome nor ugly. Mustapha blended in and had a nonthreatening demeanor. A dangerous person would always feel that he had the advantage in a confrontation with Afridi's enforcer. That person would be wrong. Mustapha killed without conscience and was deadly with a knife at close quarters. He was also a skilled sniper who had learned his trade in Afghanistan and Iraq.

Afridi didn't recognize the two other men in the motel room. They were over six feet tall and thickly muscled, with the scowl worn by bouncers who guard nightclub doors. The men stood up when Mustapha ushered his boss into the room.

"You know what happened?" Afridi asked.

Mustapha nodded. "Rafik told me. The detonators malfunctioned."

"This was not an accident. Either the man who sold the detonators to Reynolds was FBI or he was co-opted by the FBI. In either case, the FBI knew about our plan in advance. Someone betrayed us."

"Do you know who?" Mustapha asked.

"No, but there are four people who could have. Ali Bashar was the only member of the cell who worked with the bombs."

"I can't see him as a spy for the Americans, Imran. I know his background. He was recruited from a remote village and was sent directly to the camp. If he had contact with the CIA, someone in his village would have noticed. After the camp, Bashar was sent to the safe house in Karachi. After that, he was on the freighter, and from there he went straight to the safe house in Maryland."

"Someone could have gotten to him at FedEx Field while he was working," Afridi said.

"But how would they know he was a member of our cell? If he was turned, it was because the traitor identified him."

"An excellent point. In any event, he's in custody and we have no way of getting to him."

"Who else do you suspect?"

"Jessica Koshani knew that FedEx Field was our target."

"Did she know any other important details, like the date of the operation or the identity of the person who sold Reynolds the explosives?"

"No, but her death is suspicious."

"Wasn't Koshani murdered by that escaped serial killer?" Mustapha asked.

"That might be what the CIA wants us to think. Koshani was in Washington to testify before the Senate Select Committee on Intelligence. She was staying at a house owned by

Senator Carson. Koshani was blackmailing the senator to find out what the Americans knew about our plan. She phoned me on the afternoon of the day she was killed. The senator had just left after telling her that the FBI still had no idea where the attack was going to take place or when it would occur.

"It's possible that Carson went to the CIA or FBI and confessed that Koshani was blackmailing him. After Carson left, agents could have tortured her for details of the plot and faked Clarence Little's MO."

"Even if she was tortured by the CIA, she couldn't have told them enough information to get them to the person who supplied the detonators," Mustapha pointed out.

"Someone else may have done that, and Senator Carson might know who it is."

"It will be difficult to get to a United States senator," Mustapha said.

"Are you telling me you can't do it?" Afridi challenged.

"I'm saying it will be difficult, but I will find a way if it becomes necessary. Who is your last possibility?"

"Steve Reynolds. It has always seemed convenient that he was in that alley when the imam's student was attacked. He could have been in deep cover and the attack could have been a setup to get him in contact with the imam. Also, Reynolds found the man who sold the dynamite and detonators."

"I can question him," Mustapha suggested.

"Question him, then kill him."

"What if he isn't the traitor?" Mustapha asked.

"Kill him anyway. Reynolds has outlived his usefulness."

• • •

The house where Reynolds was staying was a forty-five-minute ride from the motel. They were several blocks from the rental when Mustapha told the driver to slow down so he could scout the surrounding area. As they drew closer, Mustapha tensed.

"Keep going," he said. "Something is wrong."

Chapter Thirty-four

Without warning, Mother Nature threw a switch, and fall turned to winter. Keith Evans and Maggie Sparks were a block away from a small, two-story Cape Cod in an unmarked car. The wind-chill factor had pushed the temperature into the thirties, but Keith had cranked up the car's heater, and he was sweating under his Kevlar vest.

A low chain-link fence surrounded the Cape Cod's unmowed, weed-infested lawn, and the paint on the front of the house was peeling. The rental agreement was made out to Stephen Reynolds, the name on the registration for the 2008 Volvo station wagon with the license plate number Ali Bashar had given up during his interrogation.

Keith had been sitting in front of his television eating a TV dinner and watching a college football game when Harold Johnson called him back to the office. Johnson gave Keith an arrest warrant for Reynolds, told him the suspect was armed and dangerous, and informed him that he'd have a SWAT team for backup.

A little after midnight, a pickup truck pulled into the driveway and a man fitting Reynolds's description got out, accompanied by a woman. Lights went on in the house. A half hour later, the house went dark. Keith gave the couple an hour to get to sleep before radioing the commander of the SWAT team to tell him that they were going in.

The moon was a cold sliver hiding behind thick clouds, and the only light came from the streetlights. A stiff wind smacked Keith in the face as soon as he got out of the car, and he ducked his head as he raced across the street. Even with SWAT to back him up, his nerves were getting to him. They always did before a raid, but he knew he'd be okay once the action started.

Keith and Maggie followed six members of the SWAT team up the driveway. More men were covering the back and sides of the house. The SWAT team and Maggie vaulted the low fence easily. Keith struggled and vowed to definitely put in some time at the gym.

Keith positioned himself on one side of the front door while Maggie ducked low and peeked through a gap between the windowsill and the curtain that draped the front window. She could see a sagging sofa, a television, and a cheap coffee table in the living room. A counter separated the living room from a small kitchen. There were doorways on either side of the living room, but it was too dark to see into the rooms. The team had procured a blueprint for the house when they were planning the raid, and the rental agent had identified the two darkened rooms as bedrooms.

Maggie relayed her information to the commander of the SWAT team, and he signaled two men who were holding a battering ram. Just as the ram swung back, a light came on in one of the bedrooms, and Steve Reynolds walked toward the kitchen.

The ram smashed into the door before Maggie could warn anyone, and the team rushed in shouting "FBI" with Maggie and Keith following.

Keith saw a skinny woman dressed in a T-shirt and panties step into the darkened doorway to his left, but he also saw a man speeding toward the other bedroom. Keith turned toward the man just as a body crashed into him, sending him to the floor. Before he could react, a shotgun blast whistled over his head, hitting the man in front of him. The officer pitched forward as several guns fired behind him. The weight on Keith's back eased as Maggie rolled onto the floor.

Keith pushed up and turned. The woman was sprawled on the floor, her body riddled with bullets, a shotgun inches from her hand. A SWAT team member kicked the gun out of reach. Another checked to make sure the woman was dead. Then some of the officers went to their downed comrade while others spread out to search the rest of the house.

"Holy shit," Keith whispered when he realized how close he'd come to being dead. Maggie stood unsteadily, adrenaline still coursing through her.

"Thanks," Keith said.

"Don't mention it," Maggie gasped as she bent forward and rested her hands on her knees.

Keith heard raised voices in Reynolds's bedroom, and he and Maggie walked in. A blond man clad in boxer shorts and a T-shirt was lying facedown on the floor with his hands cuffed behind him.

Keith had his boss on speed dial, and Johnson picked up after the first ring. Keith was still shaken from his close encounter with death, and he had to fight to keep his voice steady.

"We got him, Harold. There was a woman with Reynolds. She killed an officer and was killed by return fire. There are no other casualties."

"Where is Reynolds?"

"They're just taking him out."

"Stop them. I want him brought to the Department of Justice and not booked into any jail. Drive him into the basement garage."

"Okay. Hold on."

Keith was a little surprised by the change of plans, but he was sure Johnson had a good reason for having Reynolds transported to the DOJ. He pulled the SWAT team commander aside and relayed Johnson's instructions.

"Someone will be there to take custody of the prisoner. Maggie and I will wait for the morgue wagon and the team from the crime lab. And I'm sorry about your man."

While they were talking, a hood was slapped over the prisoner's head, and he was hustled out of the house. When the members of the SWAT team were gone, Keith and Maggie stepped outside into the cold night air. They stood without speaking for a while. Then Keith turned to Maggie.

"I'd be dead if it wasn't for you."

"I didn't even see the broad," Maggie joked to ease the tension. "I just thought this was a great opportunity to knock you on your butt."

Keith smiled. "You did that, all right."

Maggie returned the smile. "Think of this as payback for Webster's Corner."

During the Farrington affair, Keith had saved Maggie's life during a shoot-out at a West Virginia motel.

The couple's banter was interrupted by the arrival of the forensic experts. Keith briefed them, then he and Maggie headed downtown.

"Do you want to come in for a drink?" Maggie asked when Keith parked in front of her duplex three hours later.

Keith hesitated. The thought of being alone with Maggie made him nervous.

"Come on, Keith," Maggie insisted. "I'm too wound up to sleep and I can use the company."

"Sure. Thanks. I don't think I'd get much sleep, either."

Keith followed Maggie upstairs, his heart beating almost as wildly as it had just before he had rushed into Steve Reynolds's house. Maggie turned on the lights. It dawned on Keith that this was the first time he had been in Maggie's place.

Keith's apartment looked as though it belonged to someone who had just moved in, even though he had lived there for years. Maggie's looked like a home. It was neat and clean, with none of the pizza boxes and carry-out cartons that were scattered around Keith's living room and kitchen. The walls of Maggie's living room were decorated with abstract art. Some were lithographs, but Keith spotted two oils. The furniture was modern, and a few large pillows lay in front of a fireplace.

"This is nice," Keith said.

"It's convenient for work, and there's a park, a movie theater, and a lot of shopping nearby. What's your poison?"

"Scotch, neat," Keith said.

Maggie walked into the kitchen and Keith realized that he was terrified. He was drawn to Maggie, but they worked together, and no good could come from a relationship with a partner.

Maggie returned with Keith's drink. She stopped in front of him, but she didn't hold out the glass. They looked at each other. There were only inches between them. Maggie put down the glass and leaned in to kiss Keith. He put his hands on her shoulders to hold her back.

"Have you thought this through? We work together, I'm eight years older."

Maggie looked Keith in the eye. "Let's get this on the table. I want you. Unless I'm a piss-poor detective, I'm sure you want me, too. If you're not interested, tell me. There'll be no hard feelings. So do you want to talk about the Redskins or politics, or do you want to make love?"

Keith only hesitated a second before taking Maggie in his arms. Years of built-up tension evaporated after one long and fantastic kiss. Then they were staggering into Maggie's bedroom, shedding clothes along the way.

Keith had fantasized about making love to Maggie, but the real deal was better than anything he'd imagined. When they finally lay next to each other, all the ugliness of the night was forgotten. Keith found Maggie's hand and squeezed.

"Not bad for an old man," Maggie said softly.

Keith wished he could think of a witty comeback, but all he did was smile.

Part V

Prosecutorial Misconduct

Chapter Thirty-five

Deputy Assistant Attorney General Terrence Crawford's square jaw looked as though it had been created by a cartoonist who illustrated superhero comics. His adversaries likened his piercing blue eyes to laser beams, and his shaved head resembled the battering-ram noggins of professional wrestlers. When he wasn't prosecuting terrorists and the heads of drug cartels, Crawford was training for marathons or in the weight room in the basement of the Department of Justice working on the body he'd been building since junior high.

After being educated at the finest prep schools, graduating with honors from Princeton, and making the Yale Law Review, Terrence Crawford had scandalized his parents by choosing government work over an associate position in Wall Street's most prestigious law firm, where his father was a senior partner. Since his teens, Crawford had secretly fantasized about being a crime fighter like the superheroes he resembled, and he lived for the opportunity to send bad guys to prison.

When Jorge Marquez knocked on his doorjamb, Crawford was seated behind his desk, reading preliminary reports about the raid. Marquez was wearing a mismatched sports jacket and slacks he'd thrown on twenty-four hours ago, and he had not been home since to change. Marquez was a trial attorney in his fourth year at the DOJ. He'd worked his way up from a barrio in Los Angeles using scholarships to finance degrees from UCLA and its law school. Crawford used Marquez when he could because he respected his diligence and high IQ.

"What have you got for me?" Crawford asked.

"Scary shit, Terry. I ran Reynolds's prints. His real name is Ron Tolliver, he's originally from Ohio, *and he's dead.*"

Crawford waited for Marquez's explanation.

"Tolliver was in the Special Forces and was listed as MIA after an operation in Afghanistan. He's been officially dead for several years. We have no idea where he's been since he went AWOL. Best guess is Pakistan, because two of the detainees say he's fluent in Urdu and the FedEx plot probably originated there."

"What's he say?"

"Nothing. He hasn't said a single word since we arrested him. He's totally mute, not even a yes or a no. If it wasn't for fingerprints and the stuff we got out of the FedEx bombers, we'd have no idea who we're dealing with."

"Do we have a line on his parents, people who know him?"

"His folks live in Upton, Ohio. We have an agent on the way to interview them. From what I can tell, they're well off. Dad served in Vietnam. He's a dentist. The wife comes from money. We also discovered that Tolliver has been in trouble with the law."

After Marquez told him about the rape allegations in Ohio, Crawford stood up and straightened his tie in a small mirror that hung next to the commendations and diplomas that covered his wall.

"Let's see if I can loosen this traitor's tongue," he told Marquez before striding out of his office with the fierce countenance worn by vicious linebackers just before an all-out blitz.

Crawford opened the door to the interrogation room without knocking and studied Tolliver from the doorway. He was no longer wearing a hood, but his legs were manacled to the floor and his hands were cuffed. Crawford walked past Tolliver without a glance and sat down. He didn't begin the interrogation right away but chose to stare across the table for a while, smiling when his prisoner broke eye contact.

The interview room was small and very hot. The only furniture was the uncomfortable metal chair in which Tolliver was seated, a comfortable upholstered chair Crawford was using, and a government-issue gunmetal desk that stood between the chairs. There was no two-way mirror, but closed-circuit cameras fastened to the wall just beneath the ceiling filmed everything that went on in the room, and hidden microphones recorded every word.

"Hello, Ron," Crawford said, pausing to see if Tolliver would react. When he didn't, Crawford smiled.

"Pretty good self-control. Then again, dead men don't have physical reactions, and, according to our records, you've been dead for almost six years. We're notifying your parents about your miraculous resurrection."

When there was still no reaction, Crawford continued. "This will be one of those good news, bad news situations. Your folks will be happy to learn you're not dead, but I'm guessing that they'll puke when they learn that the fruit of their loins is a traitor who tried to top the body count of 9/11. I wonder how that will go over at the country club."

Crawford leaned forward and let his eyes bore into Tolliver's. "If you were my kid, you'd make me sick. You may think you're a grade-A martyr, but to me you're just another spoiled, self-centered rich kid. You didn't even have the guts to try to commit suicide like those poor deluded morons you talked into killing themselves in the name of Allah.

"And we know about the rape. You must be quite a man to have to brutalize a girl before you can get laid. Well, you'll soon experience the other side of that scenario. Some of the prison gangs are very patriotic, and they love traitors—and I mean that literally. So, realistically, your possible future scenarios are death row or a life of being cornholed. Personally, I hope you don't get a death sentence."

Crawford leaned back and watched Tolliver. Not a muscle in his face had twitched. Tolliver was definitely a tough guy.

"There is one way out of this mess, Ron—cooperation. The people who run you didn't take any risks, did they? They're safe and sound while you're chained to the floor, facing a life in hell. There are no female virgins where you're going, but I bet your handlers are getting laid as we speak. You're a joke to them, Ron, a dumb-ass American wannabe super-Muslim. They're probably pissed at you for failing, but I bet you made their day way back when you wandered into their psycho world. I bet they couldn't believe their luck when they stumbled on an all-American boy deluded enough to buy the bullshit they were dealing out. You think . . ."

Suddenly, the door opened and an FBI agent walked in. He looked embarrassed.

"What the fuck is this, Leveque?" Crawford barked angrily.

"He has a court order," the agent apologized.

"Who has a court order?" Crawford demanded.

The agent stepped aside, and a thickset man who was tall enough to look Crawford in the eye strode in.

"Bobby Schatz at your service, Terry," he said.

"Fuck me," Crawford replied.

Schatz was dressed in a hand-tailored navy blue pinstripe suit. A blue bow tie with white polka dots graced the collar of his white silk shirt, and the top of a folded red silk handkerchief extended upward from a pocket situated beneath the left lapel of his jacket. Schatz had straight, slicked-back hair so black that Crawford suspected that it was dyed and so heavy with gel that his hairdo resembled a lacquered cap.

"That's no way to greet a fellow member of the bar," Schatz said as he flashed a self-satisfied smile.

"You can take your ass out of here right now, Bobby, or I can have you thrown out."

"Temper, temper." Schatz held out a rolled-up document. "This is the court order to which Agent Leveque referred, and it says I get access to my client and you don't."

Crawford grabbed the papers. The more he read, the redder his face got. Crawford looked ready to explode by the time he finished.

"Satisfied?" Schatz asked.

"No, Bobby. This piece of shit tried to blow up a stadium full of decent citizens, and you're here to help him get out so he can kill more Americans."

Schatz was unfazed by Crawford's tirade. "What happened to the presumption of innocence? Were you absent the day they discussed that silly concept in your Intro to Crim Law class?"

Crawford ignored the jibe. "How did you know where to find this scumbag?" he demanded.

"Now, now, Terry, you're asking me to violate a confidence." Schatz handed Crawford a letter. "I am informing you by this letter, which I have filed with the court, that there is to be no further questioning of my client unless I am present."

Schatz surveyed the room and spotted the camera.

"I want that turned off, along with the mikes."

For a second it looked as though Crawford might assault Schatz. Then he rolled up the letter and the court order and muttered, "We'll see about this," as he stormed out of the room.

As soon as the door closed behind the lawyer, Schatz sat in the chair Crawford had vacated and smiled at Tolliver.

"Don't let Terry's bad manners bother you. He and I have been butting heads since he was a fledgling prosecutor. He's never gotten over the fact that I handed him his first defeat in court, and that wasn't the only time I kicked his ass."

Schatz laid a business card in front of the prisoner. Tolliver didn't look at it.

"Bobby Schatz at your service. Perhaps you've heard of me? I'm the best defense attorney in Washington, D.C., and this isn't the only place I practice. I've been hired by clients all over the U.S. because I take no prisoners."

"Did my parents hire you?" Tolliver asked.

Schatz stood up and walked around the desk. When he was next to the prisoner, he bent down and whispered a few words of Arabic in his client's ear. Tolliver sat up straight. Schatz smiled, walked back to his seat, and sat down.

"I have no idea whether Crawford can go up the food chain

and get another judge to block my access to you, so let's start discussing my plan to win your case."

Terry Crawford stalked down the hall to the room where Jorge Marquez was manning the camera feed and sound equipment.

"How did Schatz find out that we had Tolliver?" Marquez asked.

"He must have made an educated guess. The big question is, who hired that sleazy cocksucker?"

Crawford looked at the monitor. It was blank.

"Why did you turn off the camera?" he demanded.

"He had a court order."

"Turn it back on, and the sound equipment, too."

"But . . ."

"Just do it. We're talking national security, Jorge. Did you forget what happened at FedEx Field? This asshole tried to kill thousands of people. I am not going to take the chance of missing information that can help us stop another plot or lead us to the people who are running him."

"What if this screws up our court case?"

"It won't, because we are the only people who know the mikes and camera are still on, and neither of us is ever going to tell anyone, do you understand?"

Chapter Thirty-six

Ginny was nervous during her walk to the Department of Justice. She kept searching the crowds for Clarence Little even though Brad had assured her that the escaped serial killer was on the other side of the continent. When she entered the building through the Pennsylvania Avenue entrance, a security guard asked her for her identification. She showed him her badge before swiping it across a scanning device. Then she stepped into a glass-walled security area. When she left the area on the other side, another security guard checked to see if her face matched the photo on the badge.

Getting in today was a lot easier than getting in the first day she'd showed up for work. She didn't have a badge, so the guards wouldn't let her in, and she wasn't on any list. She had called Human Resources, but the person she'd dealt with was on vacation. Finally, Ginny had stopped a kind soul on his way into the building and explained her problem. He had taken pity on her and told her boss that a newbie was waiting on the sidewalk.

Life hadn't gotten much easier once she was inside. She had her own desk, but no computer or telephone for almost a week, and she shared an office with two other new trial attorneys. The good news was that she got along with her office mates, and the work was more interesting than her work in the big firms she had left.

Ginny had been placed in the Fraud Section, where she helped prosecute health-care scammers, telemarketing schemes, and identity theft. It wasn't as sexy as taking down organized crime figures or terrorists. Mom-and-pop credit-card fraud wasn't the subject of many big-budget movies or TV shows. Still, she felt good about protecting citizens as opposed to well-heeled corporations.

Ginny also appreciated the manageable hours she put in at DOJ. She wasn't paid as much as she'd been paid at Rankin, Lusk, but she didn't come in to work at seven and leave at ten, either, and her weekends were usually free. The people she worked with were just as bright as the Rankin, Lusk crowd, and they were definitely more dedicated. Very few of her fellow associates at her Portland and D.C. firms were enthusiastic about looking up property records at two in the morning or combing through corporate accounts for weeks on end. And her fellow prosecutors were more fun. Friday-afternoon happy hour at one of the watering holes in the neighborhood was a common occurrence, and it was not unusual to find a deputy chief mingling with the troops. On the rare occasion when the associates in her Oregon or Washington firms had been able to leave work in time for happy hour, no senior partners had deigned to rub shoulders with them.

The main drawback to working Fraud was the travel. She hadn't been sent on the road yet, but she'd been told that she could expect to go to Omaha, Nebraska, in a few weeks to work with the local United States attorney on a major health-care scam. She wasn't looking forward to being separated from Brad or living in Nebraska during the winter.

Ginny said hello to her office mates before booting up her computer. She had barely gotten comfortable when her door opened and Terrence Crawford walked in. He was dressed immaculately as usual, but there were dark shadows under his eyes, and he had the look of someone who had not slept much. Ginny's office mates were both women, and he looked at each in turn.

"Striker?" Crawford barked.

Ginny had never met Crawford, but he had a scary reputation, and she raised her hand timidly like a first-grader called on to recite to the class on the first day of school.

"Pack up your stuff," he ordered. "You're moving over to CTS."

Ginny blinked and her office mates gave her an odd look. The DOJ was organized into nine divisions, Criminal being the biggest. The National Security Division included Counterespionage (CES), the Office of Intelligence (OI), and Counterterrorism (CTS). Ginny couldn't think of a single thing in her background that qualified her to be in the Counterterrorism section.

Ginny's first impressions of her new boss were not very positive. Crawford ignored her as he led the way to the second floor, making Ginny feel like a stewardess bag the deputy assistant attorney general was reluctantly dragging behind him. Things looked up when Crawford stopped at an open door.

"This is where you'll work," he said.

Ginny peeked in. The office was empty, and it was a decent size. She hoped she wouldn't be sharing it with anyone.

"Can I ask you a question?" Ginny said.

"You want to know why you've moved, right?"

"I am curious."

"Don't you like the assignment?"

"It's definitely not that."

"Then what? Don't you think you can handle the work?" Crawford challenged.

"No, don't get me wrong. I'm really excited, but I haven't been here all that long."

"The work you'll be doing could be done by a first-year law student, and you're up here because one of the attorneys on the team that's prosecuting the FedEx bombers jumped ship without much notice to get rich at one of the big firms.

"Now get settled in. You're going to have to get a special clearance to work with us. It takes thirty days, but I'll see about getting it expedited. And I'll have an STU brought down this afternoon."

"An STU?"

"Better get up to date on the lingo, Striker. Secure Telecommunications Unit. It's a computer. Put in a key and press a button, and it scrambles everything around so you can access secure databases. I'd grab a quick lunch if I were you, because someone is going to be piling that empty desk with really boring shit in no time flat."

Chapter Thirty-seven

Dana Cutler stopped outside the door to Le Faisan d'Or and tugged self-consciously at the hem of her skirt, the bottom half of her only business suit, a charcoal black, pinstripe Elie Tahari she'd bought on sale. She was wearing the suit with a white silk blouse and a string of tasteful pearls Jake had bought her for her last birthday. Dana knew she looked good in the suit because she'd seen the way men looked at her on the rare occasions she'd had to wear it, but she never felt comfortable in a skirt because it limited her movement in a fight.

Dana was wearing her suit because a certain type of client expected her to dress in a certain way, and she'd guessed that Bobby Schatz fell into that category the moment his secretary had asked her to meet him at Washington's most exclusive French restaurant.

Dana had never met Schatz, but she'd seen him interviewed on television and read about his cases in the newspaper. And of course, she'd Googled him. All of *Exposed*'s stories about Senator Carson had carried Dana's byline, and she'd gotten a few clients from the publicity, but none as prestigious as Bobby Schatz. It would be a real coup to investigate a case for him because it would give her instant credibility with all of the heavy hitters in town. She'd also heard that he paid top dollar, and Dana could definitely use the money.

The maître d's face lit up when Dana told him that she was a guest of Bobby Schatz. He asked her to follow him, and Dana spotted Schatz when she was halfway across the dimly lit dining room. The celebrity lawyer was sitting in a booth in the back of the restaurant, sporting his trademark bow tie and wearing a satisfied grin. The media described him as self-indulgent, and photographs of his riverfront mansion and expensive cars supported the conclusion. Dana imagined Schatz leaning back after his meal and sipping a snifter of outrageously expensive Cognac before lighting up an illegally imported Cuban cigar while the maître d', who had received a shockingly large tip, ignored this violation of the D.C. antismoking code.

When the maítre d' was almost at his booth, Schatz slid out to greet his guest.

"Miss Cutler," he said, extending his hand. "I'm so glad you could join me. Have you eaten here before?"

Schatz knew damn well she hadn't.

"I'm more of a McDonald's girl. When I think of French, I think of fries."

Schatz smiled. "Then you're in for a treat."

They sat, and the maître d' presented Dana with a menu. Schatz was nursing a glass of bourbon, and Dana ordered a glass of scotch before turning to the menu. She didn't recognize a third of the items on it. Schatz noticed her furrowed brow.

"I eat here regularly, and I know what they do best," he said. "Would you permit me to order for you?"

"Sure," Dana said, relieved that she wouldn't have to guess what was going to arrive at the table after she ordered.

"Let's get business out of the way so we can enjoy our meal," he said as soon as the waiter left. "Unless you've been living in a cave in the Gobi Desert, you know that the FBI has arrested several people charged with trying to blow up FedEx Field."

"The four men who were working as vendors."

Schatz nodded. "I've got number five, and he's an interesting fellow. I guess his most interesting feature is that he's been dead for six years."

Their appetizers came when Schatz was halfway through briefing Dana on what he'd found out about Ron Tolliver/Steve Reynolds. He finished when the main course arrived.

"I assume you asked me to dinner to see if I want to investigate Tolliver's case."

"Exactly."

"You never asked me to work for you before. Why now?"

"Several reasons. First, I'm a big fan of your investigative reporting. It took guts to break the Farrington case, but it took smarts, too. This latest series on Jack Carson only served to increase my admiration for your work.

"Second, I've been told you're no-nonsense and never give up. That's what a few of your former clients said about you when I did my due diligence. All the comments were laudatory, by the way. No complaints.

"It's the fact that 'tough' was used by so many of them that convinced me to call you. You're going to need a thick skin if you take on this assignment."

"I'll be quite honest with you, Mr. Schatz . . ."

"Call me Bobby."

"Okay, Bobby. If I had to choose between helping Tolliver's defense and shooting him in the head, I'd choose to put that gutless terrorist in the ground."

"You *are* a tough guy, but don't forget that the state will do your work for you if Tolliver is convicted."

"If he tried to kill all those innocent people, I don't want to spend my time trying to keep him off death row."

Schatz's head bobbed up and down. "You may not believe this, but I share your sentiments about terrorists. If Ron Tolliver is guilty of participating in the plot to blow up the Redskins' stadium he deserves anything he gets. But you're missing the point."

"Don't give me that 'Innocent until proven guilty' bullshit."

"Ah, but it's not bullshit."

Dana smirked. Schatz raised his hand.

"Hear me out. When we broke free from the British, the colonists believed that government could be evil because they had been oppressed by a dictatorial government that did not respect their rights. People were imprisoned for political reasons, their homes were searched on the whim of a government official; they had no faith in the fairness of the judicial process. That lack of faith led to revolution.

"There are many, many countries in this world where the rule of law does not exist. Those are the countries where fear and violence are a common part of everyone's life and the people rise up and overthrow the government. America is different. We don't believe in revolution. We believe that differences with our government should and, most important, can be resolved in a court of law. That is why it is so important to give the best trial to the most heinous criminals, the criminals we would all execute personally without blinking an eye. When average citizens see these monsters receive due process, it reaffirms their belief that if they or their loved ones were ever arrested for shoplifting or driving under the influence, the system would treat them fairly."

Dana smiled. "Now I see why you win so many acquittals. But I am curious. You have an investigator, right?"

Schatz nodded. "Ben Mallory."

"Then why not use him?"

"Normally, I do use Ben to investigate my cases. We've been together for years, and he's a terrific investigator. But Ben's brother was working in the Twin Towers on 9/11, and he didn't make it. Ben just couldn't bring himself to work on this case, and I couldn't ask him to do it. That's why I need you, Miss Cutler, and I'm willing to pay top dollar to get you on board.

"If Ron Tolliver goes down, it should be because the government convinces twelve citizens that there are no reasonable doubts about his guilt and not because his lawyer was stuck with a mediocre investigator who missed evidence that pointed toward his innocence. What do you say?"

Chapter Thirty-eight

Dana entered the elegant reception area of Bobby Schatz's law office at 9:00 on the dot. Everything from the original oils on the wall to the expensive Persian carpet and fine furniture told potential clients that they better be able to afford a six-figure retainer if they wanted Schatz to represent them.

The receptionist was stunning in an understated way that was more *Vogue* than *Penthouse.* She flashed a perfect smile as Dana approached her desk.

"Good morning, Miss Cutler," she said before Dana could introduce herself. "My name is Cassie. If you'll come with me, I'll take you to see Mr. Schatz. He's expecting you."

Dana followed Cassie down a narrow hall past the open doors of offices occupied by earnest young men and women Dana assumed were Schatz's associates. Dana turned down an offer of tea or coffee before Cassie ushered her into her boss's corner office. As expected, there was a wall of fame displaying headlines from the attorney's most famous cases, as well as framed awards and pictures of Schatz with movie actors, television personalities, presidents, and lesser but well-known politicians. The windows behind Schatz presented a view of the Capitol dome at one end of the Mall and the White House at the other.

"Sit. We've got a busy morning ahead of us and only a little time for me to brief you," Schatz said. Dana liked the fact that there was no small talk. "In one half hour, you and I are going to walk over to the Department of Justice to have the pleasure of having our balls busted by Deputy Assistant Attorney General Terry Crawford, who is heading up the prosecution of our client. I will hand him motions for discovery, and he will laugh at us and treat us like shit, while making no effort to disguise the pure joy he gets out of trampling on the constitutional and statutory rights of those unfortunate enough to find themselves in the federal criminal injustice system."

"It sounds like you've dealt with Crawford before."

"Many times, unfortunately. Terry is a complete asshole, but you should never underestimate him. He is also very smart and very, very cunning. The only saving grace of having him as an opponent is that he is so driven to screw all defense attorneys that he occasionally makes mistakes."

"If you know we're not going to accomplish anything, why do you want me along?"

"Do you have a good memory, Dana?"

"It's decent."

"Good, because your job will be to observe. While we are with Terry, or any of his cronies, let me do the talking. You do the listening. It's not out of the realm of possibility that Terry will do something as a result of his zeal that may, in the future, lead to a motion charging him with prosecutorial misconduct. If I file such a motion, I'll need witnesses."

"You got it. So when do I get to interview our client?"

"That's not going to happen."

Dana frowned. "Some of the best leads I've gotten have come from the defendant."

"I'm sure that's true, but Ron is off-limits to you."

"And why is that?"

"Ron Tolliver does not trust anyone. I've tried to get him to talk to me about the case, and he refuses."

"Why don't you let me give it a shot?"

"Maybe later, but I'm trying to build rapport with him. I also want him to see me as his only point of contact with the world outside his prison. And don't worry; you'll have plenty of tasks that will occupy your time."

Schatz glanced at his diamond-studded gold Rolex. "It's time to enter the dragon's den, Cutler. Put on your armor and follow me."

"Striker, grab a pad and pen and come to my office," Terrence Crawford barked over the intercom.

Ginny had been arranging thousands of pages of investigative reports into neat piles before punching holes in them so they would fit into a three-ring binder. She had been at this task for three days and was so relieved to escape from it that she was actually grateful to Crawford, who had been treating her like a secretary when he wasn't ignoring her.

Ginny started to ask Crawford what he wanted her to do, but the intercom went dead. Ginny sighed and pulled a yellow legal pad out of the bottom drawer of her desk. When she reached Crawford's office, he was reading a brief.

"Sit," he said, pointing at a chair in a corner of the room without looking up.

Ginny waited for Crawford to explain why he had summoned her. When five minutes passed, Ginny had had enough.

"What is it you want me to do, Mr. Crawford?"

The deputy AG looked at Ginny as if he hadn't realized she was in the room. Then he directed a malicious smile at her.

"In five minutes, Bobby Schatz is going to come in here and demand all sorts of things, which I am not going to give him. When he comes to grips with the fact that I'm not going to budge, Schatz is going to run to court and accuse me of everything from pederasty to rape. As with any accused, I will fare better in court if I can produce a witness who can testify that I did none of the acts Schatz will dream up."

Ginny was about to reply when Crawford's intercom buzzed and his secretary announced the arrival of Schatz and his investigator. Crawford told her to send them in. A moment later, the door swung open and the secretary stood aside to admit Bobby Schatz. A second later, Dana Cutler followed him into the office. Crawford was looking at Schatz, or he would have seen Ginny's jaw drop. Dana's eyes locked in on her friend, but her expression gave away none of the surprise she felt.

"Hey, Bobby, come on in," Crawford said as he walked around his desk and shook hands.

"Thanks, Terry. I'd like you to meet my investigator, Dana Cutler."

"A pleasure."

Crawford did not introduce Ginny, but he did motion Schatz and Dana toward a comfortable couch that stood against the wall under a framed copy of the Constitution.

"So, Bobby, what can I do for you?" Crawford asked as soon as he'd retaken his seat.

"I'm interested in discovery, Terry. For starters, I'd appreciate a look at the affidavit you used to get the warrant to search my client's house."

"I'm sorry, I can't help you there."

"Why not? I'm entitled to see it, and I'll need to read it if I'm going to challenge the search."

"My problem is that I can neither confirm nor deny the existence of such warrants."

"You're joking!"

"The Foreign Intelligence Surveillance Act is no joke, Bobby. If a search warrant affidavit for Tolliver's house was obtained from the FISA court, it would be classified, and I wouldn't be able to even acknowledge its existence."

"If you're going to use evidence from the search you conducted using a FISA warrant, you have to tell me."

Crawford shrugged. "It's early days, Bobby. I have no idea what evidence I'm going to use."

"Stop screwing around. You know a Federal District Court judge is going to tell you to give me the affidavit. We're talking about the Fourth Amendment here."

"Maybe a judge will agree with you. File a motion and we'll hash this out in court. But I seem to remember hearing that there isn't a single case where a FISA affidavit has been disclosed to a defense attorney." Crawford grinned. "Maybe you'll set a precedent. What else would you like?"

"I'd like to see the statements made by the four men who were arrested at FedEx Field."

"I'm not at liberty to confirm or deny that such men exist."

"Terry, pictures of the arrest have been on YouTube, Facebook, CNN, and every media outlet in America and abroad."

"Then serve a motion for discovery on YouTube."

"Cute, but you know this is bullshit," Schatz said.

"Hey, I don't make the rules. Call your congressman and get him to repeal FISA. Me, I'm just an employee of the federal government, and my boss tells me I have to follow the law, which does not allow me to confirm or deny the existence of these so-called arrestees."

"Can you give me the names of their attorneys?" Schatz asked.

"I'm not at liberty to discuss that."

"This isn't a game, Terry. My client is facing serious jail time."

Crawford sat up and leaned forward. His face was tight and his body language signaled that he had shifted from taunting Schatz to real anger.

"We lost three thousand people on 9/11. There were over ninety thousand people in FedEx Field on Sunday, and your client wanted to kill them all, so I won't be too upset if he has to serve serious jail time."

"You're assuming he had some part in the plot."

"Oh, he did."

"You haven't told me one thing that leads me to believe he was involved with the suicide bombers."

Crawford got hold of his emotions and leaned back in his chair. "You'll get discovery at the appropriate time and not a second before. If you don't like my position, file a motion."

Schatz looked as though he was about to say something else, but he changed his mind and stood up.

"Thanks for taking the time to see us," he said.

"Sorry I couldn't be more help," Crawford lied.

Seconds after the door closed behind Schatz and Dana, Crawford broke into a huge grin.

"I hope you remember what you just saw, Miss Striker, because that is the way to kick ass and take names in the doing-justice business."

Ginny nodded and kept her opinion of what she had just seen to herself. Everything Crawford had done went against her basic sense of fair play. She knew that Crawford had complied with the law, but the end result was that Schatz would have no information he could use to defend his client. Ginny had no sympathy for terrorists, but a court would have to decide whether Tolliver was a terrorist. What if he was innocent but he couldn't defend himself because his lawyer had no information about his case?

Ginny was also upset by Crawford's attitude. A man's life might literally be at stake. Crawford was treating the case as if it concerned only him and Bobby Schatz, but the case really revolved around the ability of the government to prove Tolliver's guilt beyond a reasonable doubt. Ginny was appalled by laws that hid evidence and begged for an unjust result and by a prosecutor who treated a matter this serious as a game.

"Can he do that?" Dana asked when they were out of the building and headed back to Schatz's office.

"Oh, yeah. The federal rules are barbaric. Most prosecutors don't follow them to the letter, but under them we aren't entitled to see the statements of a witness until after he testifies, which means you probably aren't going to have any time to investigate before I cross.

"Then there's the Federal Intelligence Surveillance Act. The government attorneys go to the FISA court, which is made up of federal judges. Their proceedings are secret, and it's almost impossible for a defendant to find out the basis for the search or even that a search occurred unless they decide to use evidence they got using the warrant. And even then, there's a declassification process that can prevent a defendant from ever knowing the real basis for the warrant.

"What's worse, the government is allowed to conduct searches and wiretaps under FISA without satisfying the normal Fourth Amendment requirement of showing probable cause that a crime has been committed when it's trying to get a warrant.

"On top of that you have CIPA, the Classified Information Procedures Act, which sets out procedures when a defendant wants discovery of evidence that's classified. The defendant can't get classified evidence unless a judge finds that it's relevant, and the judge makes that finding in secret. If the government objects after a judge finds the evidence is relevant, the court enters a nondisclosure order and tries to figure out an appropriate sanction for the government's failure to disclose the evidence it's decided is relevant to defending the case. And even when there is no nondisclosure order, the defense attorney can only see the evidence if he has a security clearance, and the defense attorney is usually prohibited from showing the evidence to the defendant. If the judge decides that the defendant can see the evidence, he provides it in a sanitized form like a summary or a redacted document."

"What about the government's obligation to give the defense evidence in its possession that can clear him?" Dana asked.

"In the *Moussaoui* case, the defense wanted to interview terrorists who were detained in U.S. custody outside the country to develop witnesses who would testify that Moussaoui's involvement with al-Qaeda was limited. The court wouldn't let the defense interview the potential witnesses. The best they got were summaries of intelligence reports they would have been allowed to read to the jury if the case had gone to trial.

"The whole thing stinks to high heaven, but our client is caught up in post–9/11 hysteria, and that gives a guy like Crawford an opportunity to trample on his rights that he'd never have if Tolliver were charged with bank robbery."

"What are you going to do?" Dana asked.

Schatz shrugged. "I'll scream and holler and file motions and hope that Crawford gets overconfident and screws up."

Chapter Thirty-nine

The next morning, Ginny arrived at the DOJ bright and early. She was taking off her coat when Terrence Crawford pushed a multitiered cart into her office. Ginny was surprised to see her boss doing a job that would normally be assigned to a secretary.

"Great news," Crawford said. "I was able to rush through your security clearance, which means you are now able to organize these top-secret files."

Crawford scanned the office. When he spotted Ginny's hole punch, he grinned maliciously.

"Good, good," he said. "You've got a hole punch and I've provided you with binders and tabs. When you've got the case file organized, bring it to my office. Say by tomorrow afternoon."

"Tomorrow, but . . ."

"No buts. There's a team of lawyers waiting for this material. I imagine this job will evoke fond memories of your days at Rankin, Lusk—the all-nighters, the Saturdays and Sundays at the office when normal people were at the beach or lying around at home doing the *Times* crossword.

"Well, enough of this idle chatter. I'm taking up valuable time."

Crawford sped away before Ginny could protest any further. She was appalled by the joy he seemed to take in her discomfort. What a prick! She wondered if Crawford had any redeeming qualities. She sure couldn't think of even one.

Ginny walked over to the cart. Its three shelves were loaded down with banker's boxes. In addition to the boxes, three-ring binders were stacked on the bottom shelf. Ginny counted twenty boxes in all. She lifted the cover of one of them. It was filled to the top with paper. She groaned. This was going to take forever; only she did not have forever, she had until the next afternoon.

The first thought that sprang into her head was *coffee*. She was going to need a lot of it. On the way down to the basement cafeteria, something occurred to her. Security clearances had been discussed by Ginny's coworkers on a few occasions, and Ginny had the impression that they took a while to get. On the day Crawford moved her over to Counterterrorism, he had mentioned that he was going to try to expedite the process, but he seemed to have pushed her clearance through in record time. She wondered why.

Ginny filled a thermos to the top with coffee and carried it back to her office. Just thinking about the daunting task she was facing was exhausting. She poured out a cup of caffeine and took a stiff drink. Then she carried the first box to her desk and pulled a stack of paper out of it so she could see what she was dealing with. It didn't take her long to realize that she was looking at 302s—the FBI equivalent of a police report—in the FedEx case. She was still pissed off at Crawford but not as pissed off as she had been. Working at Justice might not pay as much as Rankin, Lusk, but no one at Rankin, Lusk would have the inside scoop on one of the biggest terror cases in American history.

Ginny read the first report. It was an interview with a person who worked at a concession stand at the football stadium. The interview concerned a fellow worker, but the name of the subject in whom the interviewer was interested was redacted. Ginny flipped through a few of the other reports. Names and other information—like an address in one case—were also blacked out. News stories on television and in the papers had reported that hawkers for several concessions were believed to be suicide bombers who were arrested before they were able to detonate their bombs. Ginny assumed that the terrorists were being held at a secret prison somewhere. She wondered what that would be like and she shuddered. She had read stories about waterboarding, and she'd seen the pictures from Abu Ghraib prison. She was certain that she couldn't stand up under that type of pressure. Something else about the prisoners being held at a secret prison bothered her, only she couldn't put her finger on it, so she got back to work.

A lot of the 302s in the first two boxes recounted interviews with people who worked at concession stands at FedEx Field. Ginny built a tower out of these reports on a corner of her desk. She would put them in a binder in alphabetical order when she had collected all of these interviews and the reports that concerned them.

Ginny was reading a report of an interview with a woman named Ann O'Hearn when she noticed that Keith Evans and Maggie Sparks were the agents who had conducted the interview. She smiled. It made this tedious work easier when she could connect with someone involved in the investigation.

Later on, Ginny came across a series of reports about a man named Lawrence Cooper who owned the concession stands where the suicide bombers had been employed. It came as a shock when she found out that he had been murdered. She thought about that. The terrorists had to figure out a way to get their people into FedEx Field. Maybe Cooper was part of the plot or a dupe who had been talked into hiring the suicide bombers. Maybe he was killed to prevent him from telling anyone who had arranged for him to hire the four bombers. Ginny felt proud of herself when she read a report by a detective who had drawn a similar conclusion.

By the time six o'clock rolled around, Ginny's head was swimming, her stomach was rumbling, and the lines on the reports were starting to blur. After calling Brad to tell him that he shouldn't wait up for her, Ginny went down to the cafeteria. It was good to get away from the banker's boxes, even if it was only for the time it would take her to buy her dinner. She carried a sandwich, two bags of chips, and more coffee back to her office.

Twenty minutes later, Ginny was finished with her sandwich and one of the bags of chips. She tossed her trash in the can under her desk and opened the next banker's box. It contained transcripts of the interrogations of the suicide bombers. Ginny was surprised at how little most of the bombers knew. They were all from small villages and were educated in madrassas where they studied the Koran and little else. Their only exposure to a wider world had been in a training camp in Somalia, a day or two in a safe house in Karachi while they waited to be smuggled out of Pakistan, and their work in FedEx Field.

One prisoner, AB, was the only bomber who appeared to be of above-average intelligence. While reading the transcript of his interrogation, Ginny found out how the FBI had learned Ron Tolliver's license plate number. An autopsy report let Ginny know that AB had committed suicide.

The next set of 302s dealt with the way Ron Tolliver had been tracked down, the raid on his house, and his transportation to the Department of Justice. Ginny sat up straight. That's what had bothered her before. The suicide bombers had been captured at FedEx Field and immediately transported to a secret prison. Why was Ron Tolliver taken to the DOJ? If he'd been imprisoned in the secure facility where the other members of the cell were being held, Bobby Schatz would never have been able to find him. Ginny puzzled over this problem for a while, then gave up.

By eleven, Ginny had developed a dull headache and her vision was blurred. She decided that she would finish reading the last pile of paper in the banker's box on her desk, then call it a night. She was halfway through her last stack when she found a typed transcript that looked out of place among all the 302s. After finishing the first page, she realized that she was reading the transcript of Terrence Crawford's interrogation of Ron Tolliver.

Crawford started off by insulting and threatening the prisoner. Ginny wasn't surprised. If she studied a genome of Crawford's DNA, she was certain she wouldn't find the gene for subtlety. From the one-sided nature of the conversation, Ginny concluded that Tolliver had not been intimidated.

Ginny turned the page and smiled when Schatz appeared on the scene, brandishing his court order and demanding that the cameras and microphones be turned off. She could imagine what Crawford looked like when he was forced to leave the room.

By the time she had flipped to the next page, Ginny's smile had morphed into a frown. The transcript should have ended when Crawford left the interrogation room, but it went on for many more pages. It was clear that the microphones had been off for a while, because the conversation between Schatz and Crawford ended abruptly as soon as Schatz made his demand that his attorney-client conference not be recorded. But the transcript continued in the middle of one of Schatz's sentences. Someone had turned on the microphones again, and Ginny bet that it was her boss.

Was it legal for Crawford to listen in on a conversation between an attorney and his client? It had been made crystal clear in law school that the attorney-client privilege was a sacred cornerstone of the judicial system. Competent representation of a client was almost impossible if a client didn't feel she could speak freely to her lawyer. Ginny could not imagine that there was an exception to the rule that would permit Crawford to eavesdrop on the discussion between Schatz and Tolliver.

Ginny turned to her computer and logged on to Westlaw, a tool for legal research. It didn't take long to find cases that held that the Sixth Amendment to the United States Constitution provided a right to counsel for defendants in criminal cases and that a defendant's rights under that amendment were violated if a prosecutor eavesdropped on an attorney-client meeting.

In *Coplon v. United States*, the defendant was convicted of giving United States intelligence reports to a Russian agent. The D.C. Court of Appeals reversed the conviction presuming prejudice when the defendant's telephone conversations with her lawyer were monitored after her arrest.

In *Caldwell v. United States*, a government agent managed to get himself employed by the defendant's lawyer. The agent learned confidential attorney-client communications, which he revealed to the United States attorney. The appellate court held that this intrusion was so serious that the defendant didn't have to show actual prejudice to get the case reversed.

By the time Ginny logged off, she was convinced that taping an attorney-client conference was an act of prosecutorial misconduct so serious that a defendant didn't even have to show that the taping prejudiced his case to win a dismissal.

Ginny was no longer tired. Her mind was racing. She finished reading the transcript, then she set it aside and read the rest of the documents in the box. Most of the reports she had reviewed in this box and the other boxes had some relationship to each other, but none of the other documents in the box with the transcript had anything to do with the interrogation of Tolliver or the attorney-client conference between Tolliver and his lawyer. So what was this ticking time bomb doing in the banker's box? The only conclusion Ginny could draw was that the transcript had been included with the other documents by mistake.

Ginny's heart was pounding. What should she do? If she made the violation public, she could lose her job. At minimum, it would destroy any chance of advancement she might have in the DOJ. But she couldn't just put the transcript in a binder and let someone else worry about it. She was certain that would be a violation of her ethical responsibilities. She would have to tell someone about it, but whom?

Crawford was her boss, but he was probably the person who had intentionally violated Tolliver's rights. Crawford would not want the transcript read by anyone. He might even destroy it. Then it would be her word against his, and she knew who would come out on top in that scenario if she didn't have proof that the transcript existed.

Proof! If she made a copy of the transcript, she would have proof that Crawford had violated Tolliver's constitutional rights. Crawford could argue that Ginny had faked the transcript but Schatz, and maybe even Tolliver, could tell a judge that the transcript was, word for word, what they had said in the interrogation room.

Ginny picked up the transcript. She felt sick to her stomach. She knew what she had to do, but she was paralyzed. After a few moments, she took a deep breath and forced herself to her feet. There was a copier down the hall. She walked toward it feeling a little like a death-row inmate on the way to her execution. She looked around nervously, ears alert for any sound, but it was so late that the only people on the floor would most likely be members of a cleaning crew or security guards. Even so, she couldn't risk being seen by a witness.

Ginny ducked into the room with the copier. She thought about turning on the lights but decided against it. The machine was close enough to the door so she could read the controls in the light from the corridor. The copier had been turned off for the night. Ginny flipped a switch and waited for the copier to warm up. She had just put the transcript in the copier and pressed the button to activate it when she heard footsteps. Her heart rocketed into her throat.

"I thought I heard a noise."

A security guard was standing in the doorway.

Ginny forced a smile. "Hi, Ray," she said to Ray Boyle, a heavyset man in his midfifties with whom Ginny had exchanged pleasantries on a few of the occasions when she had worked late.

"You're putting in the hours."

"Crime never sleeps, so someone has to protect the likes of you," Ginny said.

Boyle laughed. "I can take care of myself. You should head home and get some rest."

"I'm out of here as soon as I make these copies."

"Well, good night," Boyle said as he walked off. Ginny's knees buckled, and she took a deep breath to calm herself. When she looked at the copier, she saw that the job had been completed. She took the original and the two copies she had made and returned to her office. She put the copies in separate envelopes and put the original at the bottom of the pile she had made out of the materials in the banker box. She would put the 302s in a binder in the morning. That would give her the night to think about what she would do with the original.

Ginny let herself in the apartment as quietly as possible and tiptoed into the bedroom so she wouldn't wake up Brad. It didn't work. When she was halfway to the closet, he mumbled, "Hi."

"Did I wake you?" Ginny asked as she stripped off her clothes.

"Not really. I can never get comfortable if you're not in bed."

Ginny washed up in the bathroom; then she slipped under the covers.

"You're burning the midnight oil," Brad said. "What have they got you working on?"

"Crawford has me organizing reports for the FedEx trial team."

"That sounds interesting."

"It's not. It's scut work. A secretary should be doing it, but I have the privilege because I have a Top Secret clearance."

"Congratulations. Say, can you find out if the government is really keeping aliens in area fifty-one?"

"Yes, but I can't tell you because *you* do not have a Top Secret clearance."

"So that's the way it's going to be, huh?"

"I can't help it if you're unimportant."

Brad slapped Ginny playfully on her rump. "This marriage is definitely on the rocks," he said. Then he rolled over and snuggled with Ginny. They held each other quietly for a while. Then Ginny took her head off Brad's shoulder and looked at him.

"There's something I want to ask you," she said.

"Shoot."

"Let's say you were working on a case at Reed, Briggs and you discovered some information that would win the case for the other side."

"What kind of information?"

"Something illegal that the firm had done. Maybe you found proof that a partner had falsified evidence. What would you do?"

"If it was really serious, I guess I'd call the bar and ask for an ethics opinion."

"What if they told you that you had an ethical duty to make the violation known but you knew that going public would probably lose the case for a client and get you fired?"

"Whoa, that's a tough one, but I guess the bottom line is that you have to do the right thing. My folks call it the mirror test. You always have to live with the consequences of your actions, so you have to be able to look at yourself in the mirror. If you think about doing something and you know that the end result is that you won't be able to hold your head up and look yourself in the eye, then you don't do it. It's pretty simple."

"In theory, but not so simple sometimes in real life."

"I made the choice to pursue the *Little* case even after Susan Tuchman told me I'd be fired if I did."

"But you didn't care if she fired you. You hated working at Reed, Briggs."

"That's true."

"What if you loved that job? What if it was the only job you ever wanted and you knew you'd lose it if you kept investigating Little's case?"

Brad went quiet. Ginny had just asked a really hard question, but he thought he knew the right answer.

"Maybe I thought I'd love the job, and maybe I did love it up until I had to make my choice, but I don't think I would love a job if I had to do something illegal or unethical to keep it.

"Now, what prompted these questions?" Brad asked. "Are you in some kind of trouble at work?"

"Not yet, but I could be."

"Talk to me. Tell me what's bothering you."

"I wish I could, but this is a problem I'm going to have to solve on my own. Now I've got to get to sleep or my eyes will fall out of my head."

Ginny kissed Brad and rolled over. She was dead tired, but she was too wound up to sleep. The job at the Department of Justice was not her dream job. She had taken it because she was fed up with corporate law and prosecuting criminals sounded interesting. So far, the job had been a mixed bag. Some of the things she'd done were challenging, while other tasks were sheer drudgery, like the task Crawford had assigned her. To be honest, working for Crawford, an overbearing egotist, was as bad as working for Susan Tuchman at Reed, Briggs and almost as bad as working for Dennis Masterson at Rankin, Lusk. Still, she wanted to keep her job at Justice, but she wouldn't be able to if she told Bobby Schatz about the transcript and Crawford discovered that she was responsible for the leak. Ginny was still undecided about what she should do when exhaustion finally dragged her into a troubled sleep.

Chapter Forty

Dana was frustrated. Bobby Schatz wouldn't let her talk to their client, and Terry Crawford wouldn't give Schatz any discovery. Every time she asked Schatz what he wanted her to do, he would tell her to relax. But relaxing was not in Dana's repertoire.

Dana did have other cases, and she spent time on them, but business was still slow, and she found herself with a lot of spare time. Finally, out of boredom, Dana made a list of the things she knew about Ron Tolliver's case. It was a very short list, but there was one item on it she thought she could pursue, although she had no idea whether her investigation would be of any benefit to the defense.

Dana knew where Tolliver had been arrested, and she rode Jake's Harley to the place. A FOR RENT sign had been hooked onto the chain-link fence that surrounded a weed-choked yard. Dana doubted anyone would be renting until the yellow crime-scene tape disappeared. She parked at the curb and made her way to the front door. Because the house was still officially a crime scene, all she could do was circle the house, looking in the windows. The only thing she learned from that exercise was that the interior of the house looked like hell. Dana wasn't surprised. She knew from her experiences with the D.C. police that SWAT teams didn't tidy up after a raid.

Dana canvassed the neighbors, but that didn't turn up anything useful. Tolliver and a woman had moved in a few months before his arrest, but they'd kept to themselves to the point where the neighbors didn't even know their names. The neighbor across the street had seen Tolliver go and come on a number of occasions, but he'd only seen the woman in Tolliver's company. The neighbor on Tolliver's right had seen him leave and return but had never exchanged words with him or the woman. Before she left, Dana checked the FOR RENT sign and wrote down the name, address, and number of the real estate agent who was handling the property.

The real estate offices of Kendall & Marquoit were on a corner in a commercial area of Bethesda, Maryland. A receptionist guided Dana to the office of Mary Ann David, a handsome blonde in her midforties. David greeted Dana with a smile and offered her a seat.

"Myra said you're interested in our rental on Pendleton Place, Miss Cutler."

"Yes, but not in the way you think. I'm an investigator, and I'd like to talk to you about the man who rented the property."

David looked concerned. "I've already told the FBI agents everything I know."

"I'm working for Bobby Schatz," Dana said, handing the agent one of the business cards Schatz had printed for her. "He's Mr. Tolliver's attorney."

"Who?"

"Ron Tolliver is the man who rented from you."

"I rented that house to Stephen Reynolds."

Dana nodded. "Reynolds is an alias. His real name is Ronald Tolliver."

"I don't know if I should discuss anything with you without asking the agents if it's all right."

Dana flashed her warmest smile. "Mrs. David, you don't have to get the FBI's permission to talk to me, and I'd hate to inconvenience you by having to subpoena you to court.

"Look, I'll level with you. My boss can be a bit of a prick at times. I'm only interested in background material. I'll probably never see you again. But Mr. Schatz will go nuts if I tell him you wouldn't talk to me. You look like you're pretty busy. I'm sure you don't want to get subpoenaed to court and have to sit in the hall outside a courtroom all day only to answer a few innocuous questions under oath that you could have answered for me today."

David looked alarmed. "Are you threatening me?"

"Hell, no. I believe in live and let live. I know that the stuff you tell me won't be important enough to make you a witness. It's Mr. Schatz. If I tell him you wouldn't talk to me, he'll assume you know something important, and the next thing you know, a process server will ambush you outside your house, and Mr. Schatz will make you sit in the corridor all day out of spite. I've seen him do this before. So, what do you say? I've got a few harmless questions, then I'll be out of your hair."

David sighed. "What do you want to know?"

"How many times did you meet Mr. Tolliver?"

"The first time was when he came to this office and told me he wanted to rent two properties."

"Two?"

"Yes."

"Did he have specific places in mind?"

"Yes, the house on Pendleton and the one that burned down."

"Tell me about the house that burned down."

"It's out in the country on Saffron Lane. The FBI told me that they thought your client torched it."

"Can you give me the address?"

David ran her fingers over her computer keyboard and found the address.

"Did Tolliver tell you why he needed two places?"

"He said he had a construction business and he needed a place for some of his workers to live."

Dana was sure she knew exactly what "work" the men who lived on Saffron Lane did.

Finding the house on Saffron Lane was easy once the wind shifted. Even after all this time, the smell of burning wood lingered in the crisp fall air. Dana wandered around the immolated skeleton, sifting through the ashes with the toe of her boot and finding nothing of value. If there was evidence linking the inhabitants of the rental to FedEx Field, it had been carried off by FBI forensic experts.

A thought occurred to Dana as she rode home. The suicide bombers had worked as hawkers for four different concession stands. The newspapers had reported that all of the concessions were owned by Lawrence Cooper, who had been murdered on the Sunday of the failed suicide mission. Cooper had to have been approached before the football season in order to place the men in the concessions.

Then there was the attack itself. The newspapers were reporting that ambulances loaded with explosives had been strategically placed around the stadium for maximum destruction. This indicated that the bombers were working with engineers and explosives experts.

This operation was obviously not a spur-of-the-moment affair. Everything about it screamed advance planning. No aspect of the plot would have been left to chance, including the place where Tolliver and the suicide bombers were going to live. The Kendall & Marquoit real estate group had been chosen for a reason, but what was that reason?

Dana parked on the side of the road and punched in Mary Ann David's number.

"This is Dana Cutler, Mrs. David. I'm sorry to bother you again, but I do have one more question. Did Mr. Tolliver tell you why he chose your firm to rent from?"

"I did ask him. We always like to know who referred a client."

"And what did he say?"

"If I recall correctly, he said we had come highly recommended."

"By who?"

"He never said."

Dana opened her front door and picked up the mail from the floor, where it had fallen after the postman shoved it through the slot. She tossed her jacket on the sofa and shuffled through the mail as she walked into the kitchen, where she fixed a cup of coffee.

Dana carried the mug downstairs to her office in the basement of Jake's house. As soon as she logged on to her computer, she went on the Internet and Googled Kendall & Marquoit. The Bethesda office was an East Coast branch of a California company. Dana Googled the board of directors and got a shock. Jessica Koshani was a director. There were many other board members. Dana ran a check on all of them. Most of the directors did not raise a red flag, but one man did. Dana scolded herself for profiling and bigotry against people with Middle Eastern names, but she felt a little less guilty when Imran Afridi turned up in an article in a Karachi newspaper that detailed Afridi's short detention and interrogation after a car bomb took thirty-six lives. The article contained a photograph. Dana decided that Afridi looked a little like Omar Sharif. After reading some more articles about Afridi, Dana called Patrick Gorman.

"Pat," Dana said as soon as the editor of *Exposed* answered his phone.

"How's the intrepid reporter?"

"I'm in need of companionship."

"Are you asking me out on a date?"

"In your dreams. No, I want you to fix me up with your friend; the one I met at the National Museum of the American Indian."

"Any special reason for the meeting?"

"Imran Afridi. He's a Pakistani businessman. I want to know everything your friend can dig up on him."

Chapter Forty-one

To avoid the appearance of impropriety, Ginny had not talked to Dana after learning that they were working opposite sides of the Tolliver case. Then Ginny made up her mind about what to do with the transcript. As soon as she reached her decision, she set up a meeting at Vinny's, a bar in a D.C. neighborhood with a high crime rate. The advantage of meeting in this dive was the certainty that no one they knew would ever come into it.

Dana had discovered the bar while she was working undercover in narcotics, and Ginny had heard about Vinny's from Brad, who had met Dana there when he had asked her to help him figure out why someone had attacked United States Supreme Court Justice Felicia Moss. Brad's description of this den of iniquity had not done the place justice.

Ginny had taken a cab to Vinny's straight from the DOJ and was still dressed in a business suit. As soon as she walked into the dismally dark interior, she felt as out of place as a Hell's Angel in a Michelin three-star restaurant. Vinny's reeked of smoke, sweat, and stale beer, and Ginny guessed that the owner used the lowest-wattage bulbs he could find to hide the identities of the degenerates scattered around the place, all of whom looked like gang members, sex perverts, or drug dealers.

Dana was sitting in a booth in the back, nursing a beer. Ginny slid onto the bench on the other side of the booth.

"Order the cheeseburger and fries," Dana said. "You won't regret it."

"Brad raved about them, so I guess they're safe, but I'd feel even safer in this place if I was packing."

Dana smiled. "Don't worry, I am." Then she sobered. "I got the feeling that you were upset when you saw me with Bobby Schatz at the DOJ. You haven't spoken to me since the meeting."

"I was concerned that people would think we were talking about the case if anyone from Justice saw us together. And I wasn't upset, but I was confused. You did lecture Brad at the China Clipper about working for Senator Carson, whom—if I remember correctly—you accused of being soft on terrorism."

Dana shrugged. "That's the thing about criminal law; most of your clients are scumbags. If I worked only for lawyers who defended the innocent, I'd starve to death. So what made you change your mind about getting together?"

Ginny looked at the tabletop. "I found something." She hesitated. Dana watched her carefully but held her tongue. She could see that Ginny was struggling.

"What was your impression of Terry Crawford?" Ginny asked.

"I thought he acted like a guy who hasn't gotten laid in years."

"I've asked around. The opinion is almost unanimous. He'll do anything to win a case." Ginny hesitated. Dana could almost feel her anguish. "I think he crossed the line with your client."

"What do you mean?"

Ginny opened her attaché case and took out a manila envelope.

"I never met with you today, and I never gave you this. Understand?"

Dana stared at her friend, confused. Ginny slid the envelope across the table and stood up.

"Aren't you staying?"

"I can't stay someplace I've never been," she answered before turning her back on her friend and walking away.

Dana waited until the front door closed behind Ginny before opening the envelope and pulling out a sheaf of papers. She read the first page and realized that it was a transcript of Terry Crawford's interrogation of Ron Tolliver. A few pages later, Dana got to the part where Schatz ordered Crawford to turn off the cameras and the microphones so he could discuss the case with his client. Dana turned the page, read a few lines, and muttered, "Holy shit!" She was no lawyer, but she knew enough law to know that she was holding the judicial equivalent of a hydrogen bomb.

As soon as she got over the shock of realizing that the transcript was Ron Tolliver's Get Out of Jail Free card, Dana asked herself whether she wanted to be the instrument of Tolliver's salvation. The man had tried to murder thousands of innocent people. How many children had been in the stands at FedEx Field?

Dana had never been in a position like this. Sure, she'd helped attorneys gain acquittals for clients she knew were guilty, but she'd never worked for a criminal like Ron Tolliver. Crawford had brought clarity to the scope of her client's crime when he pointed out that three thousand people had died on 9/11 but ninety thousand people could have lost their lives if the FedEx Field plot had succeeded.

People committed murder for many reasons, some rational,

some not, but there were usually very few victims. The worst serial killers never came close to killing thousands of people. That was the difference between the murders that the criminal justice system dealt with and the crimes of Hitler and Pol Pot. Dana did not think that Ron Tolliver was the mastermind behind the FedEx plot, but Tolliver was as culpable as the commandants of Hitler's death camps, because he was the person who carried out the orders.

Dana stared at the transcript. She was honor bound to give it to her employer. If she didn't and that fact ever got out, she would never get another client. What she really wanted to do was burn it, and that thought brought images of burning children and innocent people screaming in the grip of unbearable pain as FedEx Field collapsed under them.

Dana looked at her beer and wished with all her heart that she had something far stronger in her glass, along with an easy answer to what she should do with Ginny Striker's gift.

Chapter Forty-two

The rest of the staff had gone home, and the office, which normally hummed with activity, was eerily quiet at 9:45, when Senator Carson told Brad that he felt he had a handle on the bill they had been discussing. They continued to debate a minor point as the senator followed Brad past the empty, darkened offices to Brad's office so Brad could get some papers he needed to go over at home.

"Well, I think I finally get why you think that clause should be modified," Carson said as Brad put on his coat. Brad started to answer when he heard a door open near the senator's office. The lights were off at that end of the hall, but streetlamps cast dim rays of light through the windows in the senator's office, allowing Brad to make out a silhouette in the hall.

"Don't say anything and follow me quickly," Brad whispered as he grabbed Carson's elbow.

"What . . . ?" Carson started to ask.

The intruder turned toward the sound.

Brad slapped a hand across the senator's mouth and pointed toward the senator's office. Then he pulled Carson after him. As they headed toward the reception area, Brad racked his brain for somewhere they could hide. He was opening the door to the hall when he remembered a place he'd been taken by one of the other legislative assistants as part of a tour of the Capitol during his first week on the job.

When the Senate was questioning nominees for director of the CIA, a seat on the Supreme Court, and other important positions that could only be filled with the consent of the Senate, the public hearings were held in the central hearing room in the Hart Office Building. His tour guide had taken Brad through an unmarked door in the Dirksen Building that led into a room where important witnesses who wanted to avoid the press could wait.

Brad sped down the corridor with the senator in tow. He stopped in front of the unmarked door and heard footsteps running down the hall in their direction. Brad prayed that the door was unlocked. He turned the knob, and the door opened into a darkened waiting room. Brad pulled the senator inside and closed the door as quietly as he could. Then he edged past chairs and a side table and led the senator down a hall to a door that opened into a massive, high-ceilinged room filled with chairs for spectators. Between those chairs and a dais were a table and chairs for the witnesses and their advisers. Behind the dais were comfortable high-backed chairs for the senators, and behind the those were chairs for staff. Along the walls were long tables for the press.

Brad raced past the press tables to the other end of the room. The walls were paneled with polished wood and looked solid. Brad stopped before one of the last panels and pushed. It swung inward into a concrete corridor. A stairway led up a floor to a landing where four doors faced a narrow hall. The first two were locked. Brad started to panic. Then the third door opened into a darkened room that resembled a smaller version of a skybox in a football stadium.

Brad pulled the senator inside and locked the door. Brad motioned the senator to sit on the floor.

"Do you have your cell phone with you?" Brad whispered. Carson nodded.

"Call for help."

On the other side of the room was a large window through which the press could look down on the hearing room. Brad duckwalked across the floor, then rose up an inch and peeked through the window. A man was walking down the rows of chairs searching for them. When he reached the back of the room, he turned in a slow circle, pausing every few seconds to listen for movement. Then, without warning, he looked up at the windows in the press boxes and stared at Brad.

Brad wanted to duck out of sight, but he was paralyzed. Clarence Little smiled and started toward the entrance to the press boxes. He was halfway there when he froze and looked over his shoulder. Seconds later, he bolted out of the room through the door to the witness waiting area. A moment after Little disappeared, two members of the Capitol Police with their guns drawn burst into the room through the door the public used.

"He's gone," Brad said as he turned on the lights and stood in the window waving at the police.

"Who was following us?" Senator Carson asked.

"Clarence Little."

"So he is after you."

"Actually, he may have been looking for you."

"Why would he be after me?"

"The press has been all over you about Dorothy Crispin's murder. Well, I learned something they don't know. Crispin was a law student, but she also worked for Executive Escorts, a high-end call girl operation that Jessica Koshani owned."

Even in the dark, Brad could see the senator turn pale. "How do you know this?" he said.

"I can't tell you, and please don't pressure me, because I promised I wouldn't reveal my source. What you need to know is that the man who murdered Crispin cut off her pinkie."

"Oh, my God!"

"It's beginning to look like Clarence Little killed Dorothy Crispin and Jessica Koshani. At first, I thought that Clarence saw me drive Jessica Koshani from the airport and killed her to send a message to me, but I never met Dorothy Crispin and both women have ties to you. If Clarence isn't after me, then he's probably after you. I think it's time for you to talk to the FBI. I can understand why you wouldn't want to, but your life may depend on the FBI knowing about your links to these victims."

Chapter Forty-three

Terrence Crawford didn't get up when his secretary ushered Bobby Schatz and Dana Cutler into his office. Schatz sat opposite the AAG while Dana planted herself on a sofa that stood against the wall.

"To what do I owe this pleasure, Bobby?" Crawford asked. "My secretary says you were mysterious about the purpose of your visit."

Instead of answering, Schatz tossed a copy of the transcript of his attorney-client conference with Ron Tolliver onto Crawford's blotter. Dana watched Crawford lose color as he leafed through the pages.

"Where did you get this?" Crawford asked.

"That's not important." Schatz dropped a Motion to Dismiss for Prosecutorial Misconduct and a brief in support of the motion onto the desk. "What is important is the fact that you violated a court order and my client's Sixth Amendment rights by continuing to listen in on our conference after I specifically told you to cease taping."

"You have no legal right to this document, Schatz. It's stolen government property."

"Then why don't you have me arrested? The transcript will be the key evidence in your case. I want to hear you explain to the judge how this transcript came into existence. You may also be interested in knowing that I have an associate looking into whether this taping is a violation of the federal criminal code."

Crawford ignored Schatz and picked up the motion and the brief. Schatz sat perfectly still as Crawford thumbed through the citations to the cases that required dismissal of the charges against Ron Tolliver.

"So?" Schatz said when Crawford put down the brief.

"How did you get the transcript?" Crawford demanded.

Schatz stood up. "See you in court, Terry, where I believe the judge will be much more interested in your explanation of why you eavesdropped than how I discovered your unethical and possibly illegal activity."

Bobby Schatz waited until he and Dana had left the DOJ before breaking into a grin.

"Terry looked like he had a serious case of indigestion," Schatz said.

"What do you think he'll do?" Dana asked.

"Cave. He's got no choice," Schatz said just as Dana's cell phone rang.

Dana held up a finger and stepped into a doorway to take the call.

"I'm thinking of publishing an article about angels," Pat Gorman said.

"I haven't come across too many of them in my line of work," Dana answered.

"Well, it's about time you acquainted yourself with some of the more famous ones, like Simone Martini's *Angel of the Annunciation*."

"And where might I find her?"

"This angel is named Gabriel and *he* hangs out—quite literally—in the West Building of the National Gallery."

The National Gallery of Art, located on the National Mall, was established in 1937 by a joint resolution of Congress with funds for construction and a substantial collection donated by Andrew Mellon. The collection is housed in two buildings, the neoclassical West Building and the modern East Building, which are connected by an underground passage.

Dana located *The Angel of the Annunciation* in Gallery 3 on the main floor of the West Building. A school group had just moved on, leaving Dana in the gallery with two Japanese tourists. As soon as they finished looking at the painting, Dana walked over to the panel that presented a side view of the angel Gabriel kneeling, clothed in an ornate robe rich with textured gold.

Dana didn't know the name of the man she was going to meet, so she thought of him as Gorman's Spook. He hadn't told her his name or anything about his background the first time they had met at the National Museum of the American Indian during her investigation into the assassination attempt on Justice Moss. The only thing she knew about the Spook was that he had deep knowledge of the intelligence community.

A minute after the Japanese tourists walked away, Dana sensed someone stand beside her. The man had a pale complexion. He was wearing a ski jacket over a sweatshirt with a hood. The hood was up and Dana could just see his brown eyes and thin lips.

"Martini was one of the most influential artists in the Sienese school," said the Spook in a voice so low that Dana had to strain to hear him.

"Really," answered Dana, who couldn't care less.

"The Angel was originally half of a two-part panel he painted around 1333. Imran Afridi will never be a model for any painting of an angel."

"And that is because?"

"Afridi is from a very wealthy Pakistani family with diverse holdings. He was educated at Cambridge and returned to Karachi with a degree in finance to work in the family businesses. He lives in a walled estate in one of Karachi's wealthier suburbs and keeps a low profile. Even so, he is suspected of financing terrorist operations."

"Why hasn't he been arrested?"

"Afridi's family is very influential. They have a lot of money, which means they have several politicians in their pocket. Two of his brothers are high-ranking military. No one is going to make a move on Afridi unless the evidence is indisputable."

"Is there anything showing a connection between Afridi and the attempt to blow up FedEx Field?"

"The bombers have been thoroughly interrogated. The only person they could finger is your client and, as you know, he hasn't given anyone the time of day."

"Jessica Koshani is on a board with Afridi."

"More than one, but she was conveniently murdered before she could be questioned by the Senate Select Committee on Intelligence."

"So that's why she was in Washington."

"InCo, one of her companies, is suspected of laundering money for terrorists. She may have helped finance the FedEx operation, but there's no way to prove that, now that Koshani is dead."

"Why isn't there more intel on Afridi?"

"He's not associated with any recognized terrorist organization like al-Qaeda. My sources say that terror is a hobby for him and he likes to run the show himself, like a boy with a model train set."

"Is Afridi in Pakistan now?"

"No, he has a home in northern Virginia." The Spook gave her the address. "He was in residence on the day of the attempt at FedEx Field, and he's still there."

"That seems odd. You'd think he would want to head home as soon as the plot failed."

"Something is keeping him here, but I can't help you with that."

"Thanks," Dana started to say but the Spook was already moving to another section of the gallery, where he commenced to study *Joachim and the Beggars*, by Andrea di Bartolo.

The traffic was deadly, and it took Dana an hour and a half to find Afridi's estate. It was in the countryside, approachable by a narrow country lane and sequestered in the middle of a forest of oak and maple. Dana drove along the wall that protected Afridi's house and grounds from prying eyes. An iron gate sealed off the only entry from the road. Dana could make out a guard shack behind the gate and a guard wearing a blazer, a black turtleneck, and tan slacks. He looked fit and ex-military, and Dana bet he was armed.

Dana parked at the far end of the wall and walked a circuit around the property. There were gaps where she could see the house, but she also saw other guards, and she bet there were security measures she couldn't see. When she decided that she wasn't going to learn anything useful, Dana drove home.

A man wearing camouflage lay in a blind in the woods high up the tree-covered slope across from the entrance to Afridi's estate. As soon as Dana's car was out of sight, he lowered his binoculars and radioed in her license number. When he learned the name of the owner, he called his superior and told him that Dana Cutler had conducted surveillance of Imran Afridi's property.

Chapter Forty-four

"I have great news," Bobby Schatz told Ron Tolliver as soon as the guard closed the door to the contact visiting room. "The government is dismissing your case."

Tolliver stared at his lawyer as if he had not understood what Schatz had said. Bobby chalked it up to shock. He smiled.

"By the end of the day, you're going to be a free man, Ron."

"They're letting me out?"

Schatz nodded. "Remember our first meeting? The prosecutor was taping everything that was said in the interrogation room. When I came in to talk to you, I demanded that he stop because it's illegal for the government to record a conversation between a lawyer and his client." Schatz grinned. "We got lucky, Ron. Crawford broke the law. He kept taping our conversation. There are a ton of cases that hold that this type of conduct is presumed to be prejudicial. In your case, there's no question that your case was prejudiced, because I laid out our trial strategy during the meeting.

"This morning, one of Crawford's superiors phoned me. He's in big trouble, and the DOJ doesn't want its dirty linen aired in public, so they're not fighting my motion to dismiss. You'll be out of here today."

If Schatz thought that Tolliver would thank him, the prisoner disappointed him.

"Where am I going to go?" he demanded.

"Maybe home to Ohio?" Schatz suggested.

Tolliver looked incredulous. "Are you insane? You don't know my father. He's ex-military and a flag-waving patriot. I'd be lucky if he didn't shoot me. And if he doesn't, someone else is bound to. Everyone in America has heard that I tried to kill ninety thousand people. As soon as I step out the door, I'll have a target on my back. Every nut job will be out to kill me, and I don't think the CIA will take this lying down. They probably have a hit squad waiting for me."

"Ron, my job is to win your case. I did that. It's your job to figure out what to do with the rest of your life."

Schatz lowered his voice and leaned close to his client. "Maybe you should call your friends. They got you into this. Maybe they'll help you out."

Tolliver looked at the tabletop. Schatz could see he was thinking hard about his predicament.

"Is there anything else you'd like to discuss?" Schatz asked.

Tolliver shook his head.

"I've left clothes and money for you," Schatz said. "I wish you good luck."

Chapter Forty-five

Brad had been questioned by the Capitol Police and the FBI for hours after the incident with the intruder, and Senator Carson had told him to take the next day off. Having a lazy day at home was terrific, but it also meant that he was behind in his work when he returned to the office, so he'd had to stay late to catch up. Brad was putting the finishing touches on a memo when Senator Carson appeared in his doorway. Lucas Sharp was standing beside him.

"Good, I'm glad I caught you before you left," Carson said. "You live near here, don't you?"

"Just a few blocks."

"I'll give you a lift home. It's too late to be wandering around Capitol Hill alone."

"I don't want to be any trouble."

"Nonsense. I insist."

Brad was exhausted and grateful for the ride. The trio took the elevator to the garage in silence. Lucas Sharp led the way to a black Lincoln town car. Sharp drove, and the senator sat in front. Brad told Sharp his address just before the car pulled out of the garage. Then he closed his eyes. When he opened them, he looked at the street signs.

"I think you took a wrong turn," Brad said. "We're headed away from my apartment."

"We're going to my house first," Senator Carson said. "There are a few matters Luke and I need to discuss with you."

Brad wondered why they had to go to the senator's home to talk. He was also having trouble keeping his eyes open, and he was starving.

"Can this wait until tomorrow, Senator? I'm out on my feet."

"I wouldn't ask if this wasn't really important. I have plenty of guest rooms. You can sleep at my estate when we're through, or Luke can drive you home."

"Okay," Brad said reluctantly. He wanted desperately to head for his apartment, but you don't say no to a United States senator, especially if he's your boss. "Let me call my wife to tell her I'll be late."

"That's not necessary," Sharp said. "We won't keep you long."

There was an undercurrent of menace in Sharp's tone, and suddenly Brad felt uneasy, but he didn't insist on calling Ginny.

Everyone was quiet during the ride from the Capitol to the Virginia countryside. A little less than an hour after leaving the Capitol, the car parked in front of a white colonial mansion with a portico shaded by an overhang supported by pillars. The estate had reminded Brad of Tara from *Gone with the Wind* when he'd visited for the staff picnic shortly after he'd started working.

"My wife and the kids are in Oregon, and I've given the staff the night off, so we won't be disturbed," Carson said when Brad got out of the car.

"What do you want to talk about?" Brad asked nervously.

The senator opened the front door. "I'm interested in how much you know about Jessica Koshani's connection with Executive Escorts and how you came by the information," Carson said.

Brad hesitated. "I told you I can't talk about that, Senator."

"That's not an option anymore," Sharp said as he crowded in behind Brad and forced him into the front hall. Carson turned on the light.

"What are you talking about?" Brad asked, suddenly frightened.

Before Sharp could answer, a large man in jeans and a leather jacket stepped from behind the door and slammed a gun butt into Sharp's head. Sharp slumped to the floor. Two more armed men appeared from the shadows. One man was as massive as Sharp's assailant. The other was Brad's height and slender.

"Put your hands behind you," Mustapha said calmly. "If you resist, we'll hurt you, and the end result will be the same."

"Who are you?" Carson asked.

Mustapha answered by slamming his gun into Carson's face. The senator's knees buckled and he looked shocked. Blood poured out of a split lip.

"We aren't in the Senate. I ask the questions, and you keep your mouth shut except when you're answering them. Now put your hands behind your back."

Brad and Carson complied. One of the larger men wrenched Sharp's arms behind him and secured his wrists with plastic cuffs. The large man who had been at Mustapha's side stepped behind Brad and the senator and secured their hands. Then Brad, Sharp, and Carson were herded into the living room and lashed to straight-back chairs. Brad tested his ropes and found almost no give.

"Go outside and stand guard," Mustapha said to the man who had assaulted Lucas Sharp. He left the living room, and Brad heard the front door open and close.

"Senator," Mustapha said. "I need honest answers. If you don't give them to me here, we will kill your friends. Then we will take you to a place where we won't be disturbed and where I will have an unlimited amount of time to question you. If I have to resort to this backup plan, you will suffer an incredible amount of pain. Inevitably, you will tell me everything I want to know. Then you will die. Tell me what I want to know now, and all of you will live."

Carson was shaking. His brow was beaded with sweat.

"Before we start, I am going to entertain you and your friends with a DVD Miss Koshani recorded."

Mustapha laid his gun on an end table and picked up a remote.

"Please, no," Carson begged. "They don't have to see that. I'll tell you want you want to know. Please."

Mustapha pressed PLAY. Brad felt sick when he recognized the man wearing the dog collar. He turned his head away from the screen. Mustapha let the DVD run for a few minutes before stopping it. He turned to Carson.

"What happened at your town house on the day Jessica Koshani was murdered?"

Carson's head dropped so he was looking at his lap. "I can't," he whispered.

Mustapha nodded. The man standing behind the senator took a knife and sliced off Carson's left earlobe. The senator screamed as blood poured onto his shoulder from the wound.

"Cauterize it," Mustapha said. The large man took out a lighter and burned the wound until it sealed. Carson was screaming right next to Brad, and Brad had to fight to keep from fainting.

"Senator Carson, what happened in the town house?" Mustapha repeated.

"It wasn't me," Carson gasped. "Please don't hurt me anymore. It wasn't me."

"Explain."

Carson was weeping. His eyes were fixed on the floor. His teeth were clenched from the pain.

"Lucas did it. He killed her."

Brad looked at the chief of staff. He was glaring at his oldest friend with unconcealed contempt.

"Start at the beginning," Mustapha commanded.

"She made me come over. She asked about the plot, what the FBI knew. Nothing had changed. I told her Homeland Security knew there was something big planned but not what the target was or when the plan was going to be executed. Then she asked me about the hearing, what would happen, what questions the committee would ask. A little before noon, she told me I could go. She was staying on the second floor in the guest bedroom. She took out a cell phone and went upstairs. As I was walking to the front door I heard her talking to someone."

Carson paused and took a few deep breaths. When he started to speak again, his voice was ragged.

"I crept up the stairs. I was hoping I would learn who she was talking to so I would have leverage to get the DVD back. I heard her mention FedEx Field. Then she stopped talking and closed the phone. She must have heard me, because the next thing I knew, she was in the doorway with a knife. I was shocked. She stabbed at me and I jumped back. She ran at me and stabbed me in the side. I don't remember how it happened. It must have been reflex. I hit her. It was hard and right on the chin. She fell back and hit her head on the corner of the grandfather clock. It's solid wood, and it stunned her. I hit her again and she collapsed.

"I was in a panic. I called Luke. When he arrived, I was lightheaded and in a lot of pain. Luke applied first aid, but he said a doctor should check me out. Koshani was still unconscious when he arrived, but she was breathing. I told Luke everything: the blackmail, the DVD. He said we had to force her to tell us where she had the DVD and who had copies so we could destroy them. He told me he'd been a DA when Clarence Little was killing people in Oregon. He'd seen the autopsy reports, he'd actually seen the body of one of the victims in person, and he'd read the opinion of the Oregon judge who reversed Little's cases. The opinion described the method of torture in detail. He said he'd make it look like Little killed her."

The senator was babbling, and Mustapha listened patiently as Brad's boss threw his oldest friend under the bus.

"It wasn't my idea. I didn't even mean to hurt her. He took off her clothes and tied her to the chair. He woke her up. She was very groggy. She could barely speak. She must have had a concussion. I tried to stop him, but he cut her until she answered all of his questions. She told him where she kept the DVD. She gave him the alarm code to her house. When . . . when he was through, he killed her. It wasn't me."

Carson looked up at Mustapha. His eyes begged for mercy. Mustapha smiled and nodded to show he understood.

"Go on," Mustapha urged his prisoner.

"Luke said I needed an alibi and someplace to rest until my wounds healed. We flew to Portland on my private jet so he could get the DVD. I told him about Dorothy Crispin. He paid her to let me stay while I healed. He knew a doctor with a drug habit from his days in the DA's office. He took care of me for a price. It was Luke who called Dana Cutler with Crispin's name. He said it made the alibi more believable if a reporter discovered her name."

"Did you tell the FBI or CIA about FedEx Field?"

"No, I swear. I didn't have time. I was in Oregon. I was hiding out. If I told, they'd know I was with Koshani when she was killed."

Brad couldn't believe what he'd just heard. Carson had known about the plot to destroy FedEx Field and he'd done nothing.

"I swear I never betrayed you," Carson said. "Please, don't kill me."

Mustapha looked Carson in the eye. "You are truly pathetic. You are a pervert and a craven coward and a perfect example of the infidels who run your country."

He looked at the man who was standing behind the three captives.

"Kill them."

Chapter Forty-six

A driving rain pelted Ron Tolliver when he walked through the door of the detention center. He flipped up the hood of the sweatshirt and turned up the collar of the jacket Bobby Schatz had purchased for him. Then he checked the street for a tail. He couldn't pick out anyone suspicious, but he was certain that someone was following him.

Tolliver thought about his next move. He had money, a gun, and false ID stashed at a pawnshop that was owned by a shell corporation controlled by Afridi. Tolliver took a bus across town, then walked a circuitous path to shake the people he was certain were tracking him. He had very little confidence that he would get to the pawnshop undetected, but he had no choice.

The shop was in a section of D.C. where a white man looked out of place, so Tolliver kept his hood up and his hands in his pockets. A bell rang when he entered the store. The owner, an elderly black man with salt-and-pepper hair, dressed in a flannel shirt, a threadbare sweater, and brown corduroy pants, looked up from a stack of paperwork.

"I need my stuff and a disposable cell phone," Tolliver said.

"Are you crazy? You should have called. I'll have every fed in D.C. in here as soon as you leave."

"I need my stuff, *now*."

The proprietor hesitated, then went into the back. When he came out, he was carrying a gym bag. He shoved it across the counter.

"Now get out," he said.

Tolliver unzipped the bag and checked the contents. Then he left without another word and took evasive action until he arrived at a cheap hotel ten blocks from the pawnshop, where whores rented by the hour and winos occupied the lobby. On the way, he picked up two sandwiches, several bags of chips, and a few bottles of water at a convenience store.

Tolliver registered under a false name and paid in cash for two days. Then he paid the desk clerk $100 to forget he'd registered. When he opened the door to his room, the odors left behind by the previous occupant made him gag. Tolliver didn't bother to unpack. He threw his gym bag on a bed with a stained sheet that covered a mattress with sagging springs that had conceded the fight with gravity a long time ago.

Tolliver pulled a chair over to the room's only window and looked at the brick wall of the building across the way. The sun set. Tolliver ate one of the tasteless sandwiches. He felt completely lost for a while. Then his spirits rose. This was the way he'd felt in Afghanistan when his team had been wiped out. His head wound looked ghastly, and he'd faked death by lying perfectly still until night fell and the last of the Taliban fighters left the battlefield. When he was finally alone and had time to think, he'd been overwhelmed by depression. He'd doubted the possibility of surviving in this hostile wasteland without food or water.

But he had survived. His situation was different now. He was surrounded by enemies, as he had been in the mountains of Afghanistan, but he had a way out. Tolliver took the cell phone out of the gym bag and called Imran Afridi.

Imran Afridi was planning to return to Pakistan as soon as Mustapha told him what he had learned from Senator Carson. He was telling the pilot of his private jet to be ready to leave at a moment's notice when another cell phone rang. It was the phone with the number he had given Ronald Tolliver to call in an emergency, but Tolliver was in jail. How would he get a cell phone? Could this be a trap?

The phone rang twice more, and Afridi's curiosity overcame his sense of caution.

"Yes?" he said.

"It's me." Afridi recognized the voice instantly. "The prosecutor screwed up so they had to release me. You have to get me out of the country."

"You must have a wrong number," Afridi said, certain now that he was being set up.

"I know you're worried that someone is listening in, but I haven't been turned, and I am out. Meet me in two hours at the last place we met, and I'll explain."

Tolliver cut the connection. Afridi sank onto a chair. His stomach was churning. Tolliver was not in jail. A man arrested for attempted mass murder was walking the streets, a free man. How did such a thing happen? The answer was simple: it didn't. Prosecutors did not screw up in a situation like this unless the screwup was intentional, unless the prosecutor wanted an informant on the street as part of a setup. This was how the heads of drug cartels were brought low. A little fish was arrested and promised a deal that would lead to dismissal of his case. Then the little fish hooked a bigger fish, and so on.

A great weight fell from Afridi's shoulders. He smiled. The mystery had been solved. Ron Tolliver was the traitor, and he would pay.

Afridi summoned his head of security and told him to take some men to the C&O Canal.

Chapter Forty-seven

"Kill them," Mustapha said.

Brad was surprised that he was resigned and sad but not terrified. In seconds, he would be dead, and that meant he would never see Ginny again or have kids or take any of the trips they had planned. This was it. The last moment of his life—and the last thing he would see was the smirk on a terrorist's face.

Brad waited for the shot. There was an explosion, and Brad was showered with blood and brains. At first, he assumed the gore belonged to Lucas Sharp or the senator. Then Mustapha dived for his weapon and there was another shot. Mustapha's left kneecap shattered. He collapsed, screaming.

"How are you doing, Brad?" Clarence Little asked.

Brad's mouth gaped open, but he couldn't speak. Carson and Sharp stared wide-eyed at the most wanted man in America. Little walked over to Brad and used a handkerchief to wipe the gore off his face.

"Sorry about that. I'll get you a wet towel in a bit. And before you start worrying, I'd have to be a complete ingrate to harm even one tiny hair on your head after you saved my life. And don't worry about Ginny, either. She's certainly delectable, but she's off limits as far as I'm concerned."

Little turned to Carson then Lucas Sharp. "These two are another story. I don't like them. Especially you, Mr. Sharp. Imagine my surprise when I learned that I had been in Washington, D.C., killing Jessica Koshani. I do tend to be forgetful at times, but you'd think I'd remember traveling cross-country and playing with someone that tasty.

"Then I heard Senator Carson admit to shacking up with Dorothy Crispin on the day Koshani was murdered. I decided that things were not as they seemed, so I drove from Seattle to Portland and had a chat with Miss Crispin. In between screams, she told me that the senator had been stabbed and needed a place to hide out and recuperate.

"Like Sherlock Holmes, I have considered all of the evidence and deduced that I did not murder Miss Koshani and that the real killer is someone in this room. Unfortunately, the senator ruined my dramatic unveiling of the killer's identity by confessing before I had the opportunity to reveal my startling deductions, but you'll have to take it on faith that I really did figure out that you and your boss committed the dastardly deed."

Clarence placed the barrel of his gun under Lucas Sharp's chin and pressed his head up.

"Tell me, Luke, do you have any idea how inconsiderate it is to frame someone for murder? Gosh, there are so many consequences, I have trouble keeping count of them. But the biggie is that people who are successfully framed for murders they don't commit have to spend years in teensy, weensy cells living like animals until they are taken out to be slaughtered like a Thanksgiving turkey. Did you think about my feelings when you decided to frame me to save your pathetic boss?"

Little turned his head toward Carson. "And for the record, Jack, I agree with the raghead. You are pathetic."

While Little was talking, Mustapha had been dragging himself toward his gun. Little watched for a moment, then stood over the terrorist.

"I happen to be a big pro football fan, Osama, and your plan to disrupt the season pisses me off."

Little shot Mustapha between the eyes. Then he walked over to Lucas and pulled a hunting knife with a serrated blade out of a scabbard he had fixed to his belt at the small of his back.

"You are the second person who has framed me for a murder I did not commit. Enough is enough."

Little slashed the knife into Sharp's crotch. Brad had never heard anyone scream like that.

"Please, Clarence, don't do this," he begged.

Little considered Brad's plea. Then he nodded.

"I owe you big time, so I'll make this quicker than I would have liked. He's a murderer anyway, so I'm just carrying out his inevitable sentence."

Little walked behind Sharp, pulled up his chin and slit his throat. Brad turned away, unable to watch.

"Don't kill the senator," he begged. "You heard what he said. He was being blackmailed, he acted in self-defense. It was Sharp's idea to frame you."

Little smiled. "I have no intention of killing Jack Carson, Brad. Death is too quick for him."

Clarence walked over to the television and took out the DVD.

"We have a lot in common, Jack. I'm into S and M and bondage, too, although I prefer to be the bind*er* and not the bind*ee*. And I must say, what I saw of your adventures lacked imagination. But I could be wrong. Let's see what the public thinks when this runs on the Internet."

Clarence left for a moment. Brad heard water running. When he returned, he was carrying a damp towel and a dry one. He cleaned the blood and brains off Brad's face, then inspected his work.

"I'm going to call the police," he said when he was satisfied. "They'll set you free. All I ask, Brad, is that you tell them about the senator's confession so I can stop worrying about defending myself for a crime I didn't commit. And please tell them about Mr. Carson's part in Miss Koshani's murder and how he committed treason by telling that lady terrorist state secrets."

Little patted Brad on the shoulder. "I know I can count on you," he said, and Brad sensed an unspoken threat.

Then Little turned to Senator Carson. "When I'm settled in my new home, I'll send you my address, and you can tell me how you enjoy prison life."

Clarence pocketed the DVD. "Sorry I can't stay and chat some more, Brad, but I've got to run. Give my best to Ginny. I meant what I said in my letters. You two are the best."

As soon as Clarence was gone, Carson began to sob.

"You can't tell them," he begged. "I can't go to prison."

"You knew the terrorists were targeting FedEx Field, and you never told a soul."

"I couldn't," Carson pleaded.

"What if the plot had worked?" Brad asked. "You would have been responsible for a mass murder."

"But it didn't work. No one was hurt."

Brad felt sick to his stomach. He looked directly at his boss. "Tell me, Senator, what did you and Lucas have planned for me if I didn't tell you how I knew about Koshani and Crispin?"

"Nothing. We'd never hurt you. You've got to believe me."

"No, I don't, Senator. No, I don't."

Chapter Forty-eight

The moment Dana gave the transcript to Bobby Schatz, she was plagued by the knowledge that she would be the instrument of Ron Tolliver's release. By the time Schatz had pressured Justice into dropping the charges against his client, Dana had decided that there was only one way she could absolve herself of the guilt that was overwhelming her.

Tolliver had been booked into jail wearing a sweat suit the FBI had grabbed from his closet. Bobby Schatz had given Dana the job of buying clothes their client could wear when he was discharged from jail. Dana had sewn a miniature tracking device into a seam of Tolliver's jeans. She'd purchased it from a contact with sources in the intelligence community. When Tolliver left the jail, Dana followed in the nondescript brown Toyota she used for surveillance, using a GPS to track her target. She was carrying several weapons. She planned to end his life with one of them, but she had higher aspirations. Tolliver would be desperate to get out of the country, and he wouldn't be able to escape without help. Whom could he turn to? The Spook had told her that Imran

Afridi was a man who had made terror his hobby and insisted on running his operations personally. The chances were good that Tolliver would ask Afridi to help him get out of the country. Dana knew what Afridi looked like. If he met Tolliver, she would take out both of them.

The GPS showed that Tolliver had stopped somewhere ahead. The landscape was a bleak collection of vacant lots, shops with OUT OF BUSINESS signs in the windows, check-cashing establishments, bars, and convenience stores. On the horizon was a tall building that showed fire scars and gaping holes where window glass had once been. Next to the abandoned building was a hotel, and this is where the GPS led her.

After Dana parked in front of a shuttered Laundromat across from the hotel, she checked her automatic and the revolver in her ankle holster to make sure she would be prepared if any of the local bad guys were unwise enough to bother her. Then she hunkered down and waited for Tolliver to move.

A little after sunset, a cab stopped in front of the hotel, and Tolliver got into it. Dana followed the cab to Georgetown. It stopped a few blocks from the C&O Canal, and Tolliver got out. Luck was with Dana, and she found an empty parking space. Tolliver turned into a side street that led to the walking path that ran along the canal. Dana started after him, but then she sensed movement. A black van pulled to the curb and the doors swung open. She reached for her gun and the prongs of a Taser embedded themselves in her chest. Dana spasmed and collapsed. Seconds later, she was hustled into the van; a needle slipped into a vein, and she passed out.

• • •

When Dana came to, she was in total darkness and couldn't be sure if she was awake or still drugged. Then she felt the restraints that secured her wrists and ankles. She flashed back to the basement where the meth dealers had trapped her and panicked, fighting her restraints until she realized that her struggles were futile.

Dana squeezed her eyes shut and forced her breathing to slow. When she was calmer, she tried to figure out where she was being held, but she couldn't see much even after her eyes adjusted to the dark. There was a pillow under her head. It smelled as if it had been freshly laundered, which gave her a little hope. There was also a clean sheet under her hands.

Dana tried to figure a way out, but there didn't seem any chance of escape unless her captors made a mistake. And who were they? The lights snapped on just as she was starting to consider this question. She shut her eyes against the glare before opening them slowly. She was secured to the guardrails of a hospital bed in a concrete room with bare walls. Directly ahead was a thick steel door with a small window at the top.

The door opened and Dana tensed. A short man in a tweed jacket, brown-and-yellow striped tie, white shirt, and tan slacks walked in. He was partially bald with a bad comb-over, and his pale brown eyes examined her through wire-rimmed bifocals. Behind him were two bodyguards.

"How are you feeling?" the man in the tweed jacket asked with what appeared to be genuine concern.

"Pissed off," Dana said.

"Yes, I imagine you are," the man said in a tone intended to be comforting, "but there is an explanation for your abduction,

Miss Cutler. We knew you were following Ronald Tolliver, and we surmised that you were planning on taking action that would have endangered a very important intelligence operation. We couldn't let you do that, so we neutralized you."

"Are you going to let me out of here?"

"Definitely. You have nothing to worry about on that score, although we are going to hold you for a little while longer."

"How much longer?"

"Until we're certain that everything has gone according to plan."

"And this plan involves Ron Tolliver?"

"I'm sorry, but you're not cleared to get information about our operations."

"Whose operations?"

"Sorry again."

"Would it do me any good to ask to see a lawyer?"

"I'm afraid not." The man apologized again. "But tell me, are you hungry? I imagine you are. You might also want to use the restroom," he said, pointing to a door in one of the walls. "If you promise to be on your best behavior, I'll have your restraints removed and have dinner brought to you. So what do you say? Can we take off the restraints?"

Dana nodded. "I won't try anything."

The man smiled. "That's an empty promise. I've read your file, and I know what you did to those meth cooks. But it would be foolish to try anything with these men. You'd be risking serious injury for no good reason. I assure you that you'll be released quite soon."

• • •

By the time Dana's food was brought to her, the effects of the drug had worn off. She was sore where she'd been Tasered, and there was a knot on the back of her head where her skull had struck the pavement when she fell. Other than that, she was okay.

Dinner was an excellent steak, mashed potatoes, and mixed vegetables. There was even apple pie and coffee, so she deduced that she was a prisoner of an American intelligence agency. No one else visited her, and she started to wonder if she would really be released. At first, the isolation and quiet unnerved her. She used her free time to think about the secret operation she'd stumbled into. Obviously it involved Tolliver, but how was he involved, and was it also focusing on Imran Afridi? After a while, Dana concluded that she had no facts to work with, and she stopped guessing.

There wasn't a clock in the room, and Dana's watch had been taken from her, so she had no way to tell time. She went to sleep when she got tired and woke up when her door opened. She guessed it was morning because a guard brought in a tray loaded with orange juice, bacon, eggs, toast, and coffee.

Dana finished breakfast and waited for something else to happen. Nothing did, so she started thinking about the mystery organization that had kidnapped her. She decided that it probably wasn't the FBI. It was possible that they would kidnap a citizen, but she found that highly unlikely for a domestic law-enforcement organization. That left the CIA as the most likely suspect. They kidnapped foreign terror suspects and held them in secret prisons.

Assuming she'd stumbled into the middle of a CIA plot, what was the Agency up to? She'd been tailing Tolliver when they'd grabbed her, so they didn't want Dana to interrupt whatever

Tolliver was doing, but what was that? If she were in Tolliver's shoes, she'd be trying to get out of the country as fast as she could. Maybe Tolliver was on his way to meet Afridi. If so, Tolliver was lucky the government had caved when it had. A day or so later, and Afridi would probably have been back in Pakistan.

Dana froze. Something occurred to her. She thought back to the beginning of her involvement in Tolliver's case, and she reviewed everything she knew about it. By the time she finished, Dana had developed a theory. As soon as she was home, she would test it out, then run her idea past Ginny.

The door to Dana's room opened before she was fed another meal, and the man in the tweed jacket walked in with his bodyguards. As far as Dana could tell, he had not changed his clothes.

"You're going to be released. I hope this hasn't been too unpleasant."

"It was great," Dana answered sarcastically. "Can I book in advance for my next vacation?"

The man smiled. "It's good to see you've retained your sense of humor."

"How long have I been here?"

"Two days. You got a parking ticket, but don't worry. We've taken care of it."

"You do work for a powerful organization."

The man laughed. "I've read your file, and I have tremendous respect for you. It's unfortunate that you had to be detained. It's also unavoidable that you'll have to wear a hood when you leave, but we won't sedate you if you promise to cooperate. You'll be dropped off by your car."

Chapter Forty-nine

When Dana got home, she found copies of the *Washington Post* piled up on her doorstep. She dropped them on the kitchen table with the mail. Then she went to the bedroom, stripped off her clothes, and took a shower. Hot water pounded her body. She luxuriated in the steamy confines of the stall until she began to feel like a prune.

Dana dried off, dressed in sweats, and went back to the kitchen. She poured a mug of coffee and checked her answering machine, smiling for the first time in days when she heard Jake tell her he was headed home. She missed him terribly, and she had worried about him constantly since he'd left for Afghanistan.

Dana was about to look at her mail when she remembered the idea that had occurred to her just before her release. She looked up the number for Ben Mallory, Bobby Schatz's investigator.

"Mr. Mallory, thanks for taking my call," Dana said when she was put through. "My name is Jaime Pavel. I'm a reporter with the *Post*, and I'm researching an article about the way people who lost relatives in the Twin Towers on 9/11 are coping, years after the disaster."

There was dead air for a second. When Mallory spoke, he sounded confused.

"Why are you calling me, Miss Pavel?"

"I was led to believe that you had a brother who was working in the World Trade Center on 9/11."

"You've been misinformed," Mallory said. "My brother manages a Walmart in Kansas."

Dana apologized for taking up the investigator's time and ended the call. She looked at the clock. It was the middle of the afternoon. Ginny was probably still at the DOJ. They needed to speak, but Dana didn't want to call her at Justice, so she decided to wait and call after Ginny got home.

Dana shuffled through her mail before opening that day's edition of the *Post*. The headline TERROR SUSPECT MURDERED jumped out at her.

According to the article, the body of Ronald Tolliver had been discovered by a jogger on a footpath bordering the C&O Canal. He had been shot, and his wallet was missing. Robbery was the presumed motive. Because there was no immediate way to identify the victim, it wasn't until late last night that the authorities had discovered that the dead man had been arrested in connection with the attempted bombing at FedEx Field and released because of lack of evidence.

Dana wasn't surprised that Tolliver was dead, but who had killed him? Was it Imran Afridi or someone working for him? Was it the people who had kidnapped her? What did it matter? Tolliver deserved to die.

What with following Tolliver and then her abduction, Dana had not read a paper or heard news reports for the past three days, so she was shocked when she noticed another front-page article about the murders at Senator Jack Carson's estate. The story said that United States Senator Jack Carson, Carson's chief of staff Lucas Sharp, and Brad Miller, a legislative assistant, had been attacked by burglars in Carson's home. Dana's jaw dropped when she read that Brad and the senator had been rescued by escaped serial killer Clarence Little, who had killed the three burglars before calling 911. Lucas Sharp had died during the encounter, but it was not clear who had killed him.

Dana was thoroughly confused. Why had Little left Brad and the senator alive? Hadn't Little killed Jessica Koshani and Dorothy Crispin to terrorize Brad or the senator or both? Dana grabbed the phone and punched in Brad and Ginny's number. The answering machine told her to leave a message, and she told Ginny or Brad to call her. She was about to hang up when Ginny came on the line.

"Dana, it's me. The press has been driving us crazy, so we're screening our calls."

"Is Brad okay?"

"Not really. He's out of a job, for starters, and he's also the star witness for the prosecution in the murder and treason cases against Jack Carson."

"Carson is accused of murder and treason?"

"You didn't know?"

"I've been out of touch, and I just found out what happened."

"Where have you been? This has been the lead news story for the past two days."

Dana ignored Ginny's question. "Is Brad with you?" she asked.

"No, he's at FBI headquarters, giving a statement."

"Why are you home?"

"Crawford accused me of leaking the transcript, and I'm on administrative leave."

"We have to talk."

"About what?"

"Can I come over?" Dana asked, ignoring another question because she didn't know if someone was listening to the call.

"Don't. I'm besieged by reporters."

"I can get into the basement through the back door that opens into the alley behind your apartment building if you open it for me. I'll call when I'm a block away."

"Tell me what happened to Brad, and what's this about Senator Carson committing murder and treason?" Dana asked when they were in the apartment.

"This isn't public knowledge yet," Ginny said before relating what Brad had told her.

"Is Carson going to fight the charges?" Dana asked when Ginny was through.

"Who knows, but regardless of how the verdict comes out, Carson is ruined. Little put the DVD on the Internet yesterday evening. I watched a few minutes before turning it off. It's really gross. If that was me, I'd lock myself in my room and hide under the bed for the rest of my life.

"Now it's your turn to answer some questions. Why did you want to see me?"

"I followed Ron Tolliver when he left the jail," Dana said.

Ginny's eyes widened. "Did you see who killed him?"

"No. I was abducted before I could."

"Abducted? By who?"

"I don't know. But I suspect the CIA or Homeland Security. I also think we've been used by the same outfit that grabbed me."

"Used how?"

"Did Crawford act like a complete dick every time you dealt with him?"

"Yeah."

"He really made you dislike him, right?"

Ginny nodded. Dana switched gears.

"Doesn't it bother you that you were transferred to the Counterterrorism section of the DOJ when you'd only been at Justice for a short time and have no qualifications to work in that section?"

"It was strange, but a high school graduate would have been overqualified for the work Crawford had me doing."

"Collating 302s?"

"Yeah."

"Which put you in a perfect position to discover a transcript of an illegal recording authorized by someone you'd grown to despise."

Ginny frowned.

"About the same time you moved to Counterterrorism, Bobby Schatz offered me the position of investigator in the Tolliver case at an obscene rate of pay. Before he made the offer, I had never met the man. And to get me on board, Schatz lied about why he couldn't use his regular investigator.

"Why was he so desperate to hire me, Ginny? And why did Crawford invite you to sit in on his meeting with Schatz and me? I think Crawford wanted that transcript delivered to the defense team. He knew how honest you are. He knew you were so new to the job that you wouldn't have formed a hard and fast loyalty to Justice. He also knew that we were good friends."

"Hold on, Dana. Terry Crawford is in a lot of trouble because of that taping. He could lose his job."

"But he hasn't, has he? And I'm betting he won't."

"What you're saying makes no sense. Why would Crawford risk his career to set a terrorist free? And what if I hadn't given the transcript to you?"

"If you didn't leak the transcript, I'm betting there was a backup plan. Your other question is harder to answer, but I have a suspicion as to what the answer might be."

"Let's hear it," Ginny said.

"You read the 302s. Why did the plot to blow up FedEx Field fail?"

"The detonators didn't work, so none of the explosives went off."

"Did the agents arrest the suicide bombers before they got their trays or when they were in the stands preparing to blow themselves up?"

"They arrested them in the stands."

"Why did the authorities let the game go on? Why did they let their agents go after the suicide bombers when they would be facing certain death?"

Ginny got it. "They must have known in advance that the bombs wouldn't go off."

"Which means that the detonators were meant to fail from the get-go. And that means that the FBI knew about the plot in advance, which means that there was a mole in the terrorist organization."

"Ron Tolliver?" Ginny said.

"That's my guess."

Ginny paused and mentally reviewed everything she'd read about the case.

"Do you know how Tolliver was caught?" Ginny asked.

"No."

"It was blind luck. One of the suicide bombers had a head for numbers, and he memorized the license plate of Tolliver's car. That led the FBI to Tolliver's house. But here's the weird thing: After he was in custody, Tolliver wasn't taken to the place they were keeping the other members of the cell. That's some secret facility. I have no idea where it is. Instead, Tolliver was brought to the DOJ for interrogation. Bobby Schatz would not have been able to get to Tolliver if he was being held at a secret prison, but locking him up at the DOJ makes perfect sense if we were set up."

"The people running Tolliver had to figure out a way to get rid of the charges so he could get back on the inside of Imran Afridi's organization," Dana said. "Schatz never told me who hired him in the middle of the night and told him Tolliver was being held at the DOJ. I'm betting it was someone in the government who knew Tolliver was the mole, and I'm betting the government made a deal with Schatz."

"The plan to get Tolliver out worked, but they miscalculated, and he was killed," Ginny said.

Dana sighed. "That's probably what happened, but we'll never know the truth unless someone writes about the case in his memoirs."

"Not necessarily," Ginny said. "Let's see what happens to Terry Crawford. If he's hung out to dry, we're probably wrong and he taped the attorney-client conference out of zealousness. If good things happen to Counselor Crawford somewhere down the line, we'll know we're right."

Chapter Fifty

One advantage of being from old wealth and a graduate of the *best* schools was the ease with which one was able to gain membership in the best clubs. Terrence Crawford had graduated from Princeton and Yale and had been born into a family that traced its roots to the winning side of the American Revolutionary War, which explained why he was a member of one of New York's most exclusive clubs. The brownstone was three quarters of a block off Fifth Avenue on a side street near the Guggenheim Museum. There was no plaque affixed to the door. If you were a member of the club, you knew where it was located. If you were not a member, you did not need to know.

A servant opened the front door. It had snowed in Manhattan, and Crawford stomped on the welcome mat in the vestibule to shake off the snow that adhered to his shoes.

"Welcome back, Mr. Crawford. We haven't seen you in a while," the doorman said.

"I've been too busy to get up, Frederick."

"Well, it's good to see you again. Your guests are waiting in the library on the second floor."

It would have been too risky for the three men to get together in Washington, D.C. Meeting at Crawford's club assured that they would be shielded from prying eyes. Crawford handed Frederick his overcoat and took the stairs. Portraits of a few of the club's more venerable members graced the walls of the second-floor corridor. There were two past American presidents, a former Supreme Court justice, and the founders of two of America's largest corporations. Halfway down the hall, Crawford opened a door into a room with floor-to-ceiling bookshelves.

Crawford's guests were sitting in high-backed armchairs upholstered in maroon leather, warming themselves in front of the fire that had been laid in a stone fireplace.

"Sorry, my flight was delayed," Crawford said. "The weather."

There was a carafe of aged Cognac and an empty glass standing on an end table. Crawford saw that his guests had been imbibing, so he filled his glass and settled in a third armchair.

"To a successful end to a brilliant plan," Bobby Schatz said as he and Crawford raised a glass toward Dr. Emil Ibanescu, the deputy director of national intelligence.

"A plan that could not have succeeded without your cooperation," Ibanescu said as he raised his glass of amber liquid and returned his companions' salute. "The United States owes a debt to both of you, although, Terry, you may have to wait to receive the praise you deserve."

"I'm a patriot, Emil. I was never in this for a reward. But I know Bobby's making out like a bandit. I hear Senator Carson hired you, and I bet he's not the only scumbag who is going to throw a retainer at you, now that the media is reporting your part in gaining a dismissal for one of history's most heinous traitors."

Schatz smiled. “Come on, Terry, give me a break. There’s no one here but us coconspirators.”

Crawford laughed. “I’m yanking your chain, Bobby. If you hadn’t come in with us, we could never have pulled this off.”

“Are you certain your man is safe?” Schatz asked Ibanescu.

Ibanescu shrugged. “We can never be sure. Things go wrong all the time. I fed Carson misinformation at the meeting of the SSCI to make him think we didn’t know that FedEx Field was Afridi’s target. We wanted Koshani to think we were in the dark. Who knew Lucas Sharp would kill her? And who knew Ali Bashar had that kind of mind? All I do know is that we’ve done everything we can to make sure our man is still in place. His information saved thousands, but Afridi will try again, and we can only pray he’ll come through for us the next time.”

Crawford was about to respond when Frederick held open the door for a visitor.

“Your investigator, Mr. Schatz,” the doorman informed the defense attorney. “She said it was urgent.”

Dana walked into the room.

“What the fuck?” Crawford yelled as he jumped to his feet.

Suddenly, Frederick looked unsure of himself. He turned to Crawford. “She gave me a card. It says she works for Mr. Schatz. Is there a problem, sir?”

Crawford looked as though he was going to say something. Then he changed his mind. “It’s okay, Frederick. Thanks.”

“What are you doing here?” Crawford demanded as soon as the door closed.

“I’m here to give you gentlemen a chance to clarify a few points in my story before it goes to press in *Exposed*.”

Crawford looked horrified, Schatz frowned, but Ibanescu's face betrayed no emotion.

"What might this story be about?" Ibanescu asked.

"Right now, it's about a conspiracy between a deputy director of national intelligence, a defense attorney, and an assistant attorney general to fix a case so a notorious terrorist would get out of jail. Then there's my personal angle; the part about how a reporter was assaulted and kidnapped by intelligence agents when she got too close to the truth. I think my story will cause a stir, don't you?"

"I think any reporter who published a story like that would end up broke and discredited, or worse," Crawford said.

"Now, now, Terry," Ibanescu said. "I don't think threats will work with Miss Cutler. They might even make her more determined to publish her story. Besides, I don't think she would be talking to us if she really wanted to have her tale see the light of day."

Ibanescu turned toward Dana. "Why are you here?"

"To make certain that my friend, Ginny Striker, doesn't take the fall for you."

"How did you figure it out?" Schatz asked.

"You screwed up, Bobby. You told me Ben Mallory wouldn't work on Tolliver's case because his brother was killed in the World Trade Center bombing, but Ben's brother is alive and well and was never anywhere near New York on 9/11. Once I knew that, I also knew why a new lawyer at Justice was suddenly transferred to the Counterterrorism unit. You wanted Tolliver out of custody because he's a spy for American intelligence. That, Dr. Ibanescu, is why you convinced Schatz to take Tolliver's case and made sure Tolliver was held at a place where Schatz could get to him.

"And that's why you intentionally recorded Schatz's attorney-client conference, Terry."

"I told you we had to be careful," Schatz said after barking out a laugh. "She's too fucking smart."

"I don't think she's smart," Crawford said to Schatz. "If she was smart, she would have learned not to fuck with us after we disappeared her."

Crawford turned to Dana. "Unless you have a death wish, you'll kill your story and never tell it to another soul."

Dana glared at the prosecutor. "I think you're a chicken-shit who gets his jollies from pushing your subordinates around. But I don't work for you, and I do not like to be threatened."

"Hey, Dana, calm down," Schatz said.

"Tell us what you want," Ibanescu said calmly.

Dana continued to stare at Crawford. Then she turned away and answered Ibanescu.

"I have no problem with what you did. If it was up to me, everyone involved in the plot to blow up that stadium would be dead. But I'm not going to stand by and see Ginny Striker turned into a sacrificial lamb. You fix her problems at the DOJ and no one will ever learn how Tolliver really got out of custody."

"That's it?" Ibanescu asked.

"That's it. You fixed my parking ticket, so I've got no gripe with the CIA anymore."

Ibanescu laughed and Crawford said, "What parking ticket?"

"I'll talk to someone tomorrow," Ibanescu said. "Your friend will be fine."

"Then so will you three," Dana said.

"It's been a pleasure," Ibanescu answered with a smile. "And I mean that."

Schatz lifted his glass to toast Dana. "You are a real piece of work, Cutler."

Crawford was still fuming when the door closed behind the investigator.

Chapter Fifty-one

A little before three o'clock, Ned Farrow, the man in charge of prosecuting Jack Carson, had called Brad Miller and asked him to come to his office at the DOJ. When he walked in, he was surprised to find Keith Evans across the desk from Farrow. When he stood up to shake hands, Brad's friend looked grim.

"What's up?" Brad asked as soon as everyone was seated.

"I have news I don't think you're going to be happy to hear," said Farrow, a career prosecutor. He was pudgy and balding, and his suits always looked wrinkled. But he had an excellent reputation for tenacity and intelligence and a stellar record of convictions.

"Is that why Keith is here?" Brad asked.

"I thought it would be easier for you to take if a friend broke it to you."

"Broke what?" Brad asked as he looked back and forth between the FBI agent and the prosecutor.

"We're not going to indict Senator Carson," Keith said.

Brad stared, openmouthed. "How can you drop the case? He killed Koshani and gave her top-secret information. Not to mention putting the lives of all those people at the football game in danger."

"Carson hasn't said a word since he was arrested, so we only have your evidence to support an indictment."

"He confessed. I heard every word he said."

"He confessed after his earlobe was cut off and the wound was sealed with a lighter, Brad," Farrow said. "Think about what you would say at trial. You've testified and Bobby Schatz starts his cross. How would you answer if Schatz asked you to describe Carson's physical and mental condition when he made his so-called confession?"

Brad had a vivid memory of the scene in Carson's living room. He tried to think of a way to put a positive spin on his description, but there was no way to do it.

"If Bobby Schatz asked me that question, I would have to testify that the senator was in horrible pain. He was screaming and weeping."

"A confession elicited by torture won't fly," Farrow said. "No judge would allow your testimony.

"And even if it was allowed in, Schatz would argue that Carson hit Koshani in self-defense after he was stabbed and that Lucas tortured and killed Koshani while Carson was badly wounded. You told me that Carson said he tried to stop Sharp."

"Brad," Keith said, "the only evidence we have that Carson is culpable in Koshani's death is your statement of what he said under torture, and a lot of what he said was exculpatory."

"What about the treason charge? He told Koshani what he heard in the Senate Intelligence Committee."

"Same problem," Farrow said. "Carson will testify that he made everything up to stop being tortured. With Koshani and

Crispin dead, the government doesn't have anyone but you, and that's not going to be enough."

After his meeting with Keith Evans and Ned Farrow, Brad walked down to Ginny's office, and they took a cab to the China Clipper, where they planned to celebrate Jake's homecoming. The last time they had eaten Chinese, the newlyweds had just returned from their honeymoon and were looking forward to starting new jobs. But Brad's and Ginny's jobs had not turned out anywhere near the way they thought they would. They tried to put up a brave front when Jake and Dana sat down, but Dana was a pretty good detective, and it wasn't difficult for her to deduce that her friends were playacting.

"Are you worried about the trial?" Dana asked Brad.

"There's not going to be a trial."

"Why not?" Jake asked.

"I met with the prosecutor this afternoon. They've cut a deal with Carson."

"He's going to prison, right?" Dana said.

"No. He's going to resign, and they're not going to indict."

Dana was furious. "How is that possible?" she asked.

"The prosecutors decided that the case was too thin," Brad said.

"He confessed that he and Sharp killed Koshani," Dana shouted. "You heard him."

"He confessed after his earlobe had been sliced off and cauterized with the flame from a lighter. Ned Farrow is convinced that no judge will let me testify to anything Carson said under those conditions."

"So Carson walks?" Jake asked.

"He walks away from a prison sentence," Ginny said, "but that video will be on the Internet forever. He's giving up his Senate seat . . ."

"Which he would have lost anyway," Dana said. "He's so far back in the polls that it would have been a miracle if he got a single vote if he stayed in the race."

"His wife is divorcing him," Brad said.

"It's still not enough," Dana said.

"I agree," Brad said, "but it's the best that can happen under the circumstances."

"Maybe Clarence Little will finish what he started," Dana said.

Brad looked shocked. "Don't say that, Dana. Carson is an awful person, but I wouldn't wish Clarence on anyone."

"Speaking of Mr. Little, what's the latest on him?" Jake asked.

"There is no latest. Keith Evans told me that he's disappeared without a trace."

Ginny shivered. "Hopefully he'll stay disappeared."

"He did save Brad's life," Jake said.

Brad shook his head. "Never, ever think of Clarence as a good guy. I'm glad he saved me, and I'm very thankful that he told me that he would never come after Ginny or me, but he is pure evil."

"What are you doing for a job?" Jake asked, to change the subject.

"I don't know. Ginny was fully reinstated, so we're okay moneywise for a while. I can probably get a decent job in D.C., but we're thinking of leaving."

Dana looked upset.

"I got my old job back working in the Fraud section," Ginny said, "but I'm getting the cold shoulder from a lot of people. It's unpleasant, and I've already been given some awful assignments, and I suspect it will get worse."

"You can sue the bastards if they fuck with you like that," Dana said.

"I could, but I don't want to. I'll stick it out at Justice until we decide what to do, but my days there are numbered."

"We'd miss you guys," Jake said.

"We'd miss you, too, but we've been through hell these past few years, and we'd love to lead a normal life. Ginny and I have talked about starting a family, and that's not really practical here."

"Where would you go?" Jake asked.

"We're both members of the Oregon Bar. Oregon is beautiful, and the chances of anything really exciting happening to us there are pretty small."

"Are you forgetting your adventures with Clarence Little and President Farrington?"

"That was an aberration, and we wouldn't have to practice in Portland. Ginny and I could start a law firm in a small town or the suburbs."

"With your luck, anywhere you settle will be the site of the biggest international criminal conspiracy in history," Dana joked.

"Yeah," Jake added. "The government will probably move the aliens from Area 51 there."

Ginny smiled. "If we see any aliens, we'll take pictures, sell them to *Exposed*, and retire."

"How is your business going?" Brad asked Dana.

"Great. I thought Bobby Schatz would be pissed at me, but he's referred some really good clients."

The conversation was interrupted by the arrival of their food. After everyone filled their plates, Jake talked about an assignment he'd just gotten photographing swimsuit models in Tahiti for a fashion magazine. Dana said she'd worked out her schedule so she could go with Jake as a bodyguard.

After dinner, the foursome went to the same jazz club they'd gone to the last time they'd eaten at the Chinese restaurant, to hear a quintet that had gotten a good review in the *Post*. No one mentioned jobs, serial killers, or crime for the rest of the evening, and Brad and Ginny were in a better mood by the time they returned to their apartment.

Brad had been downtown meeting with the prosecutor, then he'd picked up Ginny, and they had gone to the China Clipper. So neither of them had checked the mail. Brad sorted through it while Ginny looked over his shoulder. He shuffled through a bunch of bills and flyers before a postcard froze the blood in his veins.

"Oh no," Ginny said.

Brad swallowed hard. The front of the postcard showed a beach in Acapulco. On the back Clarence Little had written, "Having a wonderful time. Wish you were here."

There were brownish-red stains on a corner of the card. Brad was certain that if they were analyzed, they would turn out to be human blood.

Epilogue

Rafik Nasrallah thought about his move for three minutes. Then he took the pawn. Imran Afridi tensed as if low-voltage electricity had passed through him. He hunched over the board, concentrating on the square where the pawn had been and Rafik's knight now stood. Rafik knew that his friend was trying to convince himself that his position was not as bad as it seemed. After five minutes, he accepted reality and his shoulders sagged. Rafik knew that Imran would play on. All the last move had given him was an edge, but with accurate play, it would be enough.

Rafik took no joy in winning, as he might have before the FedEx debacle. Three months before, when Imran believed his plan could not fail, a rare victory over the chessboard was something Rafik would savor, but he had been beating his old friend regularly since Imran had returned from America.

Imran was depressed. He could not concentrate, he had no patience. That is why he misread positions and made foolish errors of judgment. Imran had told Rafik that he was being followed. He was certain that his phone was tapped. More than once when Rafik had come to visit, Imran had asked if he had noticed a black Audi outside the wall of his estate. Rafik had not seen a black Audi or any other suspicious vehicle. What he had seen was his friend's steady mental decline.

Imran rarely left the grounds anymore. His businesses were suffering. He no longer held the parties for which he was famous. Rafik saw no traces of women. There had always been women before, but Imran had confided to his friend that he did not trust women he did not know well, women who could be spying on him for the CIA or Pakistani intelligence.

"Well done," Imran conceded fifteen moves after the capture of the pawn.

"I was lucky," Rafik said. "You were distracted."

"It's the weather. It's unsettling."

The weather in Karachi had been depressing for the past four days; a warm, slashing rain had kept everyone indoors praying for clear skies and the sun to raise their spirits. But Rafik knew it was the failure of Imran's grand scheme that was really bringing him down.

"What is really worrying you, Imran? I know it's more than the weather."

Imran smiled sadly. "You know me too well. And you're right. I keep waiting for them to come for me. I cannot believe that I am safe."

"You are Allah's faithful servant, and he will keep you safe," Rafik assured his friend. "I was certain you would be arrested when you told me you were going to stay in America, but Allah saw you home, and he will protect you."

Imran thought about his last day in America. "I was getting ready to leave when Tolliver called me. He must have thought that we are complete fools. The traitor wanted me to fly him out of the country. He probably expected us to trust him with the plans for our next operation."

"You're certain he was working with the CIA?"

"He had a weapon. My men had to kill him before I could question him. But there can be no question, Rafik. The man was in custody because he tried to kill ninety thousand people. The CIA doesn't open the prison doors for someone like that. I don't care what legal error the prosecutor made. Someone in Tolliver's position would have 'committed suicide' or been killed 'resisting arrest' before he would be set free.

"And why was he even in a jail instead of one of the CIA's secret prisons? Why was Tolliver permitted to have a lawyer? It was a setup."

"You're right," Rafik conceded. "And it's my fault. I should never have told you to use him."

"You did nothing wrong. He fooled everybody; you, me, the imam. If anyone is to blame, it is I. I made the final decision." Imran sighed. "Anyway, it is over. The plan was a total failure."

Imran looked exhausted, and Nasrallah left so his friend could turn in early. The ride through the quiet streets in the back of his chauffeured bulletproof Mercedes was conducive to thought. Rafik was relieved that he had been instrumental in foiling Imran's insane plot. He loved Imran, but he had worried about him since Cambridge, when his friend began talking about jihad. He had not known what to do until the men approached him. Rafik had been using cocaine; he was involved with prostitutes; he was heavily in debt to the casinos of London and terrified of what his father would do if his sins were discovered. These men promised him a fresh start, and he was only too eager to escape from the pit of addiction and sin into which he had fallen.

As soon as he agreed to provide the occasional tidbit of information, the debts had miraculously disappeared.

Rafik had hoped that he would never have to pay his new debt. Then Imran, inspired by 9/11, started talking about mass killings. Imran's plans made Nasrallah's stomach turn. He was sick of violence in the name of God. He was tired of seeing good Muslims portrayed as insane killers by the Western press because of the acts of a few deranged men. Rafik had reached out to his handlers as soon as he was certain there was more than simple talk involved.

Rafik often wondered what Imran would do if he learned that his best friend was working with British and American intelligence. Tolliver had been a godsend; the ideal fall guy. Nasrallah hoped that the failure of the FedEx plot would dampen Afridi's desire for jihad. He did not want to betray him again. But he would if it meant saving the lives of innocent people.

Acknowledgments

If I kept my mouth shut about the number of people who helped me with the research and writing of *Capitol Murder*, everyone would think I was a genius, but the truth is that I could not have written *Capitol Murder* without a lot of help from a lot of wonderful people who were willing to take time from their busy days to give me the information I needed to make the book work.

Much of the book takes place in the United States Senate, and I have to thank my friend United States senator Ron Wyden for not only letting me hang around his office for several days and giving me access to his staff so that I could pester them with questions but also for personally taking me on a tour of the Capitol dome. Special thanks go to Jennifer Hoelzer, who helped set up my interviews, took me all over, and generally made my visit to the Senate a success. Thanks also to Chief of Staff Jeffrey Michels and staffers Joel Shapiro, Jayme White, Isaiah Akin, and Lisa Rockower. Finally, a warm thank-you to David Najimi, who conducted the dome tour, and was then kind enough to e-mail me the answers to specific questions. I wanted to put a scene in the dome, but it didn't work out. Be sure to ask your congressperson to arrange a tour the next time you are in D.C. It is really interesting.

Many scenes in the book take place in the Department of Justice. I want to thank Assistant United States Attorney Charles Gorder for helping make my visit there possible, and for answering my questions about various aspects of the federal criminal justice system. Tremendous thanks to Jeff Breinholt, who showed me around the DOJ, and thank you to Erin Creegan and Steve Ward, who answered my questions about the routines of DOJ attorneys.

Thanks to Guy Berliner for showing me how the concessions at FedEx Field work, and thanks to Mike Unsworth of the Portland Police Bomb Squad, Medical Examiner Karen Gunson, Steve Perry, Dennis Balske, Steve Wax, Krista Shipsey, Anass Shaban, and Gina Farag.

Additional thanks to Mitch Berliner, Andy and Ami Rome, Daniel Margolin, Robin Haggard, and Carolyn Lindsey.

Capitol Murder is my tenth book with HarperCollins, and I am very grateful for the support of Jonathan Burnham, Brian Murray, the sales force, and the art department, all of whom have made my long tenure with the house so enjoyable. I want to give special thanks to my wonderful editor, Claire Wachtel, and publicist par excellence Heather Drucker.

I thank my agents Jean Naggar, Jennifer Weltz, and everyone else at the Jean V. Naggar Literary Agency in every acknowledgment, but I've got to. Jean, Jennifer, and the rest of the crew are amazing, and I wouldn't even be writing this book if it hadn't been for them.

And last but never least, I thank Doreen, who is gone but who still inspires me.

About the Author

Phillip Margolin has written fifteen *New York Times* bestsellers, including his latest novels, *Supreme Justice* and *Fugitive.* Each displays a unique, compelling insider's view of criminal behavior, which comes from his long career as a criminal defense attorney who has handled thirty murder cases. Winner of the Distinguished Northwest Writer Award, Margolin lives in Portland, Oregon.